"We have the ch
fantasy, with no repercussions.

He stared at her. "Are you talking about what I think you are?"

There was no mistaking the heat in his eyes, and Eileen's body responded to it, throbbing with pent-up needs.

"If you don't take advantage of this chance, you'll regret it forever." She certainly would. She couldn't imagine a better setup than this one to satisfy her craving for anonymous sex.

"So all you want from me is—"

"This moment. I'm not looking for Mr. Right. I'm asking you to be Mr. Right Now." The situation was perfect—it was after hours, the office was deserted and he was a gorgeous telephone repairman she would never see again. She slid her gaze down to the telling bulge below his tool belt. He was interested. She *knew* he was.

"Look, it's up to you," she said innocently. "If you're game, I'll be in my office."

Dear Reader,

Seduced by a gorgeous stranger—is any sexual fantasy more delicious? Yes, I realize that we all have a weakness for certain superheroes, men who champion the rights of the downtrodden and make the world a safer place. That's all very admirable, but that's not what makes every female in the vicinity start to drool. It's the mask, the mystery...and, okay, the tight pants.

A guy with mystery on his side has a real advantage. Unfortunately, it's a tough advantage to keep, because inevitably the mask slips. Or sometimes the man rips off the mask on purpose, knowing that mystery can only take a relationship so far. That's the case with the hero in this story, Shane Daniels. Luckily, Eileen Connelly certainly seems to react well to the unmasking—as well as the uncovering of certain *other* parts....

Join me for another blazing sensual adventure!

Tantalizingly yours,

Vicki Lewis Thompson

Books by Vicki Lewis Thompson

HARLEQUIN BLAZE

HARLEQUIN TEMPTATION

AFTER HOURS

Vicki Lewis Thompson

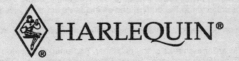

HARLEQUIN®

TORONTO • NEW YORK • LONDON
AMSTERDAM • PARIS • SYDNEY • HAMBURG
STOCKHOLM • ATHENS • TOKYO • MILAN • MADRID
PRAGUE • WARSAW • BUDAPEST • AUCKLAND

To Judith Nolan, my buddy Down Under,
for your most excellent cyber-support
during the creation of this book.
Jude, this one's for you!

ISBN 0-373-79106-2

AFTER HOURS

Copyright © 2003 by Vicki Lewis Thompson.

Visit us at www.eHarlequin.com

Printed in U.S.A.

Prologue

NO GOOD PROSPECTS. As Eileen Connelly sat in a downtown Phoenix bar soaking up the air-conditioning while waiting for her friends Suz and Courtney, she played what had become her favorite game recently—pretending to troll for cheap sex.

If she had the nerve to proposition a stranger, which she probably didn't, was there anyone in the vicinity she'd choose? Not tonight there wasn't. She had her requirements—a rugged physique and dark good looks for starters. Plus he would need to be someone she'd never see again. That was all part of the fantasy.

Adventure, sexual and otherwise, had dominated her thoughts lately. As a little kid she'd had a reckless streak, but her parents had almost divorced when she was ten. After that she'd decided security was more important than adventure. No teenage rebellion for her. She'd gone on to law school, pleasing both parents, and focused on steady career growth. She'd had few relationships with men, and those had been G-rated.

Yet something seemed to have snapped once she'd passed the big three-oh this year. Apparently she'd been good for too long, because suddenly she was deliberately taking risky cases at work and seeking thrills in her spare time. Last month she'd gone white-water rafting, and on Saturday she'd taken a real leap and tried skydiving.

These adventures she could talk about with her friends,

but as for sex with a stranger? Forget about it. Despite knowing Suz Clements since junior high and Courtney McRae since their first pre-law class together at ASU, Eileen wasn't about to reveal her fantasy to them. They were both on the conservative side and would try to talk her out of it.

Courtney came into the bar first, pushing her dark hair away from her face. Last week she'd indulged in a new cut that left her bangs draped over one eye, and she didn't seem used to the change. "Hi!" She hung her lightweight jacket over the back of a chair, stowed her briefcase under the table and sat down. "Man, it's hot out there. Ordered yet?"

"Waiting for you."

Courtney made a face. "I had to stay late. So, you look like you're still in one piece. Did you jump on Saturday or chicken out?"

"I jumped. It was awesome. Too bad it's so damned expensive."

"God, you couldn't pay me to leap from a plane."

"I wish they *would* pay me." Eileen remembered the adrenaline rush as she'd stepped out of the open door into nothingness. "That would be extremely cool."

"You're becoming very nutty." Courtney said it with a smile that didn't quite disguise her concern. "I get chills just thinking of you launching yourself into thin air."

"I was perfectly safe. Listen, the happy-hour special is raspberry margaritas. Let's get a pitcher for the three of us."

"Sounds a hell of a lot better than skydiving."

"That's because you've never tried it." Eileen signaled a waitress and gave her their order.

"And I never will." Courtney leaned both arms on the table and shook her head. "I'll bet Benjamin had a fit, not to mention your parents."

"Uh, I didn't tell them."

"You didn't tell your parents?"

"Or Benjamin."

"Ah-ha. So that's how you got away with it. Well, I can understand not telling your folks and having them freak. I admit they're overprotective. But you told Benjamin about the rafting, so why not this?"

"Because he didn't react well to the raft trip, so why stir up trouble?"

Courtney gazed at her. "Shouldn't he be aware that you're turning into a daredevil? What's next, bungee-jumping?"

"Maybe." Eileen hadn't decided between that and hang-gliding. "But it doesn't matter, because once Benjamin and I move in together, I will give up that kind of thing. That's why I'm getting it out of my system now."

Courtney looked unconvinced. "I don't know if it works like that."

"Sure it does. This is a phase, that's all. Soon I'll— Hey, here comes Suz." She waved at her friend, who was blond like Eileen but wore her hair in a short boyish cut. Eileen had felt extremely lucky when she'd introduced her two buddies to each other ten years ago and they'd hit it off.

The three of them had become a unit during college, and the friendship had lasted through graduation, job hunting and broken hearts. They'd lived together for a while, but then Suz and Courtney had each moved in with boyfriends. Suz was still with hers, but Courtney wasn't. She hadn't suggested sharing an apartment with Eileen, though, because everyone expected Eileen to move in with Benjamin when her lease was up.

Eileen expected it, too. Time had flown by, and her parents wanted grandchildren. She was the sole candidate to give them that, which was fine because she'd always envisioned a husband, a home and kids in her future. Ultimately she needed that kind of stability. She just had to get past this thrill-seeking phase of hers first. And sex with a stranger kept nudging its way to the top of her to-do list.

"How's a pitcher of margaritas sound?" Courtney asked.

"Great." Suz, an advertising rep for the *Arizona Republic,* shoved her briefcase under the table to join Courtney's and Eileen's. She looked uncharacteristically awkward doing it, using only her right hand and keeping her left in the pocket of her linen slacks.

Courtney hadn't seemed to notice, but Eileen had her suspicions. She gazed at her friend. "What's up, Suz?"

Suz looked innocent. "Not much. How was the skydiving?"

"Amazing." She glanced at Suz's right hand. "Nice manicure."

"Thanks," she said casually. "I like this magenta." But she only spread out the fingers of her right hand, while keeping her left in her pocket.

"Okay, Suz," Eileen said, watching her closely. "Spill."

Suz grinned as she pulled her hand out of her pocket to display a glittering diamond. "Chad proposed!"

Pandemonium erupted at the table as the three friends squealed, embraced and even got a little teary. Suz was the first to become engaged.

"Eileen, you're next," Suz said sometime after they'd started in on their second pitcher of margaritas.

"We'll see." But Eileen thought so, too. Even though she'd been careful not to promise Benjamin exclusivity, she hadn't dated anyone else in quite a while. Benjamin wanted her to move in with him. After that, knowing Benjamin and his timetable, the next step would be a proposal. Suz's engagement brought the concept of marriage a lot closer than it had been an hour ago.

No doubt about it, commitment was closing in on her. As she contemplated a lifetime with Benjamin, she suddenly knew what she had to do. Before she agreed to forsake all others, she wanted the ultimate adventure—sex with the perfect stranger.

1

IT WAS NOW OR NEVER. Traynor and Sizemore, the law firm that employed both Benjamin and Eileen, had sent Benjamin to Switzerland for six days. That left Eileen free to enact her sex-with-a-stranger fantasy without any danger of him finding out.

Although she wasn't breaking any agreement between them, she didn't want to have sex with someone else right under his nose. Benjamin's last-minute trip to Switzerland was like being handed an engraved invitation to take care of unfinished business. Sure, she was scared, but that was part of the excitement.

She was also incredibly turned on by the idea of choosing a sexual partner she'd never met before and would never meet again. Unfortunately, she'd seen Benjamin off at Sky Harbor last night at seven, nearly twenty-four hours ago, and since then she'd made no real progress toward her goal. The condoms she'd stashed in her purse this morning in preparation for some wild and crazy adventure were still there, untouched.

From her second-floor office window, she'd spent at least a half-hour watching a good-looking guy down below working with a street-repair crew. She'd just mustered up her courage to go down and speak to him when he'd paused to spit tobacco juice into the gutter. Then the overnight mail courier had looked like a possibility until she'd checked out his wedding band. Her bad luck had continued when the muscled hunk she'd made eye contact with on her lunch break had been joined shortly thereafter by his gay partner.

Scoping out handsome strangers had cut way down on her efficiency at the office today. She'd deleted a valuable file from her hard drive while daydreaming about sex, and now she was stuck at her desk after hours trying to reconstruct it from her scribbled notes.

She could give up the handsome stranger project right now and no one would be the wiser. *No,* damn it, she wouldn't forget it. If she did, she'd end up like Meryl Streep in *The Bridges of Madison County.* She'd rather succumb to temptation before the wedding, not years after when the guilt would probably kill her.

On the drive to the airport Benjamin had reminded her that when he came back at the end of the week, he expected an answer to his question about living together. And he was a damned good catch. He was a cinch to make partner at Traynor and Sizemore a good year ahead of Eileen because he worked harder than she did. He kissed ass better, too. Well, metaphorically speaking. In bed, he wasn't particularly imaginative, poor guy.

He'd promised that once Eileen shifted her belongings over to his luxury apartment, he'd morph into a more spontaneous lover. She thought it was possible. Some people needed security to let loose, and Benjamin seemed to fit in that group. And maybe it didn't matter whether he became more sexually impulsive. She didn't want to put too much importance on one trait.

She'd dated enough guys to know that she'd never find anybody higher on the compatibility scale than Benjamin. Yep, they had the compatibility thing down...except Benjamin didn't like risks and he wasn't into sexual fantasies. He'd told her flat out that he didn't have fantasies, didn't need them, and wondered about the people who did. That had shut her up fast.

Considering his attitude, she wasn't about to tell him about the fantasy that had gripped her from the age of eighteen. That was the year Michael Keaton as Batman had stepped through the open window of Kim Basinger's darkened apartment. Eileen remembered the hot stab of desire she'd felt while sitting in the theater. What would it be like to have an anonymous man in her bedroom? She wanted that thrill for real.

But she'd been in her good-girl mode at eighteen, not wanting to rock the boat. Her parents' marriage had stabilized by then. At the age of ten she hadn't understood what had caused the problem, but looking back on it now, she was pretty sure another woman had been part of the equation. Her dad had also bought a Corvette and had tried out local stock-car racing.

But all that was over now. Her parents' marriage was solid. But Eileen had learned from the experience that adventures need to take place before marriage, before the serious business of creating a family. If she could complete her sex-with-a-stranger project this week, she'd be ready to give Benjamin an answer on Saturday.

However, she'd have to concentrate on the project after she'd finished keying in these notes. Maybe her sexual fantasy was a priority, but keeping her job ranked right up there, too. She wasn't willing to trade security for adventure. She wanted both.

By seven, she was the only person left in the suite of offices. Not surprising. The Diamondbacks were playing a three-game series at home, and she was one of the few who didn't have season tickets. Benjamin had suggested they buy some for next year after she moved in with him. Maybe it was his version of a promise ring, to have tickets for next season.

Around seven-thirty, she opened her desk and pulled out the raspberry mocha energy bar that would substitute for dinner. She'd taken the first bite when she heard a clanking noise in the reception area.

Could be the cleaning service, except...that sounded like a power screwdriver, not a vacuum. She tried to imagine why a thief would be using a power screwdriver, or even what there was to steal in the reception area.

She'd have to investigate, but she didn't want to be stupid, in case an intruder was really out there. All she had in the way of a weapon was her collapsible umbrella, a holdover from the monsoon season which had pretty much ended a couple of weeks ago.

But as she gripped the umbrella's plastic handle and pushed back her chair, she remembered about the phone system upgrade. Two days ago everyone had received a memo, but she'd been too involved in her sexual search to think about it again. Some communications company was installing the system tonight, after regular hours, to keep from interrupting business.

She listened for conversation that would confirm that the telephone guys were out there. When no one said a word, she figured out, being fairly smart and a law-school graduate, that one person was working alone. Smiling, Eileen leaned back in her chair, idly caressed the umbrella in her hand and pretended this was her Michael Keaton moment.

Roll the cameras. The sexy lady lawyer would wander into the reception area, and... No, first she'd unfasten the top three buttons of her blouse. *Then* she would wander into the reception area.

Kneeling on the floor next to the phone jack would be a gorgeous man wearing a tight T-shirt, soft jeans, work boots and a tool belt. The tool belt would ride low on his hips and would contain…lots of tools.

She would clear her throat. He would glance up. Or…wait. She'd walk right up beside him, and he'd look over and notice shapely legs placed conveniently at his eye level. Slowly his gaze would travel upward, appraisingly, until he was staring into her baby blues, mesmerized. No words would be necessary. He would know what to do. And she would let him do it.

In reality, the guy in the reception area probably had a wife, six kids, and a beer belly. Or it wasn't a guy at all. No reason a woman couldn't be installing the new system. The way Eileen's luck had been running today, the installer would definitely be a woman.

The fantasy had been fun for a while, though. As long as she didn't go out there, she could hold on to it. But she needed to make her presence known. The memo had requested that all personnel vacate the premises by seven. The installer expected an empty suite of offices, and he or she might not appreciate being startled by an employee who'd forgotten about the memo.

With a sigh, she put the umbrella back in her bottom desk drawer, wheeled her chair away from her desk and prepared to go out and burst her fantasy bubble.

SHANE NICHOLS TOOK OFF the faceplate on the telephone jack and inspected the wiring. Looked like it would support the added lines the client had requested, no problem. Funny, he'd been hoping for more of a challenge. He'd forgotten how much he loved the hands-on part of this business.

To think at one time he'd been eager for Mercury Communications to take off so that he could hire other people to do the actual installations. His dream had come true, leaving him stuck behind a desk while everybody else had the fun of going out on jobs. His job was now all about drumming up business and keeping current clients happy. Even when he left the office, he felt obliged to keep his pager and his cell with him at all times, in case a client had an emergency.

Both were nestled in his tool belt right now. He'd built his business on personal service, and in the beginning he'd loved that aspect. But little by little, like a creeping kudzu vine, the personal service aspect had obliterated his free time. If he didn't deal with problems himself, especially for long-standing customers, they accused him of being a big shot who didn't have time for them.

To be fair, there might be other aspects of the business he could let go of, but he didn't know how. He'd handled everything himself for so long that he couldn't imagine turning decisions over to someone else, someone without his background, someone who would probably screw it up. He'd created a monster.

At least tonight he could have fun with an installation, although he'd probably be interrupted by calls. Lou had been assigned this job, but Lou's wife had unexpectedly gone into labor with their first kid. Lou needed to be with her.

Shane had leaped at the chance to take over and install the new system at Traynor and Sizemore. He must have sounded way too cheerful about giving up his evening, because Lou had asked him if something was wrong.

Hell, yes, something was wrong. His life was a mess, and he had only himself to blame. He'd created a company that now controlled his life. He'd sell it, but then he'd worry about how his employees would be treated. They were all terrific and wouldn't be happy about a new owner.

He'd never imagined that success could be such a pain

in the ass. The piles of paperwork on his desk grew taller every day, too. Mercury consumed so much of his time that he had no hobbies, no social life, barely even watched TV. His parents and brother had been after him about how hard he worked, and he kept promising to cut back, somehow. They were empty promises.

If this installation hadn't forced him out of the office tonight, he might still be working at his desk, computer turned on, files open everywhere. Innovations in communications networks happened constantly, and he had to keep up if Mercury was to stay competitive.

But tonight he could forget about everything but upgrading the system for Traynor and Sizemore. The silence in the office building soothed him. Ironically for a guy who peddled phones, he'd started to hate the sound of the damn things ringing.

Now that it was too late, he knew what he wanted. His perfect life would include living in a small town, working a nine-to-five job for somebody else, and simply enjoying himself in his free time. More specifically, he wanted to enjoy himself in a particular way, i.e., with some special woman.

He'd even imagined what she'd look like. She'd be a blue-eyed blond, because he was a sucker for blonds, blonds with hair down past their shoulders. He didn't require centerfold measurements, but he'd like her to have a figure that would look good in the lingerie he'd buy for her.

Not too long ago he'd seen a woman who matched that description in this very building, which was probably why he was thinking about the subject now. He'd had a tantalizing glimpse of her through an open door on his way back to Traynor's office to discuss the installation. She'd been concentrating on her work and hadn't looked up.

Because she was a lawyer, she'd satisfy another requirement of his: she'd be smart. But one glance couldn't verify whether she had a sense of adventure, and he wanted that in a woman, especially when it came to sex. He harbored his share of fantasies, and most of them were unfulfilled.

Maybe he was asking too much of one woman and nobody would be able to fit his admittedly ambitious specs. But he'd never know if he didn't go looking. With the demands of his company, he'd had precious little time to do that.

He was so lost in his daydream of the perfect woman that when someone coughed, he jumped and dropped his cordless screwdriver. Looking up, he did a classic double take. Standing just inside the hallway was his blue-eyed blonde, the same woman he'd seen so briefly through an office doorway. She stood posed in a way that showed off a Victoria's Secret figure. And she was smiling.

EILEEN'S HEART BEAT fast enough to make her ears ring. On the far side of the reception area stood a red metal dolly loaded with boxes, presumably holding new telephone equipment. But the boxes didn't interest her. The man kneeling on the carpet beside the telephone jack did. Maybe she'd been concentrating so hard on finding the perfect stranger that she'd caused one to appear, like a genie out of a bottle.

However it had happened, there he was, her fantasy come to life. Rumpled black hair, green eyes, square jaw—and that was only the beginning. She'd put in an order for a rugged guy in jeans and a T-shirt, and he'd filled it. The T-shirt wasn't quite snug enough to suit her, but his chest created an excellent backdrop for his company logo, a Greek god with wings on his feet. Mercury Communications was spelled out in navy on a gray background. He wore no rings, wedding or otherwise.

All her specifications had been met, even to the leather tool belt strapped around his lean hips. If Benjamin's trip to Switzerland had been an engraved invitation to sin, then this man's appearance was a red carpet rolled right up to the toes of her high-heeled pumps. But she had to play it right.

She cleared her throat and hoped her voice wouldn't tremble. "Hi."

"Hi." His direct gaze disconcerted her.

"We got a memo about this installation, but the whole thing slipped my mind. I stayed late to get some work done."

"Oh."

He seemed at a bit of a loss for words, and she wondered if she could have great sex with a stranger who had zero social skills. She'd never given that angle much thought because conversation hadn't been part of her fantasy.

"I hope I didn't startle you too much," she continued, thinking that eventually he'd have to utter more than two words or this fantasy would never get off the ground.

"You did startle me." He got to his feet, picked up the cordless screwdriver and laid it on the receptionist's desk. "But not for the reason you think."

"I'm not sure what you mean." Yet she was very glad that he could form complete sentences when he chose to.

"I was just thinking about—" He paused and shook his head. "Never mind. Look, if I'm interrupting your work, I can come back in a couple of—"

"Tell me what you were thinking about." She had a hunch it would lead to something good.

"You're going to think it's a line. And I don't do lines."

Now she definitely had to hear what he'd been about to say. "Try me."

He eyed her for a moment. "Okay. It just so happens that while I was working just now, I was picturing my ideal woman."

It did sound like a pickup line, but somehow she didn't think he meant it that way. Her mouth grew moist with anticipation. "I look something like your ideal woman?"

"Except that your hair is up like that, yes, you look exactly like her."

Without giving herself any time to think, she reached up and pulled out the two tortoiseshell combs holding her hair in place.

He drew in a quick breath. "Why did you do that?"

She paused for a beat and held his gaze. "Because while I was in there working, I was thinking about my ideal man."

"That's hard to believe." But he looked very much like he wanted to believe it.

"It's true."

He shifted his weight. "Are you saying that I…"

"Yes." Amazing how the simple act of taking her hair down aroused her, just as it seemed to be arousing him. The gesture felt more intimate than stripping naked.

"So we were each thinking the same thing at the same time."

"Looks that way." She trembled as she contemplated the next step. She would have to be the aggressor. As the employee of a company licensed and bonded to work inside corporate offices like Traynor and Sizemore, he wouldn't dare step out of line unless she made him feel completely safe.

"Ideals don't truly exist in the real world," she said.

"Don't try to tell me this isn't real. And I'm pretty sure I'm not dreaming," he said with a crooked grin.

"This moment may be real. But our view of each other is likely skewed right now. We may seem to fit each other's ideal, but I'm sure neither of us is close to perfect."

"I'd never claim to be perfect. No human is—even you, I suppose." He grinned again. "But I still say you look a lot like the picture I've been carrying around in my head."

"I could say the same about you." She responded to everything about him—the sound of his voice, the scent of his aftershave, the subtle gestures he made with his hands. And he reacted to her, too. She could see it in his eyes and the flare of his nostrils.

"Look, we both have work to do," he said. "What if we go back to it, and when we're finished, we can go out, have a drink and find out a little more about each—"

"No."

He appeared taken aback for a moment. Then his gaze sharpened. "You're married."

"No, I'm not."

"Then what's the problem?"

She was grateful for legal training that had taught her how to present her case. "If we go out for a drink, if we take this in a conventional direction, we'll lose the chance to create something extraordinary right now."

He stared at her, his throat moving in a swallow. "Are you talking about what I think you are?"

She sensed tension, but excitement shone in his eyes, too. "Just so you know, I've never done anything like this in my life."

He continued to stare at her.

The trick would be convincing him she could be trusted, when he had no reason to believe that. "Look, I know what you're thinking. If anybody found out about it, you'd be fired. Worse than fired. But I promise you, no one will find out. This is between you and me. I could get in a lot of trouble, too, you know.''

''Not as much as I could.'' He sighed and shook his head. Then he chuckled softly. ''I have to admit, for a second there I was considering it. Never mind that you're a lawyer who would know all about how to sue me six ways to Sunday. Never mind that everything I've worked for could go right down the tubes.'' His green eyes blazed. ''Idiot that I am, I was still thinking about it.''

Her body responded to his admission, throbbing with pent-up needs. Her mind recognized that she still had a shot. ''Think about it some more.''

He shook his head. ''Way too dangerous.''

''What if I told you that for years I've had a fantasy of making it with a stranger? I'm not a flake. My semi-serious boyfriend has asked me to move in with him, and I plan to do that. But before I make that kind of commitment, I want to—''

''This semi-serious boyfriend—where is he?''

''Temporarily in Switzerland on business.''

''I suppose he's also a lawyer?''

''Does it matter?''

He laughed. ''Hell, yes, it matters. Getting beat up by a jealous boyfriend is one thing. Being hauled into court and deprived of a huge hunk of money is something else again, not to mention the damage to my reputation. You're asking me to run a big risk, just for—''

''For an unforgettable experience.'' She built on her knowledge that he'd been daydreaming about his ideal woman. A man who did that probably had a fantasy life. ''Don't tell me you've never imagined something like this.''

"That's not the point. Fantasy's one thing, reality is another."

"It's exactly the point. Both of us have a chance to act out a fantasy, with no repercussions. That chance doesn't come along every day."

There was no mistaking the heat in his eyes, but still he shook his head.

"If you don't take advantage of this, you'll regret it forever." She certainly would. She couldn't imagine a better setup than this one to satisfy her craving for anonymous sex.

"So all you want from me is—"

"This moment. I've already found Mr. Right, and he's away in Switzerland for a few days. I'm asking you to be Mr. Right Now." The situation made her bold, and she slid her gaze down to the telling bulge below his tool belt. At least she'd scored that much of a victory.

In the art of persuasion, timing was everything. Sometimes, you had to stop talking and give your words a chance to take effect. "It's up to you," she said. "If you're interested, I'll be in my office." Then she turned slowly and walked down the hall, issuing a silent invitation with every sway of her hips.

2

SHANE'S HEAD FIZZED and popped as he watched her leave. This couldn't be happening. Sure, phone installers liked to spin stories about sex-hungry women lying in wait for them at the job site, but most of the time the stories weren't true or they involved some nightmare psycho woman. He didn't think the lady lawyer was psycho.

Her pink cheeks and quivering hands told him that she was nervous. Nervous and determined, the way a woman might be if she had an unfulfilled fantasy and boring monogamy was just over the next hill, ready to grab her. He could understand that.

He believed her story, unfortunately, and that should make his decision easy. Serving as a one-night-stand fantasy and then disappearing into the sunset wasn't his style, especially not with a woman like this. He had a strong feeling she could be exactly the type he was looking for, and he wouldn't want to disappear.

Therefore he should get the hell out of this office. He could come back in a few hours and finish the job. After this jolt of adrenaline, he wouldn't be sleeping much tonight, anyway.

So why was he still standing here? Deep down, he knew why, other than the obvious sexual temptation. She represented a challenge, something that had seriously been lacking in his life. The business certainly no longer tested his mettle. Now it was simply a daily grind.

In essence, she'd given him exactly one chance to change her mind about moving in with her boyfriend. If he changed her mind, then he could go on to Phase Two, convincing her that he was the one she needed. Suddenly he saw his life unfolding as he'd envisioned—a wife, a home and a close family like the one he'd grown up in. His folks kept asking about his love life, or lack of one, and they'd be thrilled if he found the woman of his dreams.

Plus he had a hunch that finding that woman would force him to cut back on work. He desperately needed a playmate to jolt him out of this rut, because he hadn't been able to accomplish that by himself. All he had to do to make that a possibility, was win out over the current boyfriend.

She probably didn't consider Shane a contender, stacked against a lawyer important enough to fly to Switzerland on business. Sure, he could tell her he owned Mercury Communications and level the playing field, but he was used to working with a handicap. He performed better when the odds were against him.

Besides, he sensed the boyfriend had a handicap, too. If he'd been setting the sheets on fire with the lady lawyer, she wouldn't be searching for a thrill the minute he left town. Shane had a good opportunity to win the sexual contest, especially with this fantasy situation she'd chosen.

Was he seriously considering her proposition, then? If she blabbed about this, to anyone, she could ruin his business reputation. The responsibility for the welfare of his employees weighed on his conscience.

He thought about the way she'd looked, standing there waiting for him to make up his mind. His gut instinct told him she wouldn't blab, and that instinct had never betrayed him before. No, he couldn't use his work responsibilities as an excuse to back away from this one.

And finally he had to admit that he didn't want an excuse. She had the potential to be everything he wanted in a woman. Physically she was perfect. Added to that, she was smart enough to be a lawyer, and sexy enough to want a fantasy before she settled into a dull monogamous routine.

Slowly he unfastened his tool belt, his fingers shaking just a little, and laid it on the receptionist's desk. The minute he did that, his cell phone beeped out its cute little "bombs away" melody. It was no longer cute. He grabbed the phone out of habit, punched the button and said hello.

Sure enough, the person on the other end was one of his oldest customers, someone who'd had a problem earlier in the day but hadn't had time to call until now. Of course he'd called the minute Shane had a hot woman waiting for him just down the hall, a woman who had all the markings of happily ever after. He couldn't remember the last time he'd had a prospect like that. The customer would have to wait.

"Sorry, George," he said. "You've caught me at a really bad time. I'll get back to you in the morning. Talk to you then." He disconnected before George could give him any reason to stay on the line. Then he turned off his phone. And his pager.

Surprisingly, the world didn't come to an end when he did that. He stared at the two pieces of equipment that had been his ball and chain for way too long and felt a sense of triumph. He hadn't really lost control of his life. He'd only thought he had.

Straightening his shoulders, he turned toward the hallway. He had no condoms with him, so he'd have to be creative in how he satisfied her. But he guessed that was what she wanted, creativity.

His pulse rate jumping off the charts, he walked toward the only doorway with light spilling out onto the gray carpet. His senses recorded everything with the kind of accuracy that told him he'd always remember the sound of his footsteps on the Berber underfoot, the scent of commercial carpet cleaner he stirred on his way, and the Monet ''Water Lilies'' print in the gold frame hanging just outside her door.

In the silent office, she would hear him approaching. He wondered how that affected her, knowing that her fantasy was about to come true. Because it would come true. He planned to make this the most memorable sex she'd ever had, so memorable that she'd want to keep him around... forever.

When he walked into the room, his focus narrowed to include only the woman leaning against the front of her desk, waiting for him. His fantasy woman.

Her breathing came in quick, shallow gasps, which made the front of her white blouse quiver. She'd unfastened enough pearl buttons that the white lace of her bra peeked from under the crisp linen. The blouse had long sleeves and French cuffs held snug with the same pearl buttons, and it was tucked neatly into the waistband of a navy skirt that stopped a couple of inches above her knees.

Nylons in a subtle navy tint covered her slender legs. She wore pointy-toed heels that looked expensive. He was facing a professional businesswoman who wanted him to create havoc with her dressed-for-success presentation. She wanted her skirt up around her waist and her panties down around her ankles.

The prospect nearly destroyed his composure, but he breathed deeply and overcame the urge to lunge forward and pin her to the desk. He took a step closer and caught her scent, the sweetness of orange blossoms mingled with the tang of arousal. His mouth watered.

''So you decided to risk it.'' Her voice was husky.

"Yeah." He looked into her blue eyes and felt as if he'd gazed into them as a lover many times before, even though he didn't even know her name. But he'd find out her name. This was her office, and her name would be somewhere in it. Getting that information was important, considering he planned to take this beyond her proposed one-night stand.

He pretended to survey the office. "Nice space." She was partial to rosewood, apparently, but he was glad to see that the desk was sturdy and not some spindly antique. He'd be needing the desk.

It was still covered with files and papers and maybe she wanted it that way. Maybe she wanted to have sex on top of all that paperwork. Her computer was out of the way on a trolley beside the desk, but the phone could get upset in the process of what he had in mind. No problem. She was getting a new phone tonight, anyway.

The wooden mini-blinds covering the window behind her desk were closed tight, so she wasn't into exhibitionism. At least not this time around. Otherwise the office contained a wooden lateral file, a bookcase filled with serious-looking law books, a credenza with a vase of silk flowers and some framed photos. Two armchairs that might have been in front of her desk at one time were now up against the wall. She'd given him room to maneuver. Nice.

He noticed a couple of bare picture hooks and realized that if she'd had diplomas hanging there, she'd taken them down before he arrived. And if she'd had a nameplate on her desk, that was in a drawer now, too. She didn't want him to know who she was.

But he would find out. A woman eager for a long-awaited orgasm could be coaxed into saying all kinds of things. He would learn all he needed to learn.

So the diplomas were gone, but an impressionistic watercolor hung above the chairs. Its undulating curves and pink tones might look like nothing to the casual observer, but Shane decided the picture was definitely about sex.

"Do you like that?" she asked softly.

He decided to test her. "What's it supposed to be?"

"The title is 'Shades of Pink.' I bought it at an art fair. I suppose you can interpret it any way you want to."

"And how do you interpret it?"

She glanced at him. "I've…always thought it looked like a depiction of…an orgasm." She swallowed. "I've never told anyone that," she added quickly. "And it probably isn't at all, but I—"

"You hung it on the wall because you liked that interpretation." It wasn't a question.

"I guess so. Yes."

He took another step toward her. "That's what tonight is all about, being sexually honest, maybe for the first time in our lives."

Her breathing quickened. "Yes."

"I'll start. I've never been so turned on by a woman, or by the thought of having sex. I want to take you right now. I want to shove your skirt to your waist, unzip my jeans and brace you against that desk. I want to rip apart whatever lacy underwear is between us and shove deep."

She gasped.

"Am I shocking you?"

"No." She struggled for breath. "No. That's…that's what I want, too."

He wondered just how much of a risk taker she was. "You'd be a damned fool to let me, with no protection in sight."

Slowly she stretched her hand toward him, her fingers closed. When she opened them, a square packet lay in her palm.

He gazed at the condom and then looked into her eyes.

Her voice vibrated, almost like a cat's purr. "Be my guest."

Desire gusted through him with enough force to leave him shaking. He waited for the tremors to pass. Then he cupped her soft hand in his and lifted it, condom and all, to his lips.

First he kissed the tip of each manicured finger. Now it was her turn to quiver. Next he sucked gently on the end of her fingers, all the while watching her eyes.

Her lashes fluttered closed, and her breathing grew more ragged. "I thought...you wanted to...take me quickly."

"I do." He closed her damp fingers over the condom. "But I *plan* to take you slowly." He unfastened the pearl button at her cuff and edged the white linen to her elbow. Then he dropped kisses on the faint blue vein at her pulse. "Fast and hard is good, but slow and seductive is better. I'll let you hold the condom until I'm ready for it."

Her lashes lifted to reveal blue eyes stormy with passion. "What if...I'm ready now?"

"If you think you're ready now..." He released her hand and reached for her other one. "Just think how ready you'll be in a little while."

Reaction flared in her eyes.

"Good." He smiled as he unfastened the second cuff. "Now you're imagining the possibilities." If he had only one chance to make an impression, he would make it a beauty.

Maintaining some distance between them, he started undoing the buttons down the front of her blouse. "Have you ever been naked in this office?"

She drew in a breath. "No."

"Ever had sex here?" He pulled the unbuttoned blouse from the waist of her skirt and opened it to reveal the sweetest breasts ever molded by lace and underwire.

"No."

So lawyer-boy hadn't tapped into this particular fantasy. How could she possibly think the guy currently in Switzerland was Mr. Right? "Tonight I want both." He slipped the blouse off her shoulders and tossed it over the papers piled on her desk. "There's something about being naked in a place where people usually wear business suits."

Her voice curled around him like smoke. "It seems unreal that I'll be back to work as usual here tomorrow."

"Uh-huh." He unfastened the front hook of her bra. "I want you to think about this all day tomorrow."

She shivered. "I will."

He guided the bra straps down her arms. He'd meant to throw the bra on top of her blouse, but he became mesmerized by the sight of her breasts and the bra dropped from his fingers to the floor.

She'd spent time in the sun this summer. Golden skin gave way to cream where the bikini had barely covered her rosy nipples. Their taut promise invited the brush of his fingers. Somehow he found the strength to resist.

"Don't you…want to touch me?"

"Oh, yes. Very much. But not yet." He had a hunch that the boyfriend was predictable, so he would work not to be. Most any man when confronted with breasts like hers would dive in with pure joy. He would hold back and finish undressing this goddess. When she could hardly stand the suspense another second, he would begin to touch her.

He found the back zipper of her skirt and drew it down until the skirt slipped easily to the floor. His erection strained against his briefs as he gazed at the white lace garter belt holding up her navy stockings. It was as if she'd dressed this morning with him in mind. At every turn, she revealed more of the woman he'd been waiting to find.

She stepped out of her skirt and kicked it gently to one side. "Are you going to be naked, too?" she murmured.

He forced his attention from the garter belt and what lay beneath it so that he could look into her eyes. "Would you like that? Or do you want—"

"Yes. Take off your shirt."

Wordlessly he pulled it over his head and dropped it to the carpet.

"You look strong."

"Strong enough for what I have in mind for tonight." Holding her gaze, he knelt in front of her and ran both hands down the silky length of her leg. She was warm and quivering beneath his touch, and the scent of temptation drifted from between her thighs. Gently he eased off one of her shoes and caressed the sole of her foot.

She moaned. "I want you."

"I know." Unfastening her stocking, he leaned forward to flick his tongue over the bare skin of her leg as he rolled the stocking down her thigh and over her knee.

She trembled. "I want…"

"What?" he whispered, running his hands down her other leg and slipping off the second shoe.

"I want you to…"

"Tell me. Tell me your secrets." The mounting tension made him fumble taking off the other stocking. His tongue seemed to sizzle against her trembling thigh.

"Make me come."

His heartbeat thundered in his ears. "And how would you like me to do that?"

She cupped the back of his head and guided him to the triangle of lace and silk nestled below the garter belt. Her plea was low and urgent. "With your tongue…please…I can't wait…."

As if he could resist, once he was this close and surrounded by her scent. His mouth watered. "When you're completely naked," he whispered, nuzzling the damp silk of her panties.

She groaned. "Then get me completely naked. Right now."

Grasping the garter belt and panties together, he pulled them down in one swift move.

When she stepped out of them, he paused to sear the moment into his brain. The woman of his dreams stood before him, naked and eager, surrounded by the sedate trappings of a lawyer's office. The contrast was absolutely delicious, and he wanted to savor it before he was swept into a firestorm of need.

When he cupped her sleek bottom and sank to his heels, the thrill of the forbidden made him dizzy. She moaned again, an urgent little sound that told him she was desperate for release. Leaning forward, he slid his tongue boldly through her golden curls and tasted paradise.

The condom she held landed on the floor beside him as she gripped his head in both hands and shuddered.

He moved in closer, getting his shoulders under her thighs as he lifted her to the edge of the desk.

As he began to feast, she whimpered and tightened her hold on his scalp. Ah, she was heavenly, melting on his tongue like fine chocolate. He guided her to spread her thighs even more, and with a sigh of surrender she obliged him, stretching one leg along the edge of the desk. Papers rustled and drifted to the floor.

He caressed her with his tongue and slid his fingers deep into her wet heat, probing and stroking her to a fever pitch. Her cries grew more intense, her breathing more labored.

And then the wave broke, filling the small office with the sound of her ecstasy. His groin throbbed with nearly unbearable tension and he longed to rip off his jeans and bury his penis in her quaking vagina. But too much was at stake to risk muting any of the pleasure he wanted to give her. So he followed her all the way through her climax, lapping the nectar of her release and heightening her contractions with the rhythm of his fingers.

At last the tremors eased and her muscles relaxed. Placing his hands at her waist, he steadied her as he kissed a path over her flat stomach. Gradually rising from his knees, he lifted her onto the desk, scattering papers everywhere. The desk phone rattled, but somehow didn't end up on the floor.

She braced her hands behind her and arched her back, as if anticipating his next goal. He took her quivering nipple in his teeth and raked the firm tip gently.

"Yes," she whispered. "Oh, yes."

With one hand supporting the small of her back, he balanced the weight of her breast in the curve of his other hand as he nibbled and sucked.

"I can see us…in the glass of the picture," she murmured.

He licked his way to her other breast. "The orgasm picture?"

She whimpered as he flicked his tongue over her breast. "Yes, that picture."

"Do you like watching us?"

"Yes." She trembled as he sucked her nipple deep into his mouth.

He could sense she was ready again. Nibbling lightly at her breast, he slid two fingers down through her damp thatch of curls. "Now you can watch yourself come," he whispered against her dewy skin.

With a soft moan of assent, she opened her thighs and invited him inside. Slowly he stroked her, and she tightened around his fingers. He'd never been with a woman this hot, this excited.

He'd intended to give her the experience of a lifetime, and she was turning the tables on him. Making love to a woman like her was something he'd only dreamed of. She made him feel like the most gifted lover in the world, and yet it was her responsiveness making everything possible.

Increasing the rhythm of his fingers and using his thumb to massage her special hot spot, he gloried in every whimpered cry as she reached for another shattering climax. Within seconds, she found it, rocking her hips in time with his strokes and sending yet more papers to the floor.

As she gasped for breath, he eased her down until she was sprawled across the desk, her legs dangling off the edge. Moving between her outstretched legs, he leaned over her and braced his hands on either side of her head.

"I haven't even kissed you," he said, gazing into her heavy-lidded eyes.

She ran her tongue over her lips. "Kiss me...now."

"Tell me your name."

A spark flared in her eyes. "No."

"Mine is—"

"Come here." She pulled him toward her waiting mouth and into a kiss so deep, so erotic, that his hips began to move as his penis strained to break free of its confinement.

She drew his tongue into her mouth, sucking and toying with it until the urge to be inside her burned every other thought from his brain. Wrenching free of her suggestive kiss, he backed away long enough to get out of his shoes and shuck his jeans and briefs.

After grabbing the condom from the floor, he ripped open the package and rolled the latex over his aching penis.

She watched him, her chest heaving, her body shimmering with heat, her hair spilling over the far edge of the desk. Her gaze dropped to his groin. "Now?"

"Yes, now."

Her breath caught. "Here, on the desk?"

"Absolutely. With your ankles wrapped around my neck and your sweet bottom sliding back and forth on whatever paperwork you're lying on. You realize the ink will be smeared when we're finished."

Her chest rose and fell rapidly. "I don't care."

"I think that's what you want. A souvenir." He grasped her calves and lifted them so she could hook her ankles around his neck and he...oh, yes, now he could enter the beautiful pink gates of heaven. Hands splayed under her bottom, he watched the tip of his penis slide in, and that was almost enough to make him come.

With a low murmur of satisfaction, she propped her hands behind her head.

He looked into her eyes, and saw the excitement glittering there. "Remember this tomorrow," he said, and pushed deep.

3

THROUGH A SENSUAL HAZE, Eileen watched her fantasy man, his green eyes sparking with fire as he entered her. The sensation was all she could have wanted—the satisfaction of being filled as he moved deeper, exciting her all over again.

She'd never been multi-orgasmic, and yet he'd made her come twice and would make her come again. She was already beginning to quiver.

He eased back and pushed in again, his jaw flexing. "Promise me you'll remember this tomorrow."

"I'll remember." She would remember this for the rest of her life. The desk under her back was hard and unyielding, but she didn't care. With every thrust he brought her humming body closer to another orgasm, and she'd never had the depth of feeling that he gave her, never felt such quaking from the tips of her toes to the roots of her hair.

The fantasy must be heightening her reactions. She couldn't have found a more perfect man to act out anonymous sex with her. Nameless, with no history and no expectations, he was completely of the moment.

He could be a Greek god who'd materialized to seduce her, with his dark hair falling over his forehead, his classic features and his powerful body. And from this view he could be a centaur, half-man and half-animal, taking his pleasure from a mortal. He was definitely taking his pleasure. Lust shone in his eyes as he plunged into her, his strokes picking up speed, his chest gleaming with sweat.

The rising tide of an orgasm gripped her, ready to fling her into the whirlpool again. She panted, wanting that wild ride one more time. But he clenched his jaw and deliberately slowed his movements.

She licked her dry lips. "More," she whispered in a husky voice she barely recognized as her own. "Faster."

"Not yet." He stroked her with slow, lazy movements, holding himself back so he missed that magic spot he'd been stimulating so expertly before.

"You want…to make it…last longer?" Her blood pounded furiously in her veins, demanding a release he was denying her.

"Tell me your name."

"No."

"Tell me." He teased her with quick, shallow thrusts that stopped short of giving her what she needed.

"No," she murmured, easing her hands from behind her head as she gasped for breath and strained toward a climax. "Do you…do you think you can hold off…until I tell you? Is that it?"

"Maybe."

"I won't tell you." Leaning her head on the desk and closing her eyes, she cupped her breast in one hand and reached between her legs with the other.

He swore softly. "Don't do that."

"I don't need you to finish this." She caressed her nipple and brushed her finger over her sensitive trigger point, right above where he was sliding back and forth. She was so close, so very close….

His hold on her bottom tightened, and with a groan he plunged deep, pinning her finger in place. In an instant, she climaxed, hotly, loudly, wildly. He erupted with her, his cries mingling with hers. Her writhing body sent the telephone jangling and crashing to the floor.

And then there was silence, except for the sound of their tortured breathing. When her world stopped spinning, she gradually opened her eyes and gazed up at the ceiling. She'd never had reason to notice the ceiling of her office before. Acoustical tile. Who knew?

She imagined the picture she must make sprawled across her desk, one hand clutching her breast and the other locked between her body and the body of the man whose penis was buried inside her. She must look like the sexual adventurer she'd always wanted to be. Crumpled and smeared papers lay under her and littered the carpet around her desk. Her phone could be broken.

She'd certainly nailed this fantasy.

He stirred. Then slowly he lowered her hips back to the desk and eased her legs down until they were wrapped around his waist. He stayed firmly connected to her, though.

She took her hand from her breast and tilted her head up to look at him just as he slid her other hand from between their joined bodies and lifted it to his lips.

"I'll still give you credit for that one," she murmured.

He glanced at her, a smile curving his handsome mouth. "I'll take credit." He kissed her fingertips. Then he leaned forward and gazed into her eyes. "But the round goes to you. I was so sure you'd tell me your name if I picked the right moment."

She looked into his eyes and sadness erased the aftermath of pleasure. The fantasy was almost over. The way she had it scripted, they would never see each other again. That was for the best. Definitely. Their time together had been perfect. Even the little power struggle at the end had added flavor.

He braced his hands on either side of her and let his gaze roam over her bare breasts. "When does he come back?"

She didn't have to ask who he meant. "It doesn't matter."

He looked into her eyes again. "You plan to marry him, right?"

"I think that's what's going to happen, yes."

"And you're going to be a good and faithful wife until death do you part?"

"Yes." Put that way, it sounded beyond bleak, especially after the past hour.

"Then why not keep up our fantasy game until he comes home? One last chance to be wild before you turn into…whatever you'll be then."

"A grown-up?"

He smiled again, which made the corners of his eyes crinkle. "From here you look pretty damned adult to me." He leaned closer. "So how about it? How many days would we have? Or rather, how many nights?"

She calculated, even though she had no business even thinking about it. Today was Tuesday. Benjamin would be home on Saturday. Three more days and three more nights to experience this incredible rush.

But even thinking Benjamin's name made her feel guilty. She didn't have to worry that he'd ever suspect, though. He would never dream that she was capable of what had just happened in this office. He didn't operate in those terms, as he'd told her. And she hadn't confided her innermost secrets to him.

"Consider it." He dropped a soft kiss on her mouth. "I'm going to disappear for a few minutes. When I come back, we can decide." He slowly withdrew. "Mmm. Sure hated to do that. You feel great."

So did he, and she wasn't happy that he wasn't inside

her anymore. But the fun had to end sometime. "It's not a good idea to continue seeing each other," she said. "The whole point is that we're complete strangers."

"I'll be back in a few minutes." He rustled around picking up his clothes, and then he left the office.

Although she didn't feel the least bit like moving, she forced herself to sit up and slide off the desk. If he planned to reappear all dressed and presentable, she wasn't about to greet him stark naked. The room smelled of sex, and it looked like the set of a porno flick. She loved it. Exactly what she'd been aiming for.

As she pulled on her damp panties and located her bra, she allowed herself to consider, for just a tiny second, having more of this kind of activity. *No*, it would be a mistake. He wouldn't be a stranger any more, and they'd never have as much fun as they'd had tonight. Tonight could never be equaled, let alone improved upon.

She stepped into her skirt and pulled it up over her hips. No point in bothering with the garter belt and stockings. She was just zipping the skirt, her back to the door, when he cleared his throat behind her.

"Maybe I should wait for you in the reception area. One look at you half-naked, and I'm ready to beg."

She turned, her heart pounding in spite of her efforts to stay calm and rational about this now that it was over. No man had ever begged her for sex. With Benjamin, she was the one more likely to do the begging.

He stared at her, hunger in his eyes. "God, you're beautiful."

This was what she'd needed from Benjamin—a little sexual desperation. Yet that wasn't fair. She'd never given him a reason to be desperate.

She cleared her throat. "I'll...I'll meet you in the reception area."

He nodded, raked her with one more hot glance, and walked out the door.

She continued to dress, all the while reminding herself that she'd achieved her goal. By cutting the contact now, she could guarantee that this would be an isolated incident. Any more liaisons, and things could get messy.

Yet his intensity made her feel wanted in a way Benjamin never had. She remembered trying to tease Benjamin, pretending that she wasn't sure if she felt like handing out the sexual goods. She'd wanted to stir him up, wanted to see his need. He'd turned away, telling her he didn't play those games.

But this man would play. She finished dressing and straightened her office, shoving the smeared notes in a bottom drawer of her desk. She'd come in early in the morning and finish her work. Right now she had to figure out what the hell to do. Maybe her preoccupation with sexual fantasy only showed that she was still immature. For someone past thirty, that was embarrassing.

Putting on her navy suit jacket and grabbing her briefcase, she shut off the lights and walked toward the reception area. Déjà vu. He was on his knees working with the wiring, exactly as if nothing had happened between them.

But the look in his eyes was about four hundred degrees hotter than it had been when he'd glanced up at her an hour ago. All she had to do was say the word, and he'd go along with another three nights of fantasy sex.

But life wasn't about fantasy sex, and she knew it. Life meant sharing a mortgage with a good guy, giving her mother and dad some grandkids, having the neighbors over for a Superbowl party. Except for the little problem twenty years ago, that described her parents' life, and they still had each other, still had someone to grow old with. She yearned for that kind of security.

She wouldn't move a single step closer to adulthood by hanging out with this hottie for another three nights in a going-nowhere relationship centered totally on sex. "The answer is no," she said quietly. "I'm sorry."

Expectation died in his eyes. "So am I. I think we're good together."

"We were." She deliberately put it in the past tense to keep herself grounded in reality. "And that was the idea—a perfect sexual fantasy that began and ended tonight."

He sat back on his heels and nodded. "Yeah, I knew that was your plan, but if your boyfriend isn't due back for a few days, I'd love to spend that time with you."

"You don't have a girlfriend?" She shouldn't be asking questions like that, which only prolonged the conversation. But she couldn't help wondering.

"If I did, I wouldn't have accepted your invitation in the first place."

As that statement sank in, she flushed. The implication was obvious. He believed in fidelity, but she'd been willing to have a fling while the guy she was dating was out of the country.

She went on the defensive. "Look, I've never promised Benjamin that I wouldn't see other—"

"Hey, I wasn't judging you." He rose to his feet. "Not by a long shot. I don't know what kind of understanding you have with this guy."

"There is no understanding…yet." She'd been very careful about that, wanting to leave the door open for exactly what had happened tonight.

Yet she hadn't dated anyone else recently. Benjamin might assume that they had an understanding, which meant she'd been guilty of misleading the witness.

After all, she and Benjamin had a sexual relationship, such as it was. Some people thought that constituted an agreement. It might have, if the sex had been more exciting. Maybe once they moved in together, Benjamin would relax and have fun in bed.

Her fantasy man searched her expression. "But you expect there will be an understanding once he comes back, right?"

She nodded.

"That leaves you all of three nights to be a wild and crazy single girl." He smiled gently. "Why waste them?"

Tempted by that smile, she tried to hold on to her arguments for not doing it. "For one thing, we'd have to destroy the anonymous nature of our—"

"Shane Nichols."

She blinked. "Wh-what?"

"My name is Shane Nichols. I want you to know that. And yes, my parents are huge Alan Ladd fans, especially my dad. I was named after the character in the movie. Everybody gets around to asking sooner or later, so I'll answer that one up front. I don't even wince when somebody starts calling *Shaaane! Come back, Shaaane.* Feel free to do that if it gives you a chuckle."

Now her fantasy man had a name, one she wasn't likely to forget. As she'd known it would, the atmosphere between them changed immediately. Instead of an anonymous sexual partner, he was a guy with parents who loved an old movie enough to name him after the main character. She'd probably like his parents.

"And you're either Eileen or Mildred. I'm going with Eileen."

She felt like the person who'd just been found in a game of hide and seek. "How did you come up with that?"

He glanced at the receptionist's phone. "Psychic."

Well, of course. She should have realized he'd check the names on the labels next to each office line. She and Mildred were the only two women listed, and not many women her age were named Mildred.

She took a deep breath. No point in continuing the anonymity any longer. He'd be able to find out her last name without a whole lot of difficulty. "Eileen Connelly," she said.

He held out his hand, his gaze warm. "Pleased to meet you, Eileen."

She looked down at his outstretched hand and remembered all the interesting things he'd been doing with it recently. Her body remembered, too, and was reminding her of how much she'd liked what he'd done. Refusing to shake hands because she was afraid it would turn her on seemed childish, so she put her hand in his.

His handshake was firm and brief. "There. Was that so hard to do?"

Yes. "I didn't intend us to become—"

"I know that. I completely understand your original intent. I'm just asking you to expand your concept."

Her hand still tingled, and she tucked it in the pocket of her suit jacket. "And if I say no?"

Soft regret gleamed in his eyes. "Then I'll say goodbye, Eileen Connelly. And thank you for one of the most exciting...no, *the* most exciting night of my life. It's been an honor."

She looked into his eyes and felt her resolve slipping away. No one would have to know, especially Benjamin. She'd keep it to herself. Her mother had invited her for dinner this week, thinking she'd be lonesome without Benjamin, but she could get out of that. She wouldn't even confide in Suz or Courtney. Total secrecy would be the only way to go on something as reckless as this.

"You really have nothing to lose but a little time," he murmured. "You've already made the decision to experiment while your boyfriend's gone. Three more nights of experimentation will give you more memories to get you through the years of matrimony.''

''You make it sound like I don't want to get married. I do.''

''To this guy?''

She hesitated only a fraction of a second. ''Yes.''

''Okay.'' He looked at her as if he didn't believe it. ''But why not have some fun between now and Saturday? Meet me again tomorrow night.''

She had to remember that seeing him again could be a fantasy-killer. That was one of the risks. ''It wouldn't be the same as tonight. This was—''

''I should hope it wouldn't be the same! Been there, done that. Time for a new fantasy.'' He paused. ''Ever wanted to do it on the rooftop of a downtown office building at night?''

Her pulse leaped at the idea. Talk about a Batman-style adventure.

He smiled. ''I think that turns you on. Your eyes are going all dark and stormy again.''

''Again?'' Her response sounded husky and intimate.

''The way they were in your office, when I was—''

''Never mind.'' She couldn't let him go into detail or she'd be over there ripping at his clothes. ''I get the picture.''

''Do you? Do you see us up on that roof, with the city around us and the night sky above? It's still warm this time of year…you wouldn't get cold, no matter how much clothing you took off. Or I took off you.''

Heart pounding, she searched for the strength to resist the temptation he offered. She also wondered if he was throwing out ideas without considering the logistics. ''If you were thinking of this building, I have no idea how you'd access the roof.''

''Not this building. It's only four stories. Something higher. And you can leave that to me. I install telephone systems for a living. I can certainly arrange access to a suitable roof.''

She was getting hotter by the second. ''You've thought of this before?''

''Sure. Just never had a woman wild and sexy enough to do it with.''

Reaction zinged through her, making her throb in anticipation. He *was* her fantasy man, somebody who loved this kind of adventure. Apparently he was as immature as she was in that regard. ''I'm insane for even considering such a thing.''

''Come on, Eileen. You're the one who started this. Don't back out now. I'll pick you up in a company van out in front of this building tomorrow at six. I'll bring takeout and a blanket so we can have a picnic up there, as well as do....'' He paused to grin. ''Each other.''

A man who could tease her about sex. That alone was reason enough to take him up on his proposition. She would probably live to regret this decision, but she would regret even more living the rest of her days without spending three wild nights with Shane Nichols. She swallowed. ''Okay.''

''Okay.'' Excitement shimmered in his expression, but he remained standing quietly, as if waiting for her to make the next move.

''I'm going home now.'' She took a step toward the door.

''And I'll finish the system upgrade.''

''I'm not going to kiss you goodbye.''

''I don't want you to.''

''You don't?''

He shook his head. "What we have going is too hot for little goodbye kisses, and you know it. If you came over here to kiss me goodbye, we'd be rolling on the floor in two seconds."

He was right. She trembled with the urge to go over and unzip those soft denim jeans one more time. Judging from the size of the bulge under his zipper, he wanted that, too.

"Good night," she whispered.

"Good night."

She turned and forced herself to head toward the door.

"Eileen."

She paused, her hand on the knob.

"About tomorrow night…"

Glancing over her shoulder, she saw him standing there, so obviously aroused. Heat sluiced through her. "What about tomorrow night?"

"Skip the underwear, darlin'."

4

SHANE STARED AT THE carved mahogany door after it closed behind Eileen. Then he listened to the click of her heels echoing in the empty tiled hallway leading to the elevator. *Sex on a rooftop?*

He had no idea where he'd come up with that one. He'd had plenty of sexual fantasies, but they'd been pretty much confined to the bedroom. Okay, maybe he'd considered elevator sex, or doing it in an outdoor hot tub.

But on the *roof?* Not consciously. But desperation must have pulled this right out of his subconscious, and thank God for that, because rooftop sex had obviously appealed to her. He had a wild one on his hands.

Well, wasn't that what he'd wanted? Eileen was the answer to his prayers, especially if he could pry her away from her plan to move in with the boyfriend. Logically he should need more time with her before he could possibly know she was the one, but instinct told him that time would only confirm what he already knew in his gut.

She was the woman he'd been waiting for. Maybe working himself to a frazzle all these years had been designed to bring him to this point, face-to-face with Eileen. At the very moment when he needed to add more play in his life, she'd appeared to help him do that.

The ding of the elevator bell, muffled by the closed door, told him she was leaving the building. That was his signal to get this new telephone system hooked up so he could go home, get some rest and figure out what favors he could call in to secure himself a rooftop for tomorrow night.

He'd even told her to skip the underwear. In fact, the command had been, *Skip the underwear, darlin'*. He'd never called a woman darlin' in his life. Apparently she was bringing out his inner rogue. And he liked that.

He glanced over at the dolly stacked with boxed equipment. One of them contained her new phone, which was a good thing after the way her old one had hit the floor. He might as well take her new one in there and hook it up now. That office of hers was calling to him, anyway.

Sorting the boxes on the dolly, he pulled out the one he needed and walked down the carpeted hallway. No light on in her office this time. He stepped through the doorway and hit the switch.

The scent of her perfume mingled with the unmistakable aroma of fresh sex. But she'd cleaned away some of the evidence, stashing the crumpled papers out of sight somewhere so the desk looked neat and official with its calendar blotter and telephone positioned just so. The nameplate hadn't been returned though. She'd known he'd be in here replacing her phone with a new one, but she hadn't known then that he'd already discovered her name.

Walking around behind her desk, he glanced at the calendar blotter. She'd scribbled *Benjamin leaves* and a flight number and time on Monday. Her handwriting was almost as bad as his. Then she'd drawn an arrow across the week, ending with Saturday, when she'd written *Benjamin home* with another flight time and number.

So Shane's arch rival was named Benjamin. Obviously the guy used the whole thing, all three syllables. Damned pompous. Wait a minute. One of the office lines on the receptionist's phone had been labeled Benjamin. The guy worked right here with Eileen.

Shane left Eileen's office and went through the suite flipping on lights and checking nameplates until he found the lair of Benjamin Hobbs, official adversary. The guy had a massive black desk chair and a desk big enough for Ping-Pong. Old Benny could have major desk sex on this baby, if he were so inclined. Shane was betting that he wasn't.

Prowling the perimeter of the room, Shane took inventory of bookshelves with glass doors, English hunting prints, a framed license to practice law in the State of Arizona and a framed diploma from Harvard. The hunting prints were a cliché, but the Harvard sheepskin was impressive.

Aw, geez. On the far wall was a picture of a guy shaking hands with the governor. Had to be Benny. Yep, he'd even had the governor autograph the picture for him. What a suck-up.

Shane took the picture off the wall and studied his competition. Benjamin Hobbs had a symmetrical row of very white teeth, perfectly barbered blond hair and a nicely tailored suit. Plus he had at least a passing acquaintance with the governor. This was the kind of man women loved to bring home to momma. Shane wondered if Eileen's mother was thrilled with the prospect of a Harvard lawyer in the family.

Shane had a business degree from ASU, and although he had a good bottom line, he was still essentially a tradesman. Harvard Law School trumped that by a long shot. Then he reminded himself that despite dating Mr. Great Catch, Eileen had walked into the reception area tonight wanting something more.

He'd do his damned best to give her that something more, which meant coming up with a few dynamite sexual fantasies, starting with the rooftop. He had no idea how he'd conduct this campaign and stay up with everything at Mercury, but he'd have to find a way.

After all, it was only for three days. Once he'd eliminated Benny from the scene, he might be able to ease into a more normal dating routine with Eileen. Or not. Because there was nothing routine about this woman.

AFTER A PEPPERMINT-SCENTED bath, Eileen crawled under the covers of her queen-size bed and slept more soundly than she had in months. It was as if her body had sighed and said *finally*. She dreamed of many orgasms.

Usually she slapped the snooze button a couple of times when her clock radio clicked on, but this morning she scrambled out of bed the minute she heard Shania Twain at 5:00 a.m. What woman could sleep in when she'd decided to spend the whole day without underwear?

She'd made the decision while soaking in her small apartment tub the night before. Sure, she could dress normally and then sneak into the office bathroom to change out of the underwear before going down to meet Shane. But she was in this for the fantasy, and that seemed like the wimpy way.

If Shane could come up with the rooftop suggestion, she could darn sure go through the day without underwear. No way was she going to blink first. This was the most excited she'd been since the time she'd been waitressing at the Violet Oasis and Michael Keaton had walked in. Not in his Batman costume, of course, but still....

She wolfed down some Cocoa Puffs and a cup of instant coffee while standing at the kitchen counter in her Maxine sleep shirt that said Attitude Is Everything. A girl needed her strength for sex on the roof. Fun with sex. She'd always believed it was possible, and now it was happening.

Back in the bedroom, she ran through a few calisthenics.

She hadn't been interested in exercise since the senior George Bush had been president, but now she was thinking about her body image as she never had before. After a short workout, she jumped into the shower for a quick shampoo and another pass over her legs with the razor. The whole concept of getting ready for sex thrilled her. If she had a man like Shane around all the time, she'd invest in regular visits to a spa for waxing, massage and seaweed wraps, just because he would appreciate the results.

Benjamin had told her he thought spa visits were a waste of time and money, which sounded very grown-up. Levelheaded was what her mother had called Benjamin, which was a supreme compliment. In her mother's world, nothing was more important than that.

As her only child, Eileen had worked hard to live up to her mom's expectation that she be levelheaded, too. Law was a levelheaded profession promising good income. In fourth grade she'd dreamed of running off to Hollywood to be in the movies, but then she'd discovered what a messed-up personal life most movie stars had.

Eventually she'd concluded that it wasn't Hollywood she wanted, but the chance to live in a fantasy world once in a while. She considered it a failing, though, and had worked very hard to project levelheadedness. She'd succeeded for years. Shane might be the only person in the world who knew something about her reckless side, although Suz and Courtney were beginning to suspect, what with the white-water rafting and the skydiving gig.

Sorting through the jumble of things in her dresser drawer, she decided on a black lace garter belt and black patterned nylons. When Shane had said to skip the underwear, she didn't think he meant the seductive stuff. Soon she was standing in front of the full-length mirror in her bedroom wearing only the garter belt and stockings, and getting turned on by the idea of Shane seeing her this way on the rooftop.

Phoenix in September felt like late summer anywhere else, so she chose a lightweight black suit that didn't need a blouse underneath. Once she'd buttoned the jacket, she studied herself again in the mirror, trying to determine whether anyone could tell she had no bra on. They couldn't, she decided, unless they were extremely nosy and looked at her for a long time. The people in her office were too busy to be nosy. She'd be fine.

She believed that until she got behind the wheel of her five-speed Toyota and discovered how it felt to zip down the 101 wearing no panties. The word *risky* didn't even begin to describe it. *Stimulating* was a more apt word. As she adjusted to the sensation of working the clutch and the brake pedals while the breeze from the vents swirled up her skirt, she became giddy with the naughtiness of it all.

Good thing nobody was at the office yet, and she'd have a couple of hours to get used to sitting at her desk without underwear. Or maybe there would be no getting used to anything. As soon as she unlocked the door to the suite of offices and turned on the lights in the reception area, her attention went straight to the spot where she'd found Shane kneeling the night before, almost as if she expected to find him there again.

The wheeled dolly with its load of boxes was gone, but she couldn't look at the new phone on the receptionist's desk without remembering...everything. Taking a deep breath, she marched to her office. If she didn't get the information into her computer and printed out by nine, she'd be toast. She had to block Shane out of her mind and get cracking.

Unfortunately, that required pulling out the notes that had become crumpled and smeared during all that wild sex.

With a groan she plopped into her soft leather desk chair, which immediately reminded her of her panty-free state. Maybe this was why Benjamin didn't indulge in fantasies. Fantasies played hell with productivity.

She had a new phone, too, courtesy of the man who could give her multiple orgasms. She picked up the receiver, telling herself she was checking for a dial tone when all she really wanted was to curl her fingers around something he had recently touched.

As she breathed in the smell of fresh plastic, which shouldn't have been an aphrodisiac, a small scrap of paper fluttered to the desk. Still holding the receiver, she picked up the paper and turned it over to read the scrawled message. See you tonight.

Okay, so he had terrible handwriting. So did she. But he'd left a little note for her. She'd always longed for a guy who would leave her little notes. A man with a ton of obligations, like Benjamin, for example, wouldn't have the time. At least that's what she'd told herself. Maybe a phone installer did have the time.

See you tonight. Oh, yes, he would. She squirmed in her chair and replaced the receiver.

The buzz of the phone made her jump. It was definitely her line ringing, so it had to be somebody she knew, somebody who might be making use of the equipment he'd installed the night before to drive her crazy first thing this morning. Lust eddied through her as she picked up the receiver again.

She deliberately pitched her voice low, wanting to sound like a woman who was not wearing panties. "Hello?"

"Hi, sweetie!" her mother sang out. "Do you have a cold?"

Eileen sat up straight and tugged at her skirt, as if her mother had walked into the room and Eileen had to hide the evidence. "Absolutely not, Mom! Just need some more coffee, that's all!" She swivelled her chair to her computer stand and switched on the monitor. There, now she felt more normal, with the program loading. A computer worked whether you were wearing underwear or not.

"Well, now you sound better," her mother said. "I worry that you don't get enough sleep, and I'm sure you're not eating right. That's how you deplete your resources and cripple your immune system, you know."

"I had breakfast this morning." As usual, seconds into the conversation with her mother, she felt like a seven-year-old again. She brought up the screen she needed and started typing in her notes in an effort to feel more like an adult. She wondered how many adults still ate Cocoa Puffs. Probably lots.

"Glad to hear you had breakfast. Most important meal of the day. Listen, I'm calling there because I tried your apartment and got your machine. I figured you'd gone in early to catch up on work."

"You called my apartment at six-thirty in the morning?"

"I had something to say that couldn't be said over dinner."

"Mom, about dinner... I—"

"Never mind that now. Your father's out on the patio doing his Tai Chi, so you and I have a little privacy, which was my plan."

Alarm shot through her. "Is anything wrong?" Maybe she'd never get over that feeling of panic whenever her mother wanted to speak to her privately.

"No, goodness, no. Sorry if I scared you. I just wanted to talk to you about moving in with someone, living with each other, cohabiting, as they say. I wanted to tell you to go ahead."

Eileen's eyes crossed. "Are we by any chance talking about Benjamin?"

"Of course we are! And I finally figured out why you haven't moved in with him. I mean, Courtney lived with that musician for six months last year, although heaven knows what she saw in him, and Suz is—"

"It's not like I do whatever they do, you know."

"Well, no, but by this age, I'm sure you've considered it, and I know why you're holding off."

Because I have to have some fantasy sex first. "Why?"

"You're afraid we'll disapprove." Her mother sounded very proud of her conclusion.

"Mom, that's not why."

"Don't be silly. Of course it is."

Eileen thought about contradicting her again, but then she realized that she could end up having to explain what the real reason was. Not a good idea.

"See there," her mother said. "Your silence speaks volumes. So here's the deal. I'm fine with it, and I'm going to smooth the way with your father."

"Oh, you don't have to do that."

"I think I do, just to make sure he's ready to accept it. We don't want any nasty surprises, like him suddenly turning into a traditionalist who demands a wedding first. Once your father's on board, you can invite us over for dinner."

"Th-thanks." In reality, her dad had influenced her decision not to move in with Benjamin, but not in the way her mother thought. Eileen suspected she was more like her dad than her mom, which meant she needed to sow her wild oats before committing to a man. Otherwise she could end up ten years down the road having an affair and driving a red sports car.

"And there's the economic advantage," her mother added. "It makes no sense to pay rent on two places, and

I know your lease is up soon. So that's why I say, go ahead. Don't let us hold you back.''

"Okay. Thanks for the vote of confidence, Mom.''

"I have every confidence in you, sweetie. As for Benjamin, I'm sure he has his eye on holding office. He'd be perfect for that, and no telling how far he might go.''

"True.'' That had been another thing bothering Eileen. She would hate being a politician's wife, and Benjamin had hinted he had those ambitions. She hadn't said how that idea affected her, because unless they were living together, she really shouldn't offer an opinion.

"Well, your father's finishing up his exercises, so he'll be back in the kitchen any minute. What would you like for dinner tomorrow night?''

"I'm sorry, but I can't make it, after all. Something's come up.'' She controlled a giggle. Something had come up, all right. And she could hardly wait to watch it come up again.

"That's okay. We can move it to Friday night. I know Benjamin won't be back until Saturday, and I hate to think of you eating alone so much.''

Eileen had a sudden insight. Her mother wanted her to get married so she'd have company. Apparently she thought Eileen couldn't possibly be happy living alone, because her mother wouldn't want that for herself. "Friday night won't work, either.''

"Oh? Why not?''

She couldn't believe she was really clearing her calendar for fantasy sex with Shane. "I have a big project I'm working on, and I need to devote my evenings to it so I'll be finished by the time Benjamin gets home.'' There. That was the whole truth and nothing but the truth, even if she hadn't offered any details.

"Oh, sweetie, I can see that Benjamin's rubbing off on

you. You'll be a partner before you know it, with that attitude.''

Now she felt guilty for deliberately misleading her mom.
''I'm not sure about that. But I do need to concentrate on
this project.'' *And after that I'll be the model daughter you
always dreamed of. I promise.*

''That's fine, sweetie. We'll plan to have you and Benjamin over next week. How's that?''

''Perfect.'' Benjamin loved going to her parents' house.
Her mom treated him like royalty. Eileen found it kind of
sickening, but Suz and Courtney constantly reminded her
that if your parents liked your boyfriend, that was a huge
plus.

''Here comes your father. Gotta go. Bye-bye.'' The line
went dead.

Eileen put the receiver back in its cradle and stared at
the phone. Everybody, even Suz and Courtney, thought she
was so lucky to have the attention of a man like Benjamin,
a guy who might even be the frigging *president* some day,
and who wouldn't be excited about that?

Eileen felt like the one out of step, the one who must be
seeing things wrong. But once she had a chance to take all
Shane had to offer for the next three nights, she'd probably
be cured. It would be like the experiment she, Suz and
Courtney had conducted last year, to eat nothing but gooey
doughnuts for two whole days so they'd never want another
one.

That had sort of worked. The craving had gone away for
a long time, but now it was creeping back, at least for
Eileen. Last week she'd almost bought a raised glazed.
Three, instead of two days of doughnuts might have done
the trick though, and she was looking at three solid nights
of sex. She'd never had that much sex in her life. By Sat-

urday, she'd be totally sick of rooftop rendezvous plans and whatever else Shane might come up with.

She wasn't sick of it yet, though. Not even slightly.

THE WHOLE DAY Shane was juggling his work and trying to get an available rooftop, he kept thinking about prom night. He'd had this kind of anticipation then, too. He'd lost his virginity on prom night to a girl who'd also been a blonde. They'd gone steady after that, and, like a lot of seventeen-year-olds, Shane had thought having sex on a regular basis meant you were in love.

When she'd gone off to college in California and met somebody else, he'd discovered it hadn't been love, after all. He didn't kid himself that he'd fallen in love with Eileen, either. But the possibility was there, given enough time. She'd be easy to fall for.

He could already picture taking her home to meet his folks and how excited they'd be for him. Work had kept him from his family, too, and he wanted that to change. With Eileen in the picture, all things seemed possible.

Anticipation hung in the air as he sat in the no parking zone outside her building at five minutes to six. For the second night in a row he'd turned off his cell and his pager. Yes, he felt twinges of guilt and wondered if he'd lose any customers. George Ullman had sounded a little brusque this morning when Shane had called him back.

But he forgot all about his customers when Eileen came through the glass door in her professional little black suit. His usually calm heart started beating the bongos. God, she was beautiful, her cascade of blond hair gleaming in the late afternoon sun. With her sunglasses on and her briefcase slung over her shoulder, she looked every inch a lawyer.

But as she walked toward his van, he thought he detected an extra little jiggle under her jacket. If she'd done it, if she'd really come on this date without underwear, he might fall in love with her tonight. He grinned. A guy would be insane not to fall in love with a woman who would take him up on such a suggestion.

He jumped out of the van and came around to open the door for her. "Hi."

"Hi, yourself." She smiled at him and set her briefcase and purse on the floor of the van.

He caught a whiff of her orange blossom perfume as he helped her up into the van, and, *bam,* he started getting hard. "I didn't think about your car," he said. "Is it okay to leave it in the parking garage? I'll pay the extra charge."

She glanced down at him from the seat of the van. "No problem. You can just bring me back here…later on."

"Right." He had to stop looking at her jacket, but he was dying to know if she'd done as he asked. "Buckle up," he said. Then he closed the door and trotted around to the driver's seat. Trotting with a hard-on wasn't easy.

He climbed into the seat and glanced over at her. "It's not dark enough to go up to the rooftop yet, so I thought first we'd stop in at a little pub near there. It's a cozy place. I think you'll like it."

"All right." She still had that secretive smile on her face.

He couldn't stand it. "So, did you, uh, take my suggestion?"

"As a matter of fact, I did." She clicked her seatbelt buckle into place before looking at him. "It's been quite an interesting day."

His jaw went slack. "You've been that way all day?"

"Why not?" Her smile widened. "Isn't that what you had in mind?"

5

Shane was so rattled that he killed the engine as he started to pull out of the no parking zone. "Sorry," he muttered, and started it again. Then he forced himself to concentrate on traffic. Phoenix in the middle of rush hour was no time to space out, even if the woman sitting next to him was the sexiest, most daring female he'd ever met.

"So is this the van you drive for work every day?" Eileen asked.

"Actually, no. My buddy Lou usually drives this one. But he's taking a week off because his wife had her first baby." And he suddenly realized he was jealous as hell of Lou, who'd found a woman he loved and who now had a daughter. "Lou might even take next week off, too." Shane had decided to use the situation as his cover story if Eileen should happen to ask him about work. He wanted her to keep thinking he was only an installer.

First of all, the professional woman making it with the blue-collar guy was probably part of her fantasy. Second, he wanted to win her over because she was crazy about him and didn't care about his position in life. Stupid, no doubt, but that was the way he'd decided to play this little drama. If she ended up choosing Benny for his prospects, then she wasn't his dream girl.

"I think it's great that your company gives a man time off when his wife has a baby," Eileen said. "Whoever runs it must be a good boss."

Shane smiled at that. "He's okay, I guess, as bosses go."

"You don't like him?"

"I like him okay. But he sure works me hard. I had to move heaven and earth to make sure I wouldn't have any overtime this week."

"Well, that's because your friend's home with his wife, so your boss is short-handed, right? Listen, Shane, I would feel terrible if you got into a hassle with your boss because you were clearing time for me."

Shane stopped at a light. "Hey, it's good for the boss to know I have a life. He never seems to remember that, and I'm a sucker for working whenever he needs the extra help. It's a bad pattern to get into."

"I suppose, but jobs aren't that easy to come by these days."

"Don't worry. I won't lose my job." Even if that's what he longed to do. He'd tackled his packed schedule with gusto this morning, canceling meetings he'd once thought critical. Then he'd shocked his secretary Rhonda by giving her a stack of trade journals he usually read himself and asking her to skim through them and write him a report. He'd used the extra time to arrange for the rooftop escapade.

Amazing how the prospect of great sex could motivate him to change his ways, at least for this week. Tomorrow he'd see what else he could eliminate from the daily grind. He also have to think up another fantasy scenario, but he wasn't worried about that. His brain was being fed by his libido, and the result was energized dude. He hadn't felt this alive in years.

Near the Irish pub he'd chosen as a little teaser before the main event, a parking space opened up as if by magic when they arrived. When it was right, it was right.

"Looks cute," she said. "And I'm even Irish, if you go back a couple of generations."

"So I figured." He slid the van into the parallel parking spot in one pass and hopped out. "Let me help you down. It's a high step."

She laughed. "And we wouldn't want my skirt to hike up, now would we?"

He gazed across the seat at her. "You are something else, you know that?"

"Don't get the wrong idea. I'm not usually this uninhibited."

"A damned shame."

NOT REALLY, EILEEN thought as she eased carefully from the high seat while keeping a grip on the hem of her skirt. If she allowed her fantasy life to take over, she'd never make partner at Traynor and Sizemore. This morning she'd finished her work by nine, but just barely. And her production for the rest of the day had been way off.

Fortunately, people in the office blamed her distracted behavior on Benjamin's absence. She'd let them think that was the reason, even though she felt guilty about it. All day she'd deliberately avoided glancing into his empty office.

She'd halfway expected him to call her by now, and she'd been dreading it. For some reason he hadn't called yet, and she was happy about that. Maybe she'd be lucky enough to be gone when he finally decided to check in.

In three days she'd have her act together. She'd have ended this wild relationship and would be ready to give him the answer he wanted, the answer even her mother wanted. But for these three days, she was going to pretend to be some sex kitten out of a racy French movie.

She grabbed her shoulder bag from the floor of the van

and waited while Shane locked the vehicle. Once he'd pocketed the keys, he took her hand as they walked into the pub, sliding his fingers through hers as if he'd been doing it forever. The gesture was more companionable than proprietary, a link between equals heading out to have some fun.

Benjamin had a bad habit of steering her in the direction he wanted to go, as if she were a grocery cart he was forced to maneuver through a crowd. She'd never realized how much she disliked it until now, when she could see the difference between his way and Shane's.

And that was the last thought she'd devote to Benjamin, she decided as they found a small table in a corner and Shane pulled out a chair for her. This night wasn't about Benjamin. It was about a sexual adventure totally removed from her normal life.

"I know your boyfriend's Benjamin Hobbs," Shane said as he sat down across from her at the table.

She nearly fainted on the spot. "You *know* him?" Now there was a nightmare in the making! She'd never been to this pub, but now she glanced around, afraid she'd see a familiar face. She recognized no one, but her pulse raced anyway.

"No, I don't know him." Shane caught her hand and squeezed it. "Settle down, there. You look like you've been mugged. I didn't mean to scare you."

She managed a laugh, as if he hadn't just taken ten years off her life. "I suppose it wouldn't matter. It's not like I don't trust you to keep quiet."

"In point of fact, you don't have much to go on regarding my character. For all you know—" He paused and glanced up as a waiter appeared. "Irish coffee on ice for me," he said before turning toward Eileen. "How about you?"

"That sounds perfect. Make it two."

The waiter nodded and headed back toward the bar.

"I usually drink Guinness when I come here," Shane said, "but that seemed a little heavy for..."

She looked into his green eyes and thought about the rooftop. Her nipples tightened under her proper black suit. "Probably so," she murmured.

He leaned closer. "I'm going wild thinking about you sitting here looking so pulled together, and yet underneath—"

"Underneath I'm going wild, too."

He tightened his grip on her hand. "Good. That was part of my plan, that we'd have a drink together and build a little anticipation."

"You haven't been anticipating all day?"

"I've been anticipating ever since last night, when you walked into the reception area of Traynor and Sizemore."

"So have I." She could barely believe that she was sitting here with him, and that soon they would be taking off their clothes and launching into another incredible sexual experience.

"About knowing Benjamin's name," he said, "let me explain. I looked at the calendar on your desk when I was installing your phone. I made the assumption that Benjamin was the same Benjamin who works down the hall."

"He is." She noticed that Shane had a small mole on his left cheek and she had the strongest urge to lean over and kiss it. Maybe that wasn't wise. The hand-holding could be explained if anybody should recognize her. Shane could simply be an old friend going through a rough time. But a seductive kiss on the cheek was something else again.

"I thought I'd tell you that I'd figured out his name, so you wouldn't have to worry if you let it slip sometime."

"Like when?" she said, startled.

"Oh, I don't know. During conversation."

She lowered her voice. "I thought you might mean during sex."

Shane opened his mouth to reply just as the waiter arrived with their drinks. After the waiter deposited the drinks and left, Shane locked his gaze with Eileen's. "Trust me on this one," he murmured. "When we have sex, the only name you'll call out will be mine."

As she absorbed the intensity in his eyes, she quivered with excitement. She had to agree with him. There was zero chance she'd confuse Shane with Benjamin.

He picked up his glass mug of Irish coffee and licked off some of the whipped cream. Then he looked over at her, his eyes sparkling. "So let's talk. Do any of your fantasies involve food?"

"Um, maybe." She'd never told anyone the hot scenes that played in her mind, so telling Shane wasn't all that easy. To buy some time, she sipped her drink.

The cool whipped cream tickled her mouth and made her think of kissing him. She desperately wanted to do that. He had a great mouth, and the fullness of his lower lip made her long to nibble it.

Shane watched her and smiled. "Whipped cream's definitely on my list."

Something he'd said earlier niggled at her, and she decided to get it out in the open. "Before I tell you what's on my list, let's talk about that statement you made about me not having much to go on regarding your character."

He laughed. "I am definitely out with a lawyer tonight. Who else would have circled back to that?"

"Well, you did say it." She took another swallow of her drink.

"Sure did." He lifted their clasped hands and kissed her fingertips. "And it's true. You already know I'm the kind of guy who'll agree to have sex when he's supposed to be installing telephones. That doesn't speak particularly well of me.''

''So therefore I shouldn't trust you?''

''Fortunately you can trust me completely, but based on the evidence you have, I'm not sure you should.'' He blew out a breath. ''That was a huge chance you took last night.''

She bristled. ''You're not going to lecture me, are you?''

''No. I'm hardly in a position to do that. I'm just glad it was me you ended up with.''

''I knew it was a risky fantasy,'' she said. ''That's why I've waited so long, and why I discarded everyone I came up with. But then, when I walked into the outer office, and there you were, it seemed like…like fate or something.''

He held her gaze for a moment. ''Yeah, I think it was.''

The warmth in his eyes held more affection than lust, which threw her off balance, partly because she could feel herself responding to that affection. She hadn't factored those soft emotions into this experience, which was supposed to be all about sex. She picked up her drink to end the moment. ''So I can trust you to keep the secret?''

''Of course. Aside from giving my word, you have some leverage. If I let this get around, it could end up damaging me as much as you, and it could also hurt Mercury.''

''See, you do have some loyalty to the company. I'll bet that's because your boss is a great guy.''

''He has his moments.''

''But you wouldn't want him to find out what you were doing on top of my desk.''

''Mmm.'' Shane took a long swallow of his drink. Then he set down his mug and grinned. ''Remember that old episode of 'Seinfeld,' where George tells his boss that if the company manual had listed having sex with the maid on the desk as a no-no, then he definitely wouldn't have done it?''

''Yes! I loved that scene!'' She smiled at him. ''So you used to watch 'Seinfeld?'''

''Sure. That was before I got so busy with Mercury. Lately I'm lucky to catch the news.'' He swirled the contents of his mug. ''I need to thank you for giving me a reason to take some time off.''

''So what did you tell your boss?''

He looked into her eyes. ''That I had some urgent personal business that would occupy me for the next three nights.''

''Sounds like my excuse. My mother had planned on me coming to dinner tomorrow night. I told her I had a big project I was working on. She thinks it has to do with the firm.''

''It does.'' He leaned closer. ''The firm thrust of my cock into your—''

''Shane!'' She blushed, but the sexy words had an immediate effect, making her grow achy, moist and ready for exactly what he'd described. ''I can't believe you said that in a public place.''

He laughed. ''Have you checked out the noise level in this bar? Nobody can hear me. And you should see your eyes. You loved hearing that.''

''Maybe,'' she admitted.

Reaching out, he caressed her cheek and rubbed his thumb over her lower lip. ''That's what the next three days are all about, exploring things we've never had the nerve to try before.'' He traced a line down her throat to the first button of her suit. ''I've never said that to a woman in public before, but I wanted to say it now. I wanted to find out how you'd react.''

She trembled. "What if I'd been so insulted that I'd dumped my drink all over you?"

"I would have known you're not into that kind of fantasy." He fingered the button on her suit. "But I think you are." He came closer and his voice dropped to a whisper. "I can hardly wait to unbutton this. I still remember what your nipples feel like against my tongue. I've been thinking about it all day."

She was shaking so much that she put down her drink, afraid she'd spill it.

"You know what else I've been thinking about?" he murmured.

She shook her head, not trusting her voice, either.

"You going down on me."

She made a noise low in her throat. She'd thought of it, too. They hadn't gotten around to that in her office, but she wanted to remedy that oversight on the rooftop. She'd sat at her desk today, staring out the window while she pictured herself on her knees under the wide night sky, driving Shane crazy.

"Oh, God, don't lick your lips like that," he said. "I might come right here."

She hadn't even realized she'd been doing it.

"Finish your drink," he said. "Or not. Either way, I think we need to get out of here."

"Me, too."

"Then you're ready?"

She smiled at his choice of words. "Uh-huh."

"Now I'm so hard I may not be able to stand up and walk outside."

Knowing she had such power made her bolder. "If you'd picked a place with tablecloths, I could have taken care of you before we left."

His breathing became more labored. "Is that something you want to try another time?"

"You'd let me do that?"

His hot gaze raked over her. "Oh, yeah, I would let you do that. Now how about if you sit quietly while I get this problem under control? I'm going to pretend you're my Aunt Nelda."

She laughed. "Whatever it takes."

"She's the fiercest woman I know. I spent two weeks at her house every summer as a kid, and whenever she caught me goofing around, she could wither me with a look. And right now I'm in need of some withering."

"Right." She understood perfectly. She'd been in trouble a lot as a young kid, herself. How incredible that she and Shane were so in tune. She felt as if someone had flung open a treasure chest of possibilities. Shane was willing to be her coconspirator, her fellow adventurer. She wondered if three nights would be enough. But, of course, it had to be.

"Okay, I'm ready to head out the door, now." Shane pushed back his chair, stood and came over to help her up. "We have to get the picnic basket from the van, and then it's a short walk to the building where I've arranged for us to spend some time on the roof without being disturbed."

"Sounds wonderful." Eileen felt all warm and moist just thinking about being alone with him in such an unusual setting. But when he pulled a couple of bills out of his wallet, she woke up from her sensual fog. Expecting him to pay for everything was ridiculous. He'd already bought them a picnic supper to take along, and now she was letting him buy drinks.

She put her hand on his arm. "Let me get the drinks." Unsnapping her purse, she took out her wallet.

"Nope." He shook his head and put his money on the

table. "I'm the one who talked you into stretching this into another three nights together."

"But that doesn't mean you're obligated to pay for everything. I don't believe in that. Especially when..." She stopped herself before saying *especially when I have a better job.* She didn't know how their salaries would match up, but she'd probably come out ahead, and her prospects for the future were greater than his. But he wouldn't appreciate having her point that out.

"Especially when I don't have as much money as you?" he said quietly.

She looked into his eyes and could have kicked herself for even broaching the subject. He'd guessed what she'd been about to say, even without her saying it. And he'd guessed right. Now she'd wounded his pride.

"I'm sorry," she said. "I didn't mean it like that. I'm trying to be fair, that's all."

He angled his head toward the door. "C'mon outside with me. I think we need to talk about this."

"Okay." His response intrigued her. She couldn't remember the last time a guy had suggested talking something out. Usually the men she'd known got grumpy and pulled away.

They walked to the van and he unlocked the back doors. The van was filled with phone equipment boxes and tools, but right by the back door sat a wicker basket and a sturdy-looking burgundy quilt. Thinking about his plans for the quilt made her hope that she hadn't offended him to the point that he'd cancel their evening together.

Apparently not, because he took out the hamper. "Want to carry the quilt?"

"Sure." Giddy with relief, she stepped off the curb and moved past him to pick it up. When she turned, he'd set the basket on the pavement and moved in front of her, effectively caging her there.

"Before we go…" He swept a glance over her, his attention lingering on the quilt. When he looked into her eyes, his were smoldering with lust. "Maybe it doesn't matter."

She took a shaky breath. "No, tell me."

He hesitated, obviously considering his words. Finally he gave her a lazy smile. "Just wanted to know if this fantasy of yours is all tied in with tool belts and guys who make a living with their hands. Because if that's the way it is, I can play to that. You know, make it better for you."

She had the definite feeling he'd been about to say something else. He'd invited her out there to talk about the money issue, and he might want to know if she thought they weren't social equals because of his blue-collar status. She didn't give a damn about such things. Besides, for a three-day fling, it shouldn't be a problem anyway. He might be thinking beyond a three-day fling, though, and that worried her.

It worried her because she'd thought of it too and, wow, would that louse up her life but good. Or would it? A girl could get very confused looking into those gorgeous green eyes of his. And very, very hot.

6

SHANE DIDN'T KID HIMSELF that he'd covered his tracks with Eileen. From her expression, he could tell that she knew what he was really asking. He hadn't meant to give himself away like that. They weren't far enough along in the relationship for him to test her snob factor.

And women did have fantasies about guys who labored for a living. He'd wasn't oblivious to that. He'd seen calendars in the bookstore featuring construction workers in tight T-shirts. For that very reason, he'd decided to wear one tonight he'd accidentally washed in hot water.

She cleared her throat. "Okay, I'll admit when I first saw you, with the tool belt on and the power screwdriver in your hand, that played into one of my fantasies."

"Want me to wear it now?"

She gave him a slow once-over. "You're enough fantasy for me, all by yourself."

Right answer. He'd take it, even enjoy it. If they'd moved beyond the concept of a blue-collar guy getting it on with a professional chick, he'd be very happy. As an initial fantasy, if that's what had convinced her to try him on for size, he could live with that. Happily-ever-afters had many different beginnings.

"Let's go, then," he said softly, moving aside so she could step up on the curb again. He locked the van and joined her there, sliding his fingers through hers as they headed toward the building he'd picked out for this fantasy.

Phoenix wasn't known for its high rises, but fortunately he was good friends with the owner of this one, which stood at a respectable twenty-five stories. It was home to title companies, accounting firms and real estate offices, but no lawyers. He'd checked, trying to reduce the odds that Eileen would run into a colleague.

At this hour, though, the chances of that were slim. That's why he'd suggested having a drink in his favorite pub first. They'd killed some time and he'd been able to enjoy the thought of Eileen sitting there wearing only a suit, garter belt and stockings.

He was guessing about the garter belt, but he didn't think she'd choose pantyhose for tonight, and he could see she was wearing nylons of some sort. Thinking about her garter belt was interfering with his stride, so he put it out of his mind. They had a lobby to navigate and an elevator to ride before he could give in to his lust.

They reached the revolving door leading to the building's entrance. "This is it," he said. "Ever been here?"

"Not that I can remember."

"When we get inside, you can read the list of tenants to see if you've had dealings with any of them, in case that makes you nervous."

She glanced at him. "What if it does make me nervous?"

"I don't know. I guess we scrap the plan and go for something else."

Tilting her head, she looked up the side of the building to the top floor. The sky above was shades of pink. Soon it would be twilight, then dark. "I couldn't bear to scrap the plan," she said.

"Yeah, but you don't want to take a chance on somebody recognizing you." He almost wished she would take that chance, because then she'd have to tell Benjamin about him. He longed for the day when she told Benjamin.

"What are the odds that will happen?" She tugged him toward the entrance. "Let's go in and head straight for the elevators."

"If you say so. You go through first. Those pie-shaped spaces in a revolving door don't usually hold——"

"Sure they will."

And before he could stop her, she'd coaxed him in beside her. Mashed together, which he happened to like a lot, they took quick baby steps until they were both flung, laughing, into the small lobby, which was fortunately empty.

"That was fun." Her grin was saucy. "I wonder if it's possible to do it in a revolving door?"

"A few more revolutions and I might have been able to answer that. You were pressed up against me so tight that I——" He paused as the elevator opened. Eileen had her back to it, but he had a perfect view. "Two women in business suits just came out of the elevator," he said in a low voice. "Don't turn around. Just act as though standing here with a basket and a blanket is perfectly normal."

Eileen laughed. "You're too funny. I really don't care what they——"

"Eileen?" called out one of the women, a stylish brunette. "Eileen Connelly, is that you?"

Shock widened her eyes. *No way,* she mouthed to Shane. Then she composed herself and turned, pretending great enthusiasm. "Miranda! Fancy meeting you here."

"I'm closing the sale on the condo," the brunette said. "And my Realtor's office is upstairs." She gestured to the redhead standing next to her. "This is my decorator, Sheri Anderson. We're headed to her shop to finalize the choice of window treatments. Sheri, Eileen's my neighbor at the apartment complex."

Worried for Eileen, Shane tried desperately to think of a story that would explain why she was in the lobby of this building clutching a quilt, accompanied by a man holding a wicker picnic basket. He drew a blank.

"What a coincidence," Eileen said. "Here you are buying a new home, and Shane and I are delivering supplies for the homeless. Small world, huh?"

Shane was impressed with Eileen's quick thinking.

"Very small world." Miranda looked extremely curious.

Eileen, on the other hand, appeared cool as a frosted margarita. "Shane Nichols, this is Miranda Jarvis. Major congrats on the condo, by the way. That sounds exciting."

Shane smiled at Miranda and Sheri and tried to look like a humanitarian.

"Thanks," Miranda said. "I can hardly wait to move in, especially with all the fabulous ideas Sheri has for the place." She continued to stare at the quilt and the picnic basket. "So where are you delivering these supplies?"

"We think the office is in this building, but we may have the address wrong." Shane decided he needed to do his part to get this story airborne. "I was working at Traynor and Sizemore upgrading the phone system, and Eileen and I got to talking about the homeless problem. Like I said, we may have the wrong address."

"I haven't heard of anybody in the building taking donations," Sheri said. "But it's possible. Do you have a name?"

"The Roof Foundation," Eileen said.

Sheri shook her head. "I don't think they're here, but they might have moved in recently. It's a big building. The directory's right over there." She gestured toward the far wall.

"Right," Shane said. "We were on our way to check that."

"Well, it's all very commendable." Miranda still looked unconvinced. She kept glancing at Shane, as if trying to figure his angle. Finally she turned to face Eileen. "So, how's that great guy of yours?"

"Benjamin? He's just fine," Eileen said. "I'll tell him you said hello."

"By all means. I take it he isn't involved with this project?"

"He's just so incredibly busy," Eileen said. "No time for it."

"I can believe that. Very few men have his kind of drive to succeed. Well, we'd better be off. Good luck with finding the right office. Nice meeting you, Shawn."

Shane didn't bother to correct her. "Same here." He stood next to Eileen as the two women went through the revolving door, each in her own wedge of space. He had no idea how Eileen would react to meeting a person she knew, especially a person who obviously suspected something was going on. Miranda and Sheri might have doused his hot plans for a night of lust on the roof.

He had to leave it up to Eileen. She was the one who didn't want anyone to know about their sexual escapades. He wouldn't care who found out. "What now?"

She turned to him, her blue eyes bright with mischief. "Now we get on that darned elevator and zip to the top floor as fast as we can go, before we run into any other nosy people!"

MIRANDA JARVIS. Wouldn't you just know. As they rode the empty elevator hand in hand to the twenty-fifth floor, Eileen wondered if she'd looked as guilty as she'd felt standing down in the lobby with no underwear on and her new lover beside her. No doubt about it, Miranda had been suspicious.

Miranda would also love to drop a few casual comments

to Benjamin about this, if given half a chance. Knowing her, she might even make sure she had the chance by looking for some excuse to come to the Traynor and Sizemore offices. She had plenty of motivation, having coveted Benjamin ever since she'd met him in the parking lot of Eileen's apartment building about three months ago.

After that, every time Eileen had crossed paths with her, Miranda had mentioned what a terrific guy she thought Benjamin was, and how lucky Eileen was to date him. Miranda wasn't the only one with that opinion, but she was the only one frog-green with envy.

"Think she'll tell?" Shane asked as the elevator slipped past the twentieth floor.

"She might. She wants him."

"I could see that. Can you do any damage control before Saturday?"

As she turned to gaze at him, she realized it didn't matter if Miranda spilled everything she knew. "You know what? Benjamin would believe that I was carrying this quilt to donate to the homeless, although he might think it was a dumb idea. In his wildest dreams, he wouldn't imagine that a quilt and a picnic basketful of food equaled an orgy on the roof. Miranda might be wondering what we're up to, but Benjamin doesn't think in terms of sexual adventure."

"Okay. That's good, I guess." As he looked at her, a question lurked in his eyes.

"What?"

"I'm just wondering…oh, never mind. It's none of my business."

She could guess what he was wondering—why she was considering moving in with a guy who had very little imagination when it came to sex. But there was so much more to consider than that. Benjamin was the kind of man she'd always imagined that she'd marry. Her mom liked him, probably because they had similar personalities. He was steady, which would keep Eileen's reckless streak in check the same way her mom had kept her dad from going overboard.

Benjamin reminded her of a dependable green minivan with plenty of luxury features. Shane was a red, two-seater sports car, fun for a short distance, but not what a grown-up woman needed for the long haul. Maybe it was unfair, but even Shane's cooperation with her fantasies made her doubt he'd settle happily into marriage with anyone. He might crave constant excitement, and that was tough to pull off when you had kids in the house and in-laws popping over for a visit.

The elevator opened on the twenty-fifth floor.

"Almost there," Shane said. "But you can still back out."

She laughed and started out of the elevator. "After running around all day half-dressed? Not on your life."

"Do you want food first, or...."

Immediately a rush of moisture dampened her thighs, and her sensitive nipples recorded the rub of the black suit jacket. She wanted it off. And she wanted everything he could give her. "I want the *or* part," she said. "It's been a really long day."

"No kidding." He grinned at her as they headed toward the exit door at the end of the hall. "I like how you think."

She was ready to stop thinking completely and slip into a world of pure sensation. "Have you been up here before?"

"Today. To check it out." He pushed the release bar that opened the metal door and his shoulder muscles bunched under the snug T-shirt.

Eileen noticed. She was tuned in to every movement he

made. "What were you checking out?" She followed him into a small stairwell. "Isn't a roof a roof?"

He led her up a short flight of cement steps to another door. "Oh, this is a generic roof, but I wanted to check out sight lines. I wanted us to be able to see the city, but I didn't want the city to be able to see us." He glanced at her. "Maybe I should have asked if you were into that."

She laughed. "You mean exhibitionism? Not really. Taking a risk on being caught is one thing. Putting on a show deliberately isn't my idea of adventure."

He smiled. "Good. Mine, either." He pushed open the second door and they stepped onto a spongy white coating that covered the roof.

A twilight sky arched over them, with Venus and Mars already winking against a background of navy blue. Beyond the three-foot-high parapet, the horizon glowed brick red with the last traces of the sunset.

A large air-conditioning unit in the center of the roof hummed steadily, sending a slight vibration through the soles of her black heels. As the vibration made its subtle way through her body, teasing her with possibilities, she glanced over at Shane. "The air conditioner is a nice touch."

He grinned. "I should have known you'd love it. Most women want mood music, but you crave a giant machine that makes the floor quiver."

"The sculptures aren't bad, either." She gazed at the large venting pipes spaced at intervals over the roof, some of them taller than she was and almost as big around. "Shall I guess what they represent?"

Shane's grin widened. Then he lifted his face to the sky. "Thank you, God. Finally a woman who sees everything in sexual terms, just like me."

"You don't think I'm weird?"

"I think you're wonderful." He set down the picnic basket. "Better take a look at the scenery while you still can. I have a feeling that soon you won't care about the view."

"You are so right." She put down the quilt and walked over to the parapet. The city sprawled in all directions, right up to the flanks of the surrounding mountains. As the sky darkened, the landscape seemed to sparkle with pirate's treasure, complete with long necklaces of diamonds and rubies.

But as beautiful as the view was becoming, she wasn't here to gape at pretty lights. Because Shane had mentioned it, she glanced around at the neighboring buildings and discovered that the close ones weren't tall enough to give anyone a view of what happened here. Shane had chosen well.

Out of habit, she looked toward downtown and picked out Bank One Ballpark, where the lights were on and the sliding roof was open to the night sky. "The D'Backs are playing tonight," she murmured. Next season she'd be there sitting next to Benjamin in their assigned seats, probably engaged to be married. She wished that she felt more excited about that and less excited about what was about to happen on this roof.

"Would you rather be over there?"

She turned to him and discovered that he'd spread out the quilt not far from the air-conditioning unit, as if to maximize the quivering sensation. He definitely understood her. "No," she said. "Would you?"

"There's nowhere on earth I'd rather be than right here." His gaze was hot as he focused all his attention on her.

She absorbed that intensity the way a parched plant soaks up water. "Me, either."

"Come over here, Eileen."

To think that the night before, she hadn't wanted him to know her name. Hearing him say it now spiked her arousal and left her breathless. She walked toward him across the resilient surface. "I thought the roof would be hard."

He held her gaze. "You mean like your desk? Is that what you need to—?"

"No, of course not."

"Or maybe you don't want to admit that anything resembling a mattress is boring to you?" He stepped toward her, fire in his eyes. "Or that unusual positions up against unyielding objects make you come even faster?"

Her breathing grew shallow as she ran her tongue over her lower lip. No man had ever talked to her like this. She loved it.

"Maybe we should save the quilt for the picnic." He circled her waist with strong hands and backed her up against the metal trunk of an exhaust vent. "What do you think?"

Her heart thudded rapidly as she reached back with both hands to steady herself, pressing her palms against the warm cylinder. "What did you have in mind?"

"The same thing you have in mind, I'll bet." His voice rasped in the fading light. "With your hands behind you like that, you could be bound to the mast of a ship."

She was so excited she could barely breathe. "Did...did you want to...tie me?"

"Not this time." He held her gaze as he unfastened the first button of her jacket without looking. "But you'd like that before the week is over, wouldn't you?"

"I...I don't know." He was probing into fantasies she'd barely admitted to herself.

"You do know. Only you're shy about telling me. But before we're finished with each other, you won't be shy. For now, let's pretend I have you lashed to the mast of my ship, and I've been months at sea without a woman."

She trembled as he described an image that had haunted

her erotic dreams for years. "You've been reading my diary."

"No." He slipped the second button from its hole. "But I know who you are, Eileen Connelly."

"Because of what happened in the office."

"Yes." Another button came undone. "I've never known a woman brave enough to try on a fantasy like that with a complete stranger. You're a sexual risk taker."

"For now."

His mouth curved in a rogue's smile. "Oh, you've always wanted to take these risks. You just never let yourself before." He continued unfastening the buttons slowly, as if in no hurry to rid her of her clothes.

"Have you let yourself?"

"No." He undid the last button.

"Why?"

"It takes two to play." He dropped his gaze to her unbuttoned jacket, loosely running his fingers up and down the lapels. "I've never found a woman who would follow me to the rooftop, who wanted me to take off her clothes there and play sexual games until we wore each other out." He peeled back the material.

She swallowed as cool air touched her bare breasts.

Then he cupped them in his warm hands. "How many times today have you imagined this moment?" he murmured.

"Thousands."

"So have I." He brushed her taut nipples with his thumbs and watched the effect of his caress in her eyes. "And it's even better than I imagined."

She looked down, fascinated by the erotic picture of her unbuttoned jacket and his hands kneading her bare breasts. She'd longed for this all day.

His glance moved over her. "To think that only an hour

ago you were every inch the polished professional, sipping your civilized drink in a cozy pub. And now here you are, a wild thing braced against this metal cylinder, your proper little jacket unbuttoned, your breasts bare and quivering when I touch you, your eyes hungry for what will happen next.''

She moaned softly, impatiently.

''Don't worry.'' He stepped closer, pinning her against the metal pipe with his body. ''It's all going to happen. We're going to take this adventure to the end.''

7

SHANE KISSED HER THEN, taking her mouth with the arrogance of a captor, a captor who had his woman completely at his mercy. She *was* at his mercy, quivering with needs that had been buried, turned aside, dismissed. If he could satisfy those pesky needs, maybe he'd scorch them right out of her, which would be a blessing.

He kissed her hard, pressing her head against the metal, using his tongue to possess her mouth so completely that she lost track of time and space. Kneading her breasts with both hands, he held her in place with his hips wedged against hers. When she started to wrap her arms around him, he lifted his mouth a fraction from hers. "Hold on to the pipe. Let me run the show this time."

A thrill of the forbidden arrowed through her as she flattened her palms against the metal and surrendered to whatever he had in mind for her. She wondered if he was building her trust, leading up to the night when he'd take the bondage fantasy a step further and actually tie her in place.

If bondage felt anything like this, she wanted to try it, and she wanted to try it soon. Playing the helpless victim of his lust was more thrilling than she could have imagined. When he'd finished plundering her mouth, he raked his teeth gently down her throat, nipping at the vein pulsing at the side of her neck. Then he lowered his head and took the same bold liberties with her breasts, tugging at her nipples with his teeth until she was shaking and ready to do anything he asked.

He returned to her mouth, his lips seeking hers, his voice a low growl. "I'm going to take you now." He gripped her skirt and bunched it up around her waist. "Spread your legs for me."

Pulse racing, she did as he asked.

His mouth was hot against hers. "This is what I wanted to do in the pub, right there at the table." He kissed her hard as his hand slid between her quaking thighs.

The bold thrust of his fingers made her arch against the warm metal pipe.

He lifted his lips from hers. "I knew you'd be hot and wet. I knew you'd want this as much as I want to give it to you."

She groaned. "I do."

"I love that you didn't wear panties today," he murmured. "Here's your first reward." Moving his fingers quickly in and out, he gave her an orgasm in seconds, one that left her gasping and clutching the pipe for support.

"Good?" He slipped an arm behind her back and steadied her.

She kept her eyes closed, savoring the aftershocks. "Mmm."

"We're not done," he said softly.

She ran her tongue over her lips and opened her eyes to look into his. "I hope not."

"You're incredible." He swallowed. "I need to…can you stand if I let you go?"

Her legs trembled, and she held on to the pipe more firmly. "Yes."

He kept his gaze locked with hers as his zipper rasped in the stillness. "How do you like the roof so far?"

"I love the roof so far."

"Like that warm metal against your bare tush?" His question was punctuated by the unmistakable snap of latex.

"Uh-huh."

"Let's see how you like this." He cupped her bottom in both hands. "Wrap those long legs around my waist, sweetheart. I'm coming in." Then he lifted her off her feet.

With a moan of anticipation, she flattened her hands against the pipe and locked her feet together behind his back.

"Ah, you want this, too." He probed gently, seeking her heat.

Saliva pooled in her mouth. "You know I do."

"I've been counting the hours until I could sink into you." He adjusted his stance. "Mmm. Right there."

The blunt tip of his penis found its mark. He paused.

"Please."

"Oh, *yeah.*" With a quick intake of breath, he rocked forward and up, completing the connection.

"Oh." The delicious sensation of being filled had never been so exquisite as now, maybe because they weren't supposed to be here, weren't supposed to be doing this. The forbidden tasted heavenly.

He held her braced against the metal, his breath coming fast as his gaze roamed her face, her breasts, and finally settled at the place where her skirt rode up to display the spot where they were so intimately joined.

The denim of his fly brushed the moist curls between her thighs, and his fingers flexed against her bottom. She would never forget the feeling of this connection, so raw, so urgent, so uncivilized.

His voice was laced with tension. "You…are the most exciting…woman I've ever known."

"It's you. You're doing this to me, turning me into…"

She had no words to describe what she became when she was with him.

"Into my fantasy," he said. "I've dreamed about moments like this, but I never thought…" He groaned softly. "I wouldn't have to move to come. I could come just by looking at you."

"I like you to look." She could feel her response building, her body tightening. But her fantasy also involved action. "But I…" She paused and dragged in a breath. "I want you to move."

He smiled. "And I will. Get a grip on that pipe." Easing out, he pushed in deep again.

The friction made her whimper with pleasure.

"Does that little mewing sound mean you want more of that?" he whispered.

"Yes."

"So do I." He began to thrust deliberately.

Her body rocked against the curved metal surface, reminding her with every firm contact, with each hollow thump against the pipe, that she was having sex on a rooftop with a man she'd only met the night before, a man who wanted her half-dressed and braced against a large phallic symbol, a man who could see into her fevered brain and guess that she wanted that, too.

"Faster?" His breathing was ragged, his eyes filled with heat.

"Yes!" Caught in a frenzy of lust, she urged him on. "Faster! Oh, like that! Like that!"

He pumped wildly, panting now. "So *this* is how you like it, you hot thing, you. You sexy, wet, wonderful…oh, I can't hold back…I'm coming…I'm *coming*."

And so was she, gloriously. She cried out at the splendor of her orgasm, stunned by the majesty of the undulations rolling through her, waves that massaged his rigid penis until he groaned in delirious pleasure.

She had no idea how long they stayed propped up by the large exhaust pipe while they both let the world settle back into its regular orbit. Eventually he shifted his weight and began to lower her legs to the ground. With a few giggles on her part and chuckles on his, they managed to untangle themselves and stagger over to the quilt, where they flopped down and lay staring up at the sky.

Shane zipped up his jeans and Eileen nudged off her shoes, but that was about the extent of their activity. Both of them seemed content to lie there and bask in the glow of what they'd accomplished—outstanding rooftop sex.

"Same stars are up there," Shane said at last. "But I swear they look brighter."

She smiled in the darkness. "I was thinking the same thing."

"I wonder if this is what you'd call extreme sex."

"Sounds right to me." She'd never felt so sexually satisfied in her life. "And to think I tried to talk you out of spending the week like this."

"To think I almost turned down your first proposition."

"And if I'd remembered about the telephone installation, I wouldn't have stayed late to work. I probably would have taken stuff home instead." She lay there looking up at the vast sky with all its stars and planets, which made her think of the huge number of people in the world. She easily could have missed out on the wonder that was Shane Nichols.

"Well, you mentioned something about fate before," he said. "So maybe this was all supposed to happen."

"Maybe." And if they had been destined to meet, was it only to share these few days of incredible pleasure, then part forever?

MAYBE. SHE'D SAID THAT *maybe* fate had thrown them together. Shane decided he'd have to be content with that response. She'd brought up the idea before that fate had brought them together, and now he hoped to use it to get her into his life for many nights of wild sex, plus everything else—mortgages, 2:00 a.m. feedings, vacations to Disneyland. He still had the rest of tonight, plus two more nights, to change that *maybe* to a definite *yes*. As for him, he had no doubt. This was the woman he was destined to be with.

Yes, it had a lot to do with sex. He had it figured this way—some people put a lot of importance on it and some people didn't. Surely couples would be happier if they liked sex in the same way. He could tell that this Benjamin character had no concept that he had a bombshell on his hands, and she wasn't about to let him know, either. She would only reveal this side of herself to a man who understood her. Like him.

So he understood her sexually, but he didn't know a lot about her life apart from her sexual fantasies. By meeting the way they had, they'd reversed the usual way of getting acquainted. People generally found out the personal details first, then built up to the naked part.

He had a hunch she wanted him to concentrate on the naked part and forget about the personal details. That way they'd be close in one respect but not so close in another. Well, he had a different idea. He already knew more about her sexually than Benny. He wanted to find out everything personal Benny knew about her, as well.

He rolled to his side and propped his head on his hand to look at her. Her skirt had just naturally slipped back down to her knees, but her jacket was still open and she hadn't bothered to close it. He liked knowing that she felt relaxed enough with him, or seductive enough, to leave it that way.

She turned her head to look at him. "See what you've done? I'm shameless."

"Good. Shameless is exactly how I want you."

"You do realize that if this kind of behavior spread, our civilization would collapse."

He couldn't stop the laughter that tumbled out and wondered if that comment of hers was a Bennyism. "What makes you say that?"

"It's obvious. People would spend their entire time having sex and nothing would get done. Their judgment would be clouded, their productivity affected, their—"

"I think their productivity would go way up, because they'd be so happy all the time. I was very productive today." Or rather, he'd found a way to make his secretary more productive.

However, in one sense Eileen might be right—he could become so distracted by her that he'd let his obligations slide. After having mind-blowing sex with Eileen just now, that seemed like a good thing. He hadn't realized how much he'd needed to play, how dull he'd allowed his existence to become.

"I wasn't very productive today," she said. "Right now I wouldn't mind having a job more like yours."

She thought his was mindless, in other words. He could let that bother him, but he decided not to. "Trust me, you wouldn't want my job." Because he was having trouble seeing her expression in the darkness, he sat up and opened the wicker basket to get out the pillar candles he'd brought.

"You don't like your work?"

"I'd like it in smaller doses." He set the two pillars on glass coasters about a foot away from the edge of the quilt.

"Oh, you brought *candles*." She seemed very pleased.

"Sure." He rummaged around in the basket until his hand closed over a small cigarette lighter.

"I'm very impressed."

He flicked his thumb against the lighter. "If you're impressed with the candles, wait until you see what else is in the basket." He touched the flame to each of the candle wicks and the area took on a soft glow.

"I can hardly wait." She sat up. "I don't think anybody's ever packed a surprise picnic for me before."

"Then I'm glad I did." He'd given some thought to this meal, wanting the food to be a little bit on the fantasy side, too. First he pulled out the bottle of merlot and a corkscrew.

"And wine," she murmured. "I have a feeling you've done this kind of thing before."

He uncorked the wine with a soft pop and took out one of the two goblets he'd stashed in the basket. "It's been months since I had a picnic," he admitted, pouring her some wine. "And I guarantee it wasn't on a roof."

"Ah, but was it with a half-naked lady?"

He finished pouring his wine and glanced at her. Interesting that she should ask a question like that, as if she might be curious about his love life. Good sign.

"No, it wasn't with a half-naked lady," he said. "It was with my older brother, his wife and my little nephew Max. I think Max got naked that day and streaked across the park, but that wasn't a planned thing." The outings with his brother had been rare, and the nostalgia that gripped him when he thought of that day told him how desperately he longed for free time to spend with them. But he wanted more. He wanted a family of his own.

In the flickering light from the candles, her gaze seemed speculative, but he couldn't be sure. He'd told her something about himself on purpose, so that they could start learning about each other. "When was your last picnic?" he asked.

"I don't remember."

Either Benny didn't do picnics, or she didn't want to think about her boyfriend right now, or she'd kept herself as busy as he had. Shane decided all options were in his favor. "Then let's toast the fact that we're both finally enjoying a picnic, after all this time."

"I'll drink to that." She touched her glass to his. "Who would have imagined a rooftop would be the perfect place for it?" She took a sip of her wine.

"Both of us." He wanted to emphasize their common ground—the world of make-believe. "You caught on the minute I made the suggestion." He tasted the wine and was relieved that it was good as he'd remembered. He hadn't shared a bottle of wine with a woman in quite a while, either.

"I have to say you hooked me with the rooftop idea." She glanced around. "Total privacy, yet the thrill of being out in the open air, with a kinky sort of industrial feel to it. Very sexy."

"Glad you approve." Listening to her talk and watching the way her breasts played peekaboo with the lapels of her jacket was getting him hot again. But he wanted to make sure they ate the food he'd chosen so carefully.

The miniature wraps, about the size and shape of a vibrator, came from a deli that made their own tortillas. The filling was incredible, a combo of shredded beef, sour cream, guacamole and a few other wonderful things Shane hadn't identified. But he'd also chosen the food for its symbolic value.

"Hungry?" he asked.

"Yes." She smiled at him. "In all ways."

"Good." His penis twitched, ready for action. "Me, too. Let's eat the food I brought, and then...then we can see about satisfying that other hunger."

"I should be embarrassed to admit I want you again. After all, just a few minutes ago, we—"

"No embarrassment allowed on this roof." He handed her a red cloth napkin. "No one but us ever has to know about our secret cravings."

"It's probably the newness of the situation that's affecting us this way."

He wasn't about to agree with her on that. Instead he took the paper off the first wrap and handed it to her. "Try this."

She looked at it and started to laugh. "You picked these on purpose." She took the rolled tortilla from his outstretched hand.

"Sure did." He pulled a second napkin from the basket and laid it across his thigh before picking up his wrap.

Still smiling, she put down her wine. "Let's see if I can give this the attention it deserves."

"I have a feeling you can." His heartbeat kicked up a notch.

She held the wrap in both hands. Keeping her eyes on him, she brought it up to her mouth and licked the top, circling it with her tongue. "Mmm, tasty."

"I was hoping you'd like it." His own wrap lay abandoned, his wine totally forgotten.

"I do." She ran her tongue the length of the rolled tortilla. "Very nice."

He began to wonder if he could stand to watch this, after all. His erection was already straining the fly of his jeans.

"I'll bet the filling is good, too." She closed her mouth over the tip of the wrap. Then she began to squeeze and stroke upward with her lips while hollowing her cheeks and drawing the filling into her mouth. She paused to run her tongue over her lips. "Delicious."

He groaned. "You'd better stop."

"But I'm having so much fun. Isn't this what you had in mind?" She licked at the filling oozing out of the top of the tortilla.

"I had no idea...oh, Eileen, have a heart."

With a seductive smile, she laid what remained of the tortilla on her napkin. "Are you having a problem over here?"

"Yeah."

"Would you like me to take care of it for you?"

He wanted that so much he was trembling. And yet he'd never asked a woman for oral sex before, never admitted to being so desperate he could hardly see straight. "Yes," he murmured.

8

EILEEN COULDN'T REMEMBER having a better time with sex. All her suggestive tricks worked perfectly on Shane, an he wasn't ashamed to admit it. They were *so* going to restaurant tomorrow night. One with dim lighting and ta blecloths.

In the meantime, she was very happy about the curren circumstances. On her hands and knees, she crossed th small space separating them. "Lie back," she murmured.

He eased down on the quilt, but kept himself braced o his forearms.

"You don't look very comfy," she said.

"I don't care about comfy. I want..." He cleared hi throat. "I want to watch."

Heat poured through her. Here was a man who dive straight into sensuality without a second thought. She strad dled his knees and reached for the zipper of his fly. "The I'd better give you a good show, hadn't I?"

He swallowed. "As if you could help it."

Until this moment she'd never thought of a blow job a performance art. What a concept. With that in mind, sh took her time drawing down the zipper. "A little crampe in there, are we?"

His voice was tight with strain. "You could say that."

"Poor baby." In the light from the candles, she coul see the sizable bulge beneath the cotton of his briefs. Sh stroked her knuckle over that bulge and was rewarded with a tortured moan.

Her heart might be racing, but she unveiled him slowly, pretending perfect calm. He wasn't the least bit calm. With every movement she made, his breathing changed, until he sounded like a desperate man.

Long moments later, she freed his erection from its prison. As she curled her fingers loosely around his penis, she glanced into his eyes. "Better?"

His voice was a harsh croak. "Not yet."

"Hmm." She wrapped that silky warmth and latent power in both hands, squeezing gently.

He made a noise deep in his throat.

She looked into his eyes again. There was no mistaking the plea in their green depths. Oh, this was fun. "Yes?"

"I need…"

"What?" She caressed him lightly. "What do you need?"

"Your mouth…please. Now. I need…please…"

"As you wish." Leaning down, she pressed her lips to the velvet tip. Then she used her tongue on the underside, running it along the prominent ridge to the base.

Shane gasped.

Going for even more visual stimulation, she treated his penis to a thorough tongue bath. Then she made a cylinder of her fingers and stroked him, checking to make sure he was still watching.

He was. His jaw was clenched and his eyes looked hot enough to melt the exhaust vents surrounding them.

She repeated the tongue bath until he was slick and ready for those long, firm strokes again. He began to pant. Pausing in her downstroke, she circled the tip with her tongue and felt him shudder. "Having a good time?" She raked him gently with her teeth and decided his groan was answer enough.

At last, when he started visibly shaking from the tension, she closed her mouth over his entire length, taking him as far into her throat as she could. Then she began a steady rhythm. At that moment he was totally hers, her slave, with his body quivering helplessly beneath her and his cries turning to whimpers of need.

At the moment of his climax, he called her name. No man had ever poured so much intensity into her name, and the rich sound made her shiver with delight. He knew who she was. Finally, a man really knew who she was.

SHANE HAD EXPECTED the most terrific oral sex of his life, and Eileen had shot way past his expectations. For a long time afterward he lay like a dead man, staring up at the stars and wondering what he'd done to deserve this kind of unbelievable pleasure. He'd tried to express his gratitude, fumbling for the right words, and she'd laughed and kissed him, telling him that she'd had more fun than he had.

Not possible. No one in the universe had ever had more fun than that. More fun than that would surely kill you.

Eventually, despite initial indications to the contrary, he got his strength back. He even contemplated what sort of sexual adventure they'd have next. But first he knew they needed to finish off the food and enjoy more wine. Eileen went along with that program.

Then, to his surprise, she asked for some light snuggling instead of another round of all-out sex. So he doused the candles, gathered her close and flipped over a section of the quilt so it would loosely cover them. Lying there with her head nestled against his shoulder, he felt a deep peace settle over him.

"We can't go to sleep," she murmured.

"You can if you want. I'll stay awake." He knew he would, too. Although he was more contented than he could remember being in a long time, he was also fully alert. She energized him, making him feel so alive that he didn't want to waste a minute in sleep.

"I won't sleep," she said. "But I like lying here in our own private spot, looking up at the stars."

"Me, too. But I had the last orgasm. You're about due."

She repositioned her head on his shoulder. "Well, if we're keeping score, I had two the first time, so now we're even."

"Yeah, but in this game, the lady gets to outscore the guy any old time she wants. You know what they say, a girl can never have too many shoes or too many orgasms."

She laughed. "That's good." With a sigh, she relaxed against him. "Thank you for setting up such a great evening."

"Thank you for coming." He hadn't meant it to be funny, but she giggled anyway, which he enjoyed.

Then she was silent for a while, and soon her breathing evened out.

He spoke her name softly, and when she didn't answer, he realized that she really had gone to sleep. What trust. He'd promised that he'd stay awake so they didn't end up spending the night on this roof, and she'd taken him at his word.

His conscience pricked him a little. He'd misled her about his job, and maybe that wasn't fair. But telling her he owned the company wasn't fair, either, because after tonight he was really questioning his whole lifestyle.

He'd always been an all-or-nothing kind of guy. Either he ran the company or he didn't. He was lousy at delegating and he knew it. Even giving Rhonda extra duties today had taken real effort, so handing the operation to somebody else and giving them control over his professional reputation would be very difficult for him. And there was his ongoing concern about his employees.

But Eileen had demonstrated how beautiful life could be when you took time to savor the finer things, like her incredible body. If his campaign to get her away from Benny worked, he wondered how he'd manage both a relationship and work, especially with his current management style at Mercury.

He'd known for sometime that was a problem in his life, which might be why he'd unconsciously avoided becoming involved with anyone. Then Eileen had thrust herself into his life, and he had to deal with the problem or give her up. So he would deal with the problem somehow, because giving her up was not an option.

In the meantime, he'd hold her while she slept. He considered it a great honor to be allowed to do that. A person was at their most vulnerable while they were asleep, yet she hadn't been worried about it, maybe because she'd already made herself so vulnerable to him by revealing her love of sexual adventure. Well, so had he. They'd bared more than their bodies to each other. They'd bared their souls.

A LOW-FLYING JET woke Eileen from a dream of making love on a tropical island with Shane. She opened her eyes and glanced up to find him gazing at her, his face in shadow.

What a sex kitten she'd turned out to be, she thought with chagrin, falling asleep in the middle of their wild night. "I'm sorry," she said. "I didn't mean to doze off. Is it late?"

"Late for what?" There was a smile in his voice.

"Well, I'm sure you didn't come up here to watch me sleep. I mean, all your preparation, and I conk out on you. That's—"

"A compliment."

"Oh, sure."

"I mean it. We've only spent a few hours together, and yet you're relaxed enough to fall asleep in my arms."

"Good sex will do that."

"The right kind of good sex."

The air-conditioning unit was making the roof vibrate in a very intriguing way. The urge to have more of that right kind of good sex tugged at her, but she might have slept away the available time. "You probably need to get home. Tomorrow's a work day."

"Is that a proposition?" He rolled her to her back. "Because I could swear I heard, buried in a lot of talk, a proposition in there."

"I like the way this roof vibrates."

"See?" He sat up and pulled his T-shirt over his head. Starlight gleamed on his broad shoulders. "I knew there was a proposition in there."

Following his lead, she sat up and took off her jacket. "Just once more, and then we'll go home."

"What, you have a curfew?" He shimmied out of his jeans and briefs.

"I'm just trying to be sensible." She took note that he was already magnificently erect as she peeled off her skirt and took the garter belt and stockings down with it.

"I thought we banned that word for this week." Grabbing a condom from the wicker basket, he tore open the package and then rolled on the condom in one efficient stroke. "Didn't we?"

"I...guess we did." Knowing he was so quickly aroused by the thought of having sex with her took her breath away.

"Good. Now lie back and let that air conditioner get you worked up. We can consider it foreplay."

"I'm already worked up." But she did as he asked, and stretched out on the quilt, naked under the stars.

He moved over her, slid his fingers through hers and guided her arms over her head. "I'll just bet you are. You were born to have lots of exciting sex."

She didn't think so. Lots of exciting sex was for single people with no obligations. She figured this week would fill her quota of exciting sex, but she was too busy feeling the vibrations running through her body to contradict him.

"Let's see how worked up you are." He probed gently with the tip of his penis. "Mmm. You are one wet, hot babe. Thank you, Mr. Air Conditioner."

"It's not only the air conditioner."

"I know. It's you, a woman with a great imagination. How do you like having sex in the great outdoors?"

"I love it."

"Me, too." With one smooth stroke he entered her. Locked in tight, he leaned down to kiss her. "So many possibilities, so little time," he whispered against her mouth. "Here's one of my favorites. Slow and easy sex. Goes great with air-conditioner vibrations."

Moving his mouth gently over hers, he began a gentle rhythm that seemed perfectly tuned with the subtle quiver of the roof's surface. Nothing seemed required of her but to lie there absorbing the vibrations from below and the steady friction between her thighs. Gradually her body became pliable as soft wax.

There was pleasure, but it was muted, sweet and constant. She barely noticed when it became a little more insistent, when the vibrations from the roof seemed to have taken charge of her response. The change was gradual, but eventually her breathing was no longer steady, and the loose grip of her fingers tightened.

He lifted his mouth from hers. "I can hear a jet in the distance," he murmured. "I'm going to make you come right when it goes over."

She drew in a breath. "Airplane as phallic symbol."

"Uh-huh."

Now she could hear the jet, too, its powerful engines thrusting it through the air. Shane increased the pace, not much, but enough to tease her with the beginnings of a release. As the noise of the plane's engines grew louder, he stroked harder. Tension built relentlessly within her.

He leaned down and nipped at her earlobe. "Getting close," he whispered, tightening his hold on her hands as he moved faster within her, and faster yet. "Come for me, Eileen."

The sound of the plane had become a roar, and she was nearly there, nearly…right as the dark shadow blotted out the stars above her, she erupted, her triumphant cry drowned out by engines that made the air tremble as they rocketed overhead.

Shane slowed the pace, easing in and out as the contractions lessened and her cries became whimpers. His breath was warm against her ear. "Like that?"

She struggled for breath. "You know…I did."

He chuckled as he continued to move inside her softly. "I love improv."

And that, she thought, was the mark of a true adventurer.

SHANE TREATED HIMSELF to a climax a short time later. He'd held off, not wanting to get lost in his own response and risk lousing up the airplane image for Eileen. He'd thought of it when a plane had gone over earlier. Apparently the wind had shifted and the flight pattern into Sky

Harbor had changed in the past hour, which meant jets were being sent over their rooftop.

Apparently he'd guessed right that she'd get a thrill out of having an orgasm in concert with a flyby. He still couldn't get over how much in tune they were, sexually.

He could have spent more time on the roof, but when she insisted they go home, he didn't argue. One thing about fantasies—you didn't want them to become routine. If they stayed on the roof too long, maybe that would happen.

Then again, maybe not. He couldn't imagine sex with Eileen would ever seem dull. When only one person in a relationship had this kind of imagination, then ruts could develop, but when both people loved to pretend, they could go a lifetime without getting bored. That's what he had in mind.

When he helped Eileen into her car, he wasn't sure from her goodbye kiss whether she was beginning to think the same thing or not. At least he had two more nights to convince her. She was certainly into the adventure angle of their relationship. For tomorrow night she'd already picked out a restaurant where she'd made it clear they'd enjoy some hanky-panky under the tablecloth.

Just thinking about that on the drive home made his heartbeat speed up. Shoot, any thoughts of Eileen got him excited. He'd have trouble concentrating on work tomorrow, but he'd have to. Giving up his nights was one thing, but he couldn't let his days get away from him, too. The company still belonged to him.

Sure enough, even taking the night off looked like it would have repercussions. Back at his condo, he discovered ten messages waiting on his answering machine. *Ten.*

No doubt that was due to keeping his cell and pager turned off all evening. He thought about playing the messages. But he had a wonderful glow from being with Eileen, and he didn't want to lose it by listening to complaining customers. Instead he went to bed, feeling slightly guilty and very sexually satisfied.

BY THE NEXT MORNING, Shane's sexual satisfaction had worn off and his guilt had grown until it was the size of the jumbo jet that had flown overhead while he was giving Eileen an orgasm. After the quickest shower in history, he threw on a dress shirt and slacks. He wouldn't be seeing Eileen during the day, so he could dress in his normal clothes instead of the T-shirt and jeans she was used to. Tonight he'd dress up a little, too, for the restaurant meal.

Hurrying into his small kitchen, he listened to his messages while heating water for instant coffee and knotting his tie. All ten messages were from George Ullman, who happened to own a plant that employed five hundred people. The guy used a lot of phone equipment.

Like many of Shane's customers, he'd become used to getting Shane to listen to his problems whenever the slightest thing went wrong, even during the night shift. He'd called yesterday because he thought a problem was developing. Shane had put off taking care of it and had been unwilling to foist it off on someone else. Now the problem was a reality.

From the sound of the first couple of messages, it was a minor malfunction. It wasn't the malfunction causing the problem. Shane's unavailability was causing the problem. Each message was more frantic than the last. The tenth message indicated that Ullman was about to cancel his entire contract with Mercury Communications.

As Shane drove to work in the van he'd commandeered for this week, he tried not to panic. Ullman was a big account, no doubt about it. But he could afford to lose him and still be okay. However, Ullman also had a big mouth, and he was a member of all the service organizations in town. If he decided to start bad-mouthing Mercury, some people would dismiss it because they knew Ullman. But not everyone would.

Shane berated himself for getting into this position in the first place. But from the beginning he hadn't trusted anyone else to pamper his customers the way he did. He still didn't feel comfortable letting someone else handle problems.

For example, he could easily send one of his installers out to correct the problem, but only after Shane had taken the time to hear all about it, offer sympathy for the inconvenience and promise to be available if the repair didn't work out perfectly. That was the way to keep clients happy, in his opinion.

Come to think of it, he'd turned into a glorified complaint department. Recently, the complaint department had been closed for the first time in years. Just his luck an important customer had a complaint, and now that customer was ticked. When Shane arrived at the office, Rhonda was already there and the coffee was brewing.

Rhonda Ferguson was a single mom who'd raised three teenage boys, which Shane found amazing and admirable. Her flaming red hair came compliments of a beautician, but Shane thought the color exactly suited her personality. Her figure was due to a fondness for Ben and Jerry's ice cream, and she was unrepentant about that. She also loved reality TV and working for Shane.

"There are a ton of messages from George Ullman," she said. "I take it he didn't get in touch with you last night?" Her brown eyes were full of questions.

Although Rhonda wasn't quite old enough to be his mom, she was close to that age. At the moment he felt the way one of her kids must have when they'd been out after curfew. "Uh, no, he didn't."

She gazed at him. "I hope nothing's wrong. You don't look as if anything's wrong."

"Everything's fine." His face felt hot. Good God, he must be *blushing*. "I just turned off my cell and my pager last night. You know, took the night off."

She grinned. "I'm delighted to hear it. Did you have a good time?"

The phrase *good time* didn't begin to describe his night on the rooftop with Eileen. "Yes, I did."

"I'm not sure this is appropriate for a secretary to say to her boss, but I think you should turn your cell and pager off more often. The sparkle is definitely back in your eyes."

9

BY MID-MORNING Eileen was growing restless, wanting the day to end so that she could be with Shane again. She'd already made reservations at the restaurant she'd chosen for their next fantasy. Although she was supposed to be working, she was instead mentally reviewing her wardrobe for the perfect outfit. She wanted to make Shane drool.

Not that it was difficult to make him drool. He seemed to start drooling the minute she appeared, which was extremely gratifying. She couldn't allow herself to think of next week, when she would no longer have that kind of ego boost. Of course she'd give him up at the end of the week. Of course she would, because if she didn't, she'd have to break up with Benjamin, and there would go all her plans to live a levelheaded life.

As she sat staring at her computer screen, daydreaming the morning away, her new phone buzzed. She couldn't pick it up without thinking of Shane, which could be a real problem next week, and the week after that, and…for as long as the phone stayed on her desk, actually.

She answered with a lilt in her voice, because she thought it could be Shane. After all, he worked with telephones. If he spent as much time thinking about her as she did about him, he would have the urge to call. She would call him, except she hadn't asked for his cell number.

But Benjamin's voice came over the line, sounding as if he could be in the next office. "Miss me?"

She jumped, and then was hit by guilt the size of the Grand Canyon. "Of course!" She crossed her fingers. "My goodness, what time is it there? I always get that mixed up. Are you seven hours ahead, or—"

"I'm leaving for dinner with clients in a few minutes. It's been really hectic since I got here, but I wanted to call and say hi. I just talked to Traynor about a couple of things, and then I had Linda switch me to you. Been keeping busy?"

"Definitely. Busy, busy, busy, that's me." She felt a little better. He'd taken care of business with Traynor before getting around to her, so he wasn't horribly lonely. She'd hate it if he'd been lonely.

"That's my girl. Trust me, they notice around that place when someone takes the initiative. Listen, I have to go in a minute, but I have great news—I've finished up here faster than I thought, so I'll be home tomorrow night. Same flight, gets in at six-ten, just a day earlier. We can go out for dinner if you want."

Eileen started to panic. Maybe he *was* lonely after all. But worse than that, he'd just chopped an entire night off her time with Shane. That left only tonight. She'd imagined she and Shane had lots of time to play out their fantasies, but now...

"Eileen? You still there?"

"Yes! Yes, that's wonderful. It's just that I'd planned a...surprise for you, and now I'll have to—"

"Give it to me early," he said. "Although I can guess what it's all about. Something to do with moving into a certain apartment I'm familiar with. Am I warm?"

"No fair trying to guess, Benjamin." She heard the rattle of commitment chains and flinched. One more night of freedom. Only one.

"Well, it's time for me to head out for dinner. So take care of yourself, and I'll see you tomorrow night."

"You bet. Tomorrow night." Yikes. It seemed way too close.

"Think of where you want to have dinner. Then we'll go back to my apartment and have a little private celebration." He chuckled.

"Sure." She closed her eyes in despair. When Benjamin suggested a "private celebration," she felt nothing, nothing at all. It wasn't Benjamin's fault. Most women would be delighted to spend time in Benjamin's heavy walnut bed, even if the sex was totally predictable. Benjamin was going places, she reminded herself. He might be President of the United States some day.

"See you soon," Benjamin said.

"I'll be there. Bye." She hung up and stared at the phone that Shane had installed with his own two hands—imaginative, talented hands. She wanted those hands on her right this minute. She wanted his kiss, his teasing, his talent for giving her orgasms.

That probably made her shameless. She should be feeling great remorse, considering what she'd been doing while Benjamin was away. At the first sound of his voice she had felt guilty, but the minute he'd announced that he was coming home early, guilt had changed to anger. She couldn't justify feeling angry, but there it was. Once she'd planned this sexual vacation, she didn't want it cut short.

Shane needed to know about this turn of events. Maybe she didn't have his cell, but Mercury Communications should know how to contact him. He should be warned that tonight was the end of the line. The more she thought about that, the more upset she became.

Her telephone, along with all the others Shane had delivered, had a little sticker on the side giving the number

for Mercury. First she got up and closed her office door.
Then she punched in the number for Shane's company.

An efficient-sounding woman answered. "Mercury
Communications, this is Rhonda. How may I help you?"

"I'm with Traynor and Sizemore," Eileen said. "I need
to get in touch with the installer who put in our phones on
Tuesday night. I believe his name was Shawn? Or maybe
Shane. Yes, I think that's it. Would it be possible for me
to speak to him sometime today?"

There was a brief pause on the other end. "I think I can
find him for you. Is there a problem?"

"A small one. I thought it would be easier if I talked
directly to him, since he put in the system. I realize he may
be out on another job. Maybe I could have his pager number instead of interrupting him while he's working."

"As a matter of fact, he happens to be in the office right
now," Rhonda said. She sounded quite happy about it, too.

"Oh, good." Immediately Eileen pictured a curvy
twenty-something receptionist with the hots for Shane. And
why not? He was one hunky guy. Any woman would be
happy to have him hanging around, making jokes and giving a teasing glance with those green eyes. Eileen didn't
like to think of who might get a shot at Shane after she
bowed out.

"Just a moment, and I'll get him for you," Rhonda said.

"I'd appreciate that." Her pulse was jumping at the
thought of hearing his voice on the phone. She had a bad
case of the hots for him, herself. And they were almost out
of time for her to satisfy her lust.

"This is Shane. How can I help you?"

"Benjamin's coming home early."

"Eileen? Damn, I didn't know it was you. What do you
mean by *early*?"

"Tomorrow night at six. Listen, if you can't talk right

now, I understand. But I wanted you to know. I guess he finished his work sooner than he thought.''

"I can talk. It's okay."

"Well, I don't want to risk getting you in trouble. I told that secretary that I had a small problem with the phone system.''

"Then I'd better come over and see about that.''

"Now?" Instantly she was aroused, but even she had her limits. "Um, Shane, I don't know what you have in mind, but I'm not sure I have the courage to have desktop sex while everybody's here in the office." But if he pushed her, she might consider it.

He laughed. "I wasn't thinking about that. I was thinking more along the lines of having an early lunch together. Having desktop sex in the middle of the workday could get us *both* in a huge amount of trouble.''

"Are you sure you should be talking that way in the middle of the office? Can't the secretary—''

"Nope. Nobody can hear me. So can you get away in about, say, thirty minutes?''

"I can, but how can you just leave?" She thought he was being more than a little reckless, considering he had an employer who might not appreciate having him cut out like that.

"It's a slow day.''

"But you said one of the guys was home with his wife and new baby, and you were ending up with overtime, so I don't—''

"If Benjamin's coming home tomorrow night, I want to see you now.''

"Shane, I'm worried about your job.''

"I'll be outside your building in the van in thirty minutes. Please be there. Please." The line went dead.

Although the urgency in his voice thrilled her, she would

feel terrible if she caused him to get reprimanded, or worse, fired. But he'd hung up, giving her no more chance to argue with him. He would be double-parked downstairs in thirty minutes, and she would be there, if for no other reason than to convince him to go back to work.

She shouldn't have called him. She hadn't expected him to drop everything and come rushing over to meet her, but of course that was the kind of behavior that sent her heart into overdrive, the kind of behavior she'd never seen in Benjamin.

Maybe she was being unfair to Benjamin, though. He might have worked extra hard while he was in Switzerland, so that he could come home sooner. In his own way, he might be showing how much he wanted to be with her. If only she could get excited about his arrival, even half as excited as she was about going downstairs and hopping into Shane's van, then her life would start making sense again.

SHANE KNEW HE WAS walking on thin ice. The smart thing to do was use his lunch hour, which he never took anyway, to drive out to see Ullman and smooth over that relationship. Yes, someone had been sent out to take care of the problem, but Shane knew Ullman expected a show of concern from him, as well.

But damn it to hell, Benny was swooping in tomorrow night, and Shane didn't know if he'd have enough time between now and then to sway Eileen to his side. Creating sexual adventures for her had been the first part of his plan, but at some point he had to let her know that he also wanted what she wanted—a home and kids. His plan was being crunched, and that wasn't good.

Naturally, work was piling up on his desk, and he had another six calls to return. But he couldn't take time for them now. He had to run home and change into a T-shirt and jeans before driving to Eileen's office. Oh, and he needed to pick up condoms.

Plus he had to pacify Rhonda, who had to be wondering what the hell was going on. He walked out of his office and she looked up immediately with a cat-who-ate-the-canary expression.

"I'll be taking off for a couple of hours." He was sure he must look devious as hell.

"Okay." She continued to smile her mysterious smile. "Will you be taking your cell and pager?"

He thought about that. Eileen might get really suspicious if he didn't.

"Yes, I will, so be sure and get in touch with me if anything important comes up."

She nodded. "I'm dying to ask a question, although I'm quite positive it's none of my business."

He gave her a wary glance. "What's that?"

"Why wouldn't you want her to know you own the company?"

Shane cleared his throat, buying time. No point in denying there was a woman in the picture. Rhonda hadn't successfully raised three boys on her own by being stupid. "It's…complicated. I'll tell her, eventually, of course. For right now, I'd rather she didn't know."

"Excuse me in advance for saying so, but this change in you is utterly fascinating."

"Listen, I know it must seem like I've completely lost it, but the situation is only temporary. If you can cover for me for a little while, by tomorrow everything will be back to normal." He sincerely doubted it, but he said so anyway, more to reassure himself than her. "If anybody starts asking a bunch of questions, you can say I'm sick or something."

"Don't worry about it," Rhonda said. "I can hold things together for a few hours. You go ahead."

''Thanks.'' He left the office absolutely certain that Rhonda knew he was planning a nooner with the woman who had suddenly become a part of his life.

As he drove home, he wondered if he should simplify things by telling Eileen he owned Mercury. Then it came to him why he didn't want to do that. He felt more like himself when he was pretending to be the installer.

He didn't want her image of him to shift, because then his own sense of freedom might disappear, too. Maybe the owner of a company wasn't who he was, deep inside. If so, he needed to figure out what to do about that.

But not now. Now he had a mission. On arriving at his upscale condo complex, he made a faster clothing change than Clark Kent on a good day. Then he took time to wonder where this nooner should take place. Stuffing a condom in his jeans pocket, he ran back to the van, still debating.

There was a good hotel near her office—probably too good. She'd never let him get a room there. He couldn't take her back to his place because it was too pricey for the average telephone installer to be able to afford. Asking to go to her apartment seemed kind of cheesy.

That left the van. At a stoplight he glanced in the back. Yeah, there was room, and the quilt was still in there from last night but, geez, a *van?* And where would he park it? There wasn't enough time to drive to the outskirts of town.

Now that he'd started this middle-of-the-day program, he wondered if he'd made a big mistake. If this experience turned out to be less than wonderful for her, he'd lose ground instead of gaining it. Damn that Benny for coming home early. It almost seemed as if the guy had sensed something was going on via some trans-oceanic boyfriend alert.

Well, Shane intended to give this campaign his best shot. And—hold it, there was a guy selling bouquets on the corner. Shane beeped his horn, rolled down his window and waved money at the guy. Within a few seconds he had a multicolored bouquet of flowers sitting in the passenger seat. There. That should improve the atmosphere of the van, if in fact that's what they ended up using for their love nest.

Eileen stood outside her building in a red pantsuit. Talk about a bombshell. No briefcase this time, just her little purse. Her hair was done up on top of her head the way it had been when he'd first seen her.

At that moment he wanted her so fiercely that he would have taken Benny on in hand-to-hand combat, and he wasn't the sort of guy who believed in violence. Eileen was worth fighting for, though, and so he would fight for her in the only way he knew. He'd make love to her until she couldn't imagine life without him.

He double-parked and started to get out so he could come around and help her in. Before he could do that, she'd hurried between the parked cars and opened the van door.

She kept her sunglasses on as she gazed up at him. "I don't think you should be doing this. I—'' Her glance fell to the flowers on the seat and her expression softened. "Oh, Shane, you didn't need to buy these."

"Sure I did."

"Look, I came down because I didn't want you to stay here, double-parked, until you got yourself a ticket, but I can't live with the idea that you're putting your job in danger by taking time out of your day to be with me."

"I brought my cell and my pager." He gestured to the phone in its holder on the dash and the pager clipped to his belt. "If anybody needs me, they can contact me."

"I still think this will look very irresponsible, and if they should check your story and discover there's nothing wrong with the system at Traynor and Sizemore, you'll be toast."

Shane tried to think fast. Obviously she wouldn't take his word about his job stability. And it was stable. Too stable. That was the problem. Oh, sure, he might lose at least one big customer today by ignoring him, but probably not. He could mop up tomorrow, while she was telling Benny...whatever she'd be telling Benny.

Finally he came up with an idea. "If I got somebody from Mercury to promise you my job's okay, would you climb into this van?"

"Not if it's one of your buddies, I wouldn't."

He picked up his cell and speed-dialed the office. "I'm talking about Rhonda, the woman you talked with earlier. She knows everything that goes on around there, and she'll tell you the truth."

"Shane, I still don't think this is a good idea."

He ignored her protest and spoke into the phone. "Rhonda? Hi, it's Shane. Would you do me a huge favor and tell Eileen that my job will still be there when I get back in another hour or so?"

Rhonda sounded like she was trying hard to control her laughter. "My pleasure. Eileen's her name? Pretty name."

"So is she. Here she is." He passed the phone over to Eileen.

At first she looked as if she wouldn't take it. Then, with a sigh of disapproval, she did.

After exchanging a few words with Rhonda, she handed him the phone. "She wants to tell you something."

Shane could just imagine she did. He put the phone to his ear. "What?"

"She must be quite a woman," Rhonda said. "First she lures you away from your work, which I thought nobody could do, and now she's nice enough to worry about being too much of a distraction for you. If any of my sons finds someone that caring, I'm going to advise him to grab her. Just thought I'd mention that.''

"Thanks, Rhonda. Duly noted. See you in an hour or so." By the time he'd replaced the phone in its holder, Eileen was sitting in the passenger seat with the door closed and the flowers in her lap.

"You're a crazy man, you know that?" she said softly. "Absolutely crazy."

"And I'm guessing that's what you like about me."

"As a matter of fact, it is."

10

EILEEN LIFTED THE flowers to her nose and sniffed. She loved this casual arrangement of carnations, baby's breath and daisies bought on impulse from a street vendor much better than an elaborate box of long-stemmed roses delivered by a florist. Shane understood exactly how to please her. In so many ways.

She glanced over at him as he pulled the van into traffic. "These are perfect. Thank you." She wanted to reach over and touch him, but she wouldn't be satisfied with one touch, and no telling what a distraction would do to his concentration. Better wait until he wasn't driving in heavy traffic.

"You're welcome." His voice was drenched in sexual overtones.

The air between them crackled with anticipation. She wondered what he had in mind for this stolen hour. Whatever it was, she was ready to go along. Watching his hands on the steering wheel of the van got her hot. "I'll probably have to leave the flowers with you, instead of taking them back to the office, though."

He looked surprised. "Why can't you say you bought yourself some flowers during your lunch hour?"

"Because I never have before. They might wonder why I'd start now. I'm already getting comments about the perpetual grin on my face."

"Yeah?" He looked pleased about that. "So I guess

flowers along with the grin might be too big a hint that you're having fantastic sex."

"Yeah, it might, but you know what? I *should* buy myself flowers once in awhile. I love fresh flowers. So I'll tell everybody I'm turning over a new leaf."

"Sounds like a good idea."

She heard something underlying his easy comment, as if he intended the statement to have extra significance. "You mean about buying flowers, or turning over a new leaf in general?"

"I'm not sure. That was probably meant more for me than for you." He maneuvered around a bus. "Did you ever feel as if you're living someone else's life?"

That startled her. "You mean like right now, with this wild week we're having? Because I feel as if I've morphed into Lady Chatterly."

He grinned. "Actually, I meant the life you were living before this week. Did you feel like you were being totally yourself?"

She took a deep breath. He was veering onto shaky ground. "Shane, if you're trying to say that our wild and crazy times together are real life, I'd have to disagree. It's okay for a few days, a few nights, but you can't expect two people to be like that all the time and still carry on a normal routine."

"Are you sure? And while we're on the subject, what's so great about a normal routine?"

He was starting to worry her with this discussion, which sounded too much like the ones she'd recently carried on with herself. "Unless you're going to head to a tropical beach somewhere and live on fish and mangoes, there's the little matter of earning money."

"I'm not talking about dropping out. But it seems as if there should be more time for adventure, for play and imagination. This kind of week shouldn't have to be the exception to the rule.''

This was why he made such a good playmate, she thought. He was restless, tired of being in a rut and eager for adventure. That meant he wasn't at the stage of life when he'd welcome the idea of mowing the lawn on Saturday morning or coaching a Little League team. But that's what she wanted in a husband, a dedicated family man.

''Apparently you don't agree,'' he said quietly.

''Not if you're talking about being a free spirit, with no ties. I want a house in the near future. I want kids.''

''I didn't say I didn't want that. In fact—''

''Kids need a certain kind of stability, the kind I had growing up. I could always count on my parents to be responsible, to be levelheaded.'' Well, her mom, at any rate, and her father had followed her mom's lead.

''Does being responsible have to mean giving up on adventure?'' He flipped on his turn signal and pulled into a multi-story parking garage where he took a ticket from the attendant.

''Certain kinds, yes.''

''The kind we've been having, you mean.''

''Look, I'm allowing myself to be a little crazy for this week,'' she said, ''but that's not who I want to be for the long haul.''

''Then why do it at all?'' He cruised to the second level of the garage, and the third, passing parking spaces along the way.

''It's like the doughnuts.'' She took off her sunglasses. She'd assumed he wanted to park the van here and then grab something to eat at a nearby deli, but maybe he had something else in mind. ''Shane, are you planning to actually park in this garage?''

''Eventually. What about the doughnuts?''

"My girlfriends and I decided we were eating too many and getting way too much sugar in our system, so we spent two days eating nothing *but* doughnuts, so we'd get sick of them."

"Did it work?"

"Kind of. I think we should have gone for three days, to make sure. It's been six months, and I'm starting to crave a doughnut again."

He drove up to the sixth level of the garage, where the spaces were all empty, and chose one down at the very end. "So you think if you engage in enough sexual adventure, you'll get sick of it?"

She had to be honest. "I thought so at first, but now I'm not so sure."

He switched off the engine, took off his sunglasses and turned to her. "What do you plan to do about that?"

"I don't know." She saw the heat in his eyes and began to tremble. One look, and she was ready to strip naked for him. "Any suggestions?"

"Maybe. But we don't have much time left, so let's talk about that later." He unfastened his seat belt. "There's a little lunch place less than a block from this parking garage. If you want, we could go there for a sandwich. Or…" He cleared his throat. "The quilt's still in the back from last night."

She was beginning to understand why he'd driven to a parking spot where no one else was around. Slowly she unbuckled her seat belt. "And we can stay here and have doughnuts?"

"Uh-huh." His gaze flickered over her.

Her breathing quickened. "Okay."

His glance became several degrees hotter. "Give me a minute in the back." He climbed out of the van and locked the driver's door behind him.

She turned to look over her shoulder, and through the piles of boxes she watched as he opened the door and started rearranging things. There were no windows in the back, which meant they'd have a fair amount of privacy. Her pulse hammered at the thought that she was about to have sex with him in this van in a public parking garage, in the middle of the day.

And she was ready. Listening to him fix them a make-shift bed, she became very wet and excited. But she also knew he was taking a big risk, using a company van for this. "You could get in a huge amount of trouble if anybody found out how you're spending your lunch hour," she said.

"I don't intend for that to happen."

Then, as if to prove him wrong, his cell phone rang.

"Shane, your—"

"I hear it. Can you toss it back to me?"

Setting the bouquet of flowers on Shane's seat, she took the phone from its holder. Then she reached between the stacks of boxes and lobbed it in his direction.

He caught it in one hand, punched the on button and put it to his ear. "This is Shane."

Now that they'd arrived at this point, she prayed an emergency wouldn't call him away. She didn't know how she'd survive the frustration if he had to take her back to her office while she suffered in this aroused condition.

"Yeah, I'm in the middle of something right now, Ken." Shane winked at her. "Very sensitive stuff. Can I get back to you in about forty-five minutes?"

He was such an appealing bad boy. Eileen held her breath, hoping that Ken, whoever he was, could be put off for that long. It wasn't right, and Shane was playing with fire, but after tonight she wouldn't be a problem to him anymore.

He listened to Ken for a few seconds, a frown creasing his forehead. "Unfortunately I don't have that information in front of me. I'll be happy to get it to you shortly, though." He paused. "Yes, I understand you're trying to make a decision today. I'm sorry that I—okay, if that's the way it has to be. Call me if you change your mind." He disconnected the phone.

"That didn't go well, did it?" Eileen felt certain that whatever the phone call had been about, this Ken person wasn't happy with the response Shane had given him.

Shane set the phone down on the floor of the van and shrugged. "Can't be helped."

"Yes, it can. You can call him back and tell him you'll be available in ten minutes instead of forty-five."

"Nope." He walked around the van and opened her door.

"Shane! Be reasonable. You're going to end up getting fired."

"Eileen, trust me. I won't get fired. I have…seniority with the company. Lots of seniority."

She gazed down at him, torn between lust and her sense of duty.

He drew in a breath and lowered his voice. "Eileen, I'm a desperate man. If I can't bury my cock inside you very soon, I'm going to start howling like a coyote."

She quivered, unable to control a surge of lust. Silently he held out his hand. Unable to resist him, she put her fingers in his and let him help her down.

Keeping a tight grip on her, he locked the passenger door with his free hand and pushed it closed. Then he looked around. "The coast is still clear. Come on."

"This feels incredibly illicit."

"It's supposed to." He led her to the back of the van, where he'd created a narrow bed surrounded by boxes and tools. "That's what sexual adventures are all about. Take off your jacket before you get in," he said, his voice husky. "I don't want to take you back to your office all wrinkled."

Her breathing grew shallow as she slipped off her jacket. "Just well satisfied?"

"That's my plan."

And if she knew him, he'd carry out that plan to perfection.

He took her jacket and laid it carefully over a box. "Okay, crawl in. I'll be right behind you."

She looked into his eyes and dropped her voice to a sultry murmur. "Want to try it that way? With you behind me?" Once again, he'd turned her into a temptress.

He drew in a quick breath. "What do you think?"

"From the look in your eyes, I think you'd like that. I think you'd like that a lot."

"Get in there. We'll discuss positions once we get rid of these damned clothes."

Heart racing, she crawled up on the quilt and moved toward the front of the van. Kneeling on the quilt, she waited until he'd climbed in and closed the doors before pulling her cotton shell over her head.

"I'll take that, too." He held out his hand.

"And this?" She unhooked her bra and slipped the straps over her shoulders.

He let out a quivering sigh. "God, but you're gorgeous."

"You make me feel that way." A flush of pleasure skimmed over her body.

"I'm glad, but you being gorgeous has nothing to do with me." He took her bra and added it to her pile of clothes. "You just are."

She wondered if he thought so because she completely lost her inhibitions when they were together. He'd given her the courage to be sexually free, and every expert on the subject said that that made a woman irresistible.

She'd taken off her shoes and unbuttoned her slacks when she realized he was still dressed. "What about you?"

"My clothes won't wrinkle. I'm keeping as much on as I can, in case we're interrupted. I'll be able to get out there and divert attention while you get dressed."

"Wow. Are you a parking-garage veteran?"

"Nope." His breathing grew ragged as he watched her slide out of her slacks and panties. "First timer."

"Same here." She handed him the rest of her clothes.

His hands shook and her slacks slipped out of his fingers. "Look at me, all thumbs. It's because I'm going crazy knowing there's a naked woman in my van."

"One who wants you bad." Sitting back on her heels, she took the combs from her hair and let it tumble around her shoulders.

"I sure hope so." He unfastened his belt and unzipped his jeans. "Because you're about to get me." He shoved down his briefs and freed his erect penis.

"You're gorgeous, too," she whispered.

"Just so the equipment works for you. That's all that's important to me."

"Oh, it does that." She wished he didn't have to cover that most excellent piece of equipment. She'd never know the thrill of having him slide inside her without that barrier of latex, and she regretted that.

She watched, breathless with anticipation as he rolled the condom on. She'd taunted them both with a daring possibility, and she'd decided to follow through on that taunt. Once he'd finished putting on the condom, she deliberately turned her back to him and rose onto her hands and knees.

"Hey," she called softly, looking back over her shoulder. "It's time for a new adventure."

SHANE GULPED BACK a groan of delight. Somehow he'd have to enjoy this experience without making a lot of noise about it. There was no guarantee they'd have this level of the parking garage to themselves forever and sound echoed in a place like this.

"You're the sexiest woman I've ever known," he murmured, closing the short distance between them.

"Put me in the back of a van and take away my clothes, and this is what happens."

And he was the only man who knew that. Heart pounding so loud he was afraid the sound carried through the metal sides of the van, he cupped her smooth bottom in both hands. The intoxicating scent of her arousal told him that he didn't have to slip his fingers between her thighs to test her readiness. She wanted this as much as he did.

A red haze of need obscured all reason as he pushed into her slick, hot vagina. Forgetting the need for quiet, the need for discretion, he groaned with pleasure.

Her answering hum of delight was all the encouragement he needed. Easing in and out, he tried to keep the pace slow, but lust had him in a stranglehold. Before long his thighs slapped hers and they were both gasping for breath.

Her soft cries grew in volume.

He gritted his teeth, wanting to moan right along with her. "We should...be quiet." Ah, this was fantastic, gripping her smooth bottom as he plunged faster and faster.

Unbelievably, a buzzing sound chose that moment to come from the pager hanging on his belt, the belt that was dangling and wiggling with every thrust. To hell with it. Let them wait. Then the cell phone played its damned little "bombs away" song.

"Shane...Shane...your cell."

He blinked sweat from his eyes and kept pushing into

her glorious heat while he ignored the phone. "Don't care." He gulped for air. "Are you close?"

She moaned. "Yes."

"Me...too. Try not to...yell."

The pace was frantic now. He could feel her tighten, hear the hitch in her breathing that told him she was nearly there. One more stroke, maybe two...now...*yes.*

Her contractions and muffled cries sent him over the edge. His breath hissed through his clenched teeth as he fought to keep silent. He'd never come harder in his life than he did with her. Being quiet about it wasn't easy.

Finally the violent tremors subsided. He withdrew reluctantly, knowing he was leaving paradise. After taking care of the condom, he reached for Eileen, guiding her to his side and drawing her into the curve of his body.

He cupped her warm breasts and kissed her bare shoulder. "Thank you."

She still sounded breathless. "I loved every minute."

"Me, too. Van sex with you is incredible." He just wished her tone didn't imply that it would be a one-time deal. But she'd admitted that she wasn't getting tired of sex with him, so maybe he could get her to dump Benny, after all. Then he'd bring up the idea of marriage. If he mentioned that too soon, she wouldn't take him seriously.

"Do you think we made too much noise?"

"I haven't heard any cars come by, so even if we did, we're probably okay. I—"

At that moment the rumbling of an engine grew nearer. Eileen laughed. "Spoke too quickly."

"Drive on by, buddy," Shane murmured, stroking Eileen's breast. "Just drive on by."

Fortunately, the vehicle continued on, and the rumbling noise grew softer. But immediately after the sound faded, Shane's cell rang again.

Eileen extricated herself from Shane's arms and sat up. "Party's over," she said with a smile. "You need to answer your phone and your pager and get on with your day."

He gazed at her, all pink and tousled and looking as if she could easily go another round. He felt like opening the back door and tossing both his cell and his pager on the cement where somebody could run over them.

"Come on, Shane." She smiled at him. "The real world is waiting."

He thought the real world was inside this van, but he didn't want to argue with her. He also didn't want her to think that he was an irresponsible guy, so he reluctantly reached for her clothes.

"You're right. I do need to use my phone," he said as he handed over her clothes. "I'll order us each a deli sandwich to go. After all, I did invite you to lunch."

She wiggled into her panties. "This was the best lunch I've ever had."

He was getting hard watching her dress, so he glanced away. "Same here. And we're still on for dinner, right?"

"I wouldn't miss it for the world."

Neither would he. It looked like his last chance to accomplish his mission.

11

_____

CLUTCHING HER BRIGHT bouquet of flowers in one hand
and a bag containing her deli sandwich in the other, Eileen
walked into the offices of Traynor and Sizemore trying to
look as if she hadn't recently been having wild sex in the
back of a Mercury Communications van.

The receptionist, a small brunette named Linda, glanced
at her flowers. "Pretty."

"Thanks. I decided to start treating myself to fresh flowers more often."

"Good idea. And workouts at the gym on your lunch
hour?"

"Uh, no." Eileen felt a moment of panic. She'd repaired
her makeup and put her hair up again, but maybe she didn't
look as pulled together as she'd hoped.

"My mistake." Linda smiled. "You have such a healthy
glow, I thought you must have just stepped off a treadmill.
Don't mind me. I'm just trying to say you look great." She
pulled several messages off a spindle on her desk. "Here's
what came in while you were gone."

"Thanks." Juggling her flowers and deli bag with one
hand, she took the messages and started down the hall.
Three clients and her mother had left their numbers and
wanted an immediate response. Eileen never had this many
messages during lunch. It must be a conspiracy to remind
her of her duties.

"Mildred was looking for you a while ago," Linda called after her. "I told her you'd gone to lunch."

"Okay." As Eileen hurried down the hall to her office, she wondered how to explain the time she'd been gone. Obviously she hadn't left to eat lunch, considering that she was carrying a deli sandwich in a bag. Covering her tracks wouldn't be simple.

She could throw the sandwich away and pretend she'd already eaten, but she was starving to death. Shane seemed to have stirred up all her appetites. Not only was she dying to eat the sandwich, she wanted a raised glazed for dessert.

Dropping the deli bag, her purse and the messages on her desk, she grabbed the vase on her credenza, pulled out the silk flowers and took the vase along with the bouquet down the hall to the water cooler.

John Traynor, senior partner, passed her in the hall. "Delivery from Benjamin?" he asked with a wink.

"Um, not exact—"

"Usually I try to discourage office romances, but in this case I think it's wonderful. I see you two as becoming a real power couple." Then he turned and headed into his office before Eileen had a chance to respond.

She wouldn't have known what to say, anyway. *Power couple?* She imagined them each with little rocket boosters attached to their shoes so they could zoom through life. Oh, sure, she knew what Traynor meant. He wanted to see Benjamin get into politics, and a married man with the right wife on his arm had an edge in the polls. She probably qualified as a good candidate, being a local girl and a lawyer. Plus she had no skeletons in her closet, unless somebody found out about Shane.

Talk about giving up her sexual adventures. Anybody connected to a politician wouldn't dare indulge in fantasy sex or risk being smeared all over the tabloids. That wouldn't be a problem for Benjamin, because he didn't believe in such behavior.

As she shoved the flower stems into the water-filled vase, Eileen remembered what Shane had asked her today, whether she ever felt she was living someone else's life. When Benjamin was around, she felt that she was living his life. She hadn't wanted to admit that to Shane at the time, had barely admitted it to herself, but it was the truth.

That was the real reason she'd held off moving in with him. She'd told herself it was because she still needed to experience sex with a handsome stranger, but she'd done that now, and she still didn't want to move in with Benjamin. Once she shared his apartment, the takeover would be complete.

At one time she'd thought of a commitment to Benjamin as part of accepting her role as an adult. She'd considered it the logical step toward getting the house, the kids, the American Dream. Benjamin's more solid nature would balance her flights of fancy. Now she was beginning to wonder what that balancing act would cost her.

Back in her office, she set the flowers on the credenza and was amazed at how much life they brought to the room. She'd thought the silk ones were all she needed, but silk didn't give off a fragrance, and they didn't feel the same when she stroked them. Smoothing a finger over the ruffled surface of a pink carnation, she thought about the glorious moment when Shane had grasped her hips with both hands and pushed deep inside her.

"A little something from Benjamin?"

She turned, certain she was blushing, to see Mildred standing in the doorway. Mildred had gone to law school after raising three children and divorcing her husband. She didn't bother coloring her hair or trying to disguise a single one of her fifty-six years. Eileen expected Mildred to make partner before she did and maybe even before Benjamin.

"Actually, no," Eileen said. She started to say that she'd bought them for herself, but Mildred had a quality about her that demanded the truth. It made her a terrific lawyer. Eileen decided not to say where the flowers had come from.

Mildred's gray eyes grew speculative. "On second thought, I should have known they weren't from Benjamin. Not his style. He goes for a more formal arrangement."

"Yes."

"And perhaps you prefer something that's a little wilder?"

Eileen felt pretty certain Mildred wasn't talking about flowers anymore and she didn't quite know how to respond.

Mildred seemed about to say something more, but the buzz of Eileen's telephone interrupted the moment. "I'll catch you another time," Mildred said, and backed out of the office.

As Eileen walked around her desk and reached for her phone, she made a mental note to track Mildred down before the day ended. Maybe it was paranoia, but Mildred's office window looked out on the street where Shane had parked the van both the night before and today. Mildred was the most observant person in the office, and if Mildred suspected something, Eileen wanted to know that.

Her mother was on the phone. "The strangest thing happened," she said. "I got a call from Benjamin this morning, all the way from Switzerland."

"Really? About what?" Eileen couldn't imagine such a thing. Benjamin didn't call her mother when he was in town, let alone when he was in another country.

"Well, he said he was coming home early, and the two of you had a surprise for us. He wanted us to plan on going out to dinner with both of you on Saturday night."

"Oh." She felt outmaneuvered but, after all, she was dealing with a would-be politician. And she had told Benjamin that she had a surprise for him, plus she hadn't contradicted him when he'd assumed it had to do with moving in together.

"Are you planning to move in with him after he gets back?" her mother asked.

Now there was the million-dollar question. "I...I was considering it, but—"

"The reason I'm calling is that I've told you how I feel. I think it's a perfectly fine idea. However, I'm having more trouble with your father than I expected."

Relief flooded through her. She had an excuse to put off her decision. "Mom, that's okay. Let's not do the dinner thing on Saturday night. I'll talk to Benjamin and explain that we need to hold off for a bit."

"No, no, I don't want you to hold off. This is a good idea. Benjamin sounded so excited, sweetie. I don't want to rain on his parade. I still think I can bring your father around by Saturday night, but I wanted to give you a heads-up."

"I think we should just cancel Saturday night. I don't want to force anything." Mostly she didn't want to force herself to a point where there was no turning back. "Besides, I haven't decided yet what I want to do."

"I hope you're not letting your father's opinion sway you."

"Nope." She was desperately trying to hear her own inner voice in the midst of all the other influences swirling around her.

"Do you think there's a chance that Benjamin's surprise is a proposal?"

"Mom, I certainly hope Benjamin's not planning to propose. He hasn't even told me he loves me." She had a feeling that was another reward he was holding back until her clothes were hanging in his closet. He'd made vague statements about wanting to be sure they had an understanding before he gave his heart. Of course, she hadn't spouted any *I love yous,* either.

"Some men don't know how to express their love," her mother said. "I feel sure he cares deeply. And I'll bet you feel the same way about him."

"Mom, I—" The red light on her phone flashed, indicating she had another call. "Listen, I need to go. I'll call you Saturday, okay? We'll both know a lot more by then."

"That's fine, sweetie. Give Benjamin a hug for me."

"I will. Bye, Mom." *Maybe I will.* At the moment she wasn't feeling in a hugging mood when it came to Benjamin. He had no right to call her mother and set up a dinner without consulting her.

She took the next call, almost hoping it was Benjamin so she could tell him what she thought of his high-handed tactics. Considering her own behavior in the past two days, she had no right to be angry with him, but she was, anyway.

"This is Eileen," she said in her most professional manner.

"This is a man who wishes he had his head between your legs, so that he could kiss your sweet—"

"Shane." Moisture sluiced to the exact spot he'd been about to mention. She glanced nervously at her open door.

"Tell me you wouldn't like me to do that. Even then, I won't believe you."

She lowered her voice. "That's not the point. You're supposed to be working. I hope nobody can hear you."

"They can't. Listen, I know all we've planned for tonight is dinner, but under the circumstances, I'd like to figure on spending the whole night together."

She swallowed. "I...would like that, too."

"Good. I wanted to give you fair warning. When I pick you up at your apartment, you might want to pack whatever you plan to wear to the office tomorrow and whatever…whatever you want to wear to bed."

"Your bed?" She wondered if he'd take her back to his place. She had to admit she was curious about what it would look like.

"No. I have something else in mind."

"The van?"

He laughed. "No, not the van. That was fun for a lunch date, but I want more room to maneuver if we'll have all night to play. So I'll pick you up at your place about six?"

She gave him her home address, and phone number. "I'll be ready at six."

His voice grew silky and suggestive. "Are you ready right now?"

Yes, she was. "Stop it."

"I'll bet you're looking at the orgasm picture and remembering how I made you come on top of your desk."

Her body clenched. Much more of this conversation, and she might come again, without him even being in the same room with her. "I'm hanging up now. We both have work to do."

"I can't concentrate on anything but your hot, wet—"

"Goodbye, Shane." She hung up the phone and sat there quivering. Instead of getting tired of sex with him, she wanted it more than ever. Apparently there was a huge difference between a craving for doughnuts and a craving for Shane Nichols.

SHANE'S DESK WAS A disaster zone when he left a little before five. Even Rhonda, who had been so indulgent earlier in the day, had looked a little worried when she realized how many calls he hadn't yet returned. But he'd been busy.

Tonight was all the time he had to convince Eileen to give up on Benjamin. He'd had reservations to make and plans to concoct. On top of that, he was still wrestling with whether or not to tell Eileen he owned Mercury.

Finally he decided that couldn't be part of his pitch. That wasn't the essence of who he was, and he might be selling the company, anyway. Or not. He had a lot to work out about that, and he didn't want tonight to be all about his career angst. He wanted it to be about the passion between the two of them.

At his condo he dressed quickly and threw a change of clothes and his shaving kit into a small overnight bag. Leaving his BMW in the garage when he would be taking a woman to a nice restaurant felt weird, but he had to keep driving the van or blow his cover. On the way to Eileen's apartment building, he stopped briefly at a nearby mall for something interesting to add to their fun tonight. Then he had to face rush-hour traffic.

As he sat wedged in a major traffic jam, he punched in Eileen's number on his cell.

When she answered, sounding breathless and excited, adrenaline rushed through his system. Tonight had to do the trick. "I'm running late," he said. "Will they hold our reservation, or should you call?"

"I'll call, but don't worry about running late. So am I. I can't decide what to wear."

"Does that mean you're standing there with nothing on?" A dull ache started in his groin.

"Not quite."

He shouldn't ask. "What are you wearing?"

"Panties and bra."

He shifted in his seat. Traffic still wasn't moving, but it could start any minute, and he needed to get off the

phone—and get his mind off this particular topic—by then
"What color?"

"Black. Black silk. But I might change to red."

He drew a shaky breath. "I could help you decide when
I get there."

"I don't think so. We'd never make it to the restaurant
Bye, Shane." He heard the smile in her voice before she
hung up.

He shoved the phone back in its holder and sat there in
a state of high frustration. He had so little time to make
love to her, and he was stuck in traffic. Glancing around
he noticed a slight break between the cars on his right. I
he could get the car next to him to back up, he could
squeeze through there and take a side road. That might no
save him any time, but it sure beat sitting around getting
hard as a rock while he imagined Eileen walking through
her apartment in silk undies—red or black.

Putting on his turn signal, he tapped his horn and mo
tioned to the driver of the Honda beside him. The guy
didn't looked thrilled with the concept, but he put his ca
in reverse and backed cautiously toward the car behind him

Shane had barely enough room, but he managed to edg
the van through the opening. Then he took off down th
side street and searched out an alternative route to Eileen's
his pulse racing as he wondered if he'd get there before
she decided what to wear.

Twenty minutes later he rang her doorbell and hope
she'd continued to waffle on the underwear choice. Whil
he waited, he glanced around and took note of the well
maintained complex. Her apartment was on the secon
floor. The warm weather in Phoenix made indoor hallway
unnecessary, so the apartment doors opened to an outsid
walkway and exterior stairs.

From here he could see the parking lot and the Mercur

van sitting there. He wished he'd at least had the thing washed.

Moments later Eileen opened her door, and he cursed the traffic that had made him so late. She stood there looking wonderful, but way too dressed. He knew she wanted this restaurant fantasy, but that wouldn't happen for a while yet. He wanted to find out right now whether she'd decided to wear red or black under her black blouse and colorful full skirt.

His chances didn't look promising. Her purse was over her shoulder and she gripped her keys in one hand and the handle of a small wheeled suitcase in the other. "Let's go," she said.

"Aren't you going to invite me in?"

She smiled. "No, I'm not."

"But I've never seen your place."

"I've never seen yours, either."

"I'll show you mine if you'll show me yours." It was an empty promise. Once he showed her where he lived, he'd have to come clean about his ownership of the company.

She laughed and nudged him out of the way. "We're leaving now." She pulled the door shut with a solid click. Then she turned and locked the dead bolt.

With a sigh he accepted the fact that he'd have to wait a little longer to satisfy his curiosity and his unending lust. "I'll take your suitcase."

She relinquished the handle and walked beside him. "You look good in a dress shirt."

"You look good in that blouse and skirt, but I was hoping to catch you still wandering around in your underwear." He lifted the suitcase off its wheels and carried it down the stairs. "What color did you end up with?"

"Red."

"Oh, *man*. I love red. I can't believe that damned traffic made me miss seeing you in red underwear."

She grinned at him. "You sound exactly like a little boy who's been told he can't have a cookie before dinner."

"Or a big boy who's been told he can't have some nookie before dinner."

"If you'd caught me in my underwear, we would have had sex."

He shrugged. "So? I could use some sex."

"Anyone would think you hadn't had any in days."

"With you, hours feels like days. But that's just me. I guess you're totally cool right now."

"Guess again."

He set the suitcase down and took her arm. "Then let's go back upstairs. I want you so much I can taste—"

"What do you know?" called a woman from the parking lot in a voice he vaguely recognized. "Somebody must be making another donation to the homeless."

12

WELL, THIS CLINCHED IT, Eileen thought as she forced a smile and turned toward the woman walking from the parking lot. Fate was stepping in with combat boots to remind her that she was taking big risks with her future. "Hi, Miranda! How's the move coming along?" *And why aren't you gone yet, damn it!*

"Slow. I may have to take a few days off from work to get everything done."

Eileen knew she had to keep her tone light and friendly, no matter what. "Shane, you remember Miranda? From last night?"

"Sure. Nice to see you again, Miranda."

"Same here." Miranda looked him over. "I must say I'm impressed with your dedication to the cause, both of you. Did you find the place you were looking for last night?"

"Yes, we did, as a matter of fact," Shane said.

"Glad to hear it." Miranda glanced at Eileen, her expression making it clear she didn't buy the story about donations to the homeless. "Is Benjamin working late again tonight?"

Eileen felt the trap closing on her. After catching Eileen in a second suspicious situation with no Benjamin in sight, Miranda would drop by the office soon, no doubt about it, just to find out how much Benjamin knew.

Eileen decided she might as well give Miranda some of

the information she was fishing for. She'd get it eventually, anyway. "Actually, Benjamin's in Switzerland."

"Really?" Miranda's gaze grew even more suspicious. "How exciting for him. When's he due back?"

"Tomorrow night."

Miranda nodded. "Isn't it nice you found something to occupy your time while he's gone."

"I suppose it is." Eileen knew she'd been made. Miranda understood exactly what was going on and could hardly wait to tell Benjamin that his girlfriend had been fooling around.

"Well, I'd better be going. I have a ton of boxes to pack."

"Good luck with it," Eileen said as they headed off in different directions.

"She's going to squeal on you, you know," Shane said the minute they were out of hearing distance.

"I know."

He paused to unlock the van door. "You don't sound all that upset about it."

She wasn't, and that was strange. Here she'd planned to have this fling without Benjamin knowing, and now she almost *wanted* the chance to confront him with the information, to see how he'd react. "All afternoon I've been thinking that I'll have to tell him about you," she said. "Meeting Miranda only confirms it."

Shane went very still. "What are you planning to say?"

She looked into his eyes. "Don't worry. I won't mention either your name or your job. No details."

"What if I told you I didn't care?"

She gasped. "Shane! Of course you care. He's a lawyer, remember? I don't want him coming after either you or Mercury Communications. He couldn't sue you for fooling with his girl, but he could make things very unpleasant if he discovered you were doing it on company time. I'll make sure that doesn't happen.''

His jaw tightened. "I guess I don't like the idea of being some nameless guy you had a fling with. It makes the whole thing seem…''

She touched his cheek. "It's not like that, and you know it. I'm only trying to protect you. I don't know how Benjamin might react, and I don't want him to have a name to trace, in case he's feeling vindictive.'' She stroked the side of his tense jaw. "Are we going to dinner?''

He heaved a sigh. "Yes, we're going to dinner.'' He helped her into the van and then stowed her suitcase in the back.

After he'd climbed into the driver's seat and started the engine, he glanced over at her. "I appreciate you being concerned about my job, but I really wish you'd at least use my first name when you talk to Benjamin.''

"I'll—I'll think about it.'' She'd almost slipped and used it today, when she'd finally talked with Mildred. "I probably should tell you that there's another person besides Miranda who knows I've been involved with a man while Benjamin's been in Switzerland. But I trust her not to say anything.''

He backed the van out of the parking space and started toward the street. "Who's that?''

"Mildred, the other woman lawyer in the office. She must have noticed me getting into your van last night and again at noon today. Then she saw me with the flowers and guessed they weren't from Benjamin.''

"How would she figure that out?''

"Because when he sends flowers, they're usually…'' She paused, searching for a way to say it that wouldn't make Shane feel inadequate about his bouquet.

"More elaborate? Expensive? Classy?''

"Shane, I love that bouquet! It's as if someone plopped a big piece of sunshine and happiness in my office. I like it so much I've decided to start buying bouquets from street vendors on a regular basis, so I can have that kind of cheerful look all the time."

"I think you're just saying that to make me feel better about what was admittedly a cheap bouquet."

"I am not."

"Okay, so you're not." But he didn't sound convinced. "You still haven't told me how Mildred could tell the flowers weren't from Benjamin."

"Because the arrangements he has delivered are more...more pompous," she said at last, finding the courage to say what she really thought.

"Pompous." Shane sounded slightly happier. "Are you absolutely sure you didn't dredge up that word for my benefit? After all, you are a lawyer, and lawyers are supposed to be very good with words."

"I'm saying it because that's the way I really feel, and I'm finally admitting it. At first I was sort of impressed when I'd get one of these three-foot monstrosities. At least I thought I should be impressed, but—"

"Monstrosities! Now my mood's really improving. You may be shining me on, but I'll take it."

"I'm not shining you on." Her mother had been the one who'd loved the flowers Benjamin sent, she realized now. "The arrangements are beautiful, I guess, but they're total overkill. They'd work in the lobby of the Phoenician, but I have a small apartment and a small office. I'm talking about gigantic tropical flowers I don't even know the name of jutting up like sabers ready to poke your eye out if you aren't careful."

Shane was smiling now. "So my bouquet was a little more cuddly?"

"Definitely more cuddly." She loved to watch him smile. Watching him smile was one of her favorite pastimes, come to think of it.

"Okay, I'm happy now. Well, as happy as I can be, considering that we're not having sex at the moment."

"You're incorrigible."

"As I've mentioned before, I think that's what you like about me."

"I do." *For now.* But the fun had to end soon, no matter what happened with Benjamin. Eileen plus Shane added up to danger—a runaway train, a joyride with no brakes. The longer they stayed together, the more likely that he'd lose his job and she'd put hers in jeopardy. That was miles away from levelheaded behavior.

"So tell me about Mildred, the woman in your office. Why won't she spill the beans?"

"It turns out…" Eileen took a deep breath. "It turns out she doesn't think Benjamin and I are right for each other."

"That makes two of us."

"You don't even know him."

"No, although I'm starting to get a picture of a guy who compensates for a lack of imagination by grandiose gestures. But I don't want to talk about him. As I said, I'm not really worried about what he finds out when he gets back."

"He won't find out anything that would hurt you. I promise you that."

"He can't hurt me." Shane found a parking space in the lot beside the upscale Mexican restaurant Eileen had picked out for their adventure. He shut off the ignition and glanced over at her. "You're the only one who can do that."

Eileen felt her stomach clench. Deep down, she'd known that an attraction this strong would leave them both grieving when it was over. She'd hoped they wouldn't have to face that truth quite yet.

Another Arizona sunset washed the surrounding buildings with a deep pink. By this time tomorrow Benjamin would be home, and she'd have to decide for sure what to do. She'd have to have her head together by then, but she wasn't prepared for that moment now.

She cast around for the right words. "I don't know if Benjamin is the right person for me or not." She glanced over at Shane. "But up until Tuesday night, I had expected to marry him eventually."

"I know that," Shane said quietly.

"That might still be the way things turn out." She doubted it now, though. Even if Benjamin forgave her for the affair, she couldn't imagine resuming where they'd left off. Without meaning to, she'd given her heart to another.

Shane gazed at her without responding.

"I didn't mean for you to get hurt," she said. "I shouldn't have agreed to spending more time together. If I'd ended this after Tuesday night, then—"

"Then we both would have missed out on a lot," he said gently. "If tonight is the last time I'll ever be able to hold you, then it will hurt. I can't pretend it won't. But I wouldn't have missed this for the world."

She swallowed the lump in her throat. "But we wouldn't have to make it worse on you by going through with our plans for tonight." And worse on her, she realized. She was getting in over her head.

"Are you kidding? I want every single second I can have with you. I know there aren't any guarantees. I knew that going in. You're not telling me anything new. The only reason I said what I did is to make sure you understand that I'm not some shallow jerk out for thrills and no emotional involvement."

"I already know that. I'm not, either. Ever since Tuesday, I've tried to be that way, but it's not working."

His gaze softened. "Do you want to back out of tonight? Is this too intense for you?"

Maybe, but she couldn't give him up. Not yet. "I don't want to back out."

"I'm glad." He smiled. "Ready to go inside and have restaurant sex?"

"Yes." She unfastened her seat belt. "But first I want to do something." Leaning over, she cupped his cheek and kissed him gently on the mouth.

He seemed to understand this wasn't the prelude to a make-out session in the van. He kissed her back with the same easy pressure.

She drew back, her hand still cupping his cheek. "Thank you for all that you've given me."

"That goes double for me."

As THEY WALKED INTO the restaurant, Shane decided that, all in all, he was in fairly decent shape. Eileen was questioning her relationship with Benny, and Shane liked to think he'd been a part of creating some confusion in her mind. First confusion, then clarity—the clarity of knowing she was meant to be with him.

He didn't know what form their life together would take, and that was a good thing. Both of them had been trying to follow some socially accepted pattern, and that needed to stop right now. Correction, it had already stopped—the minute she'd propositioned him in the Traynor and Sizemore reception area. But living a more original lifestyle didn't have to mean giving up on marriage and kids. Or vice versa. She seemed convinced it was either/or, and that was another hurdle he'd confront…later. After restaurant sex.

From the minute they walked through the door, he knew why she'd chosen this place. Mariachi music was turned up to blast level and candles in red votive holders gave off barely enough light to see. Also, each table was draped with a generous red tablecloth. Around the perimeter of the room, alcoves for seating provided enough privacy to get his heart pumping. He doubted they'd end up at one of the tables out in the middle.

Eileen's attention seemed to be focused on one particularly remote alcove in the back corner. There was a reserved sign on the table, and Shane wasn't surprised when the hostess took them there.

Eileen made a little production of where each of them would sit at the table set for four. Shane ended up with his back to the room, and his imagination went wild as to how that figured into her scheme. She sat on his right, her back to the tiled wall that separated them from the next table of diners.

He gauged how difficult it would be to slide his hand under the tablecloth and up her skirt. Not so difficult, providing she cooperated with him. Because this had been her idea, he had a feeling she'd cooperate.

She grinned at him over the top of her menu. "What do you think?"

He had to read her lips to understand what she'd said. "The loud music is an inspiration."

"What?" She leaned closer.

He combed back her luxurious hair and put his mouth right up to her ear. "Those trumpets should drown out the sound of you coming."

She drew back and winked at him. "Maybe it'll be you needing the cover."

His ever-present erection made itself felt against the soft

cotton of his slacks. "I think you're the safer option," he said.

"What?"

He leaned closer. "You're a safer bet," he said, moving his lips more deliberately.

She spoke with the same slow deliberation, her full red lips looking infinitely kissable. "Maybe I don't want safe bets tonight."

But would she choose a safe bet when it came to a man in her life? He wouldn't worry about that now. Living for the moment had a lot of appeal, he decided, when Eileen had just slipped off her shoe and was rubbing her nylon-covered toes over his crotch.

A waiter appeared with glasses of water, a bowl of tortilla chips and two kinds of salsa. "Hi, I'm Rick. What can I get you to drink?" he asked in a voice loud enough to carry over the music.

Eileen continued to flex her toes against Shane's increasingly rigid penis as she responded in a similarly loud voice. "How about a couple of your great big frozen margaritas?" She glanced at Shane for confirmation.

He nodded. He would agree to anything as long as she kept massaging his crotch like that. What talented toes she had.

"Coming right up!" the waiter said.

So was he, Shane thought as the waiter hurried off.

Eileen continued to gaze at him as she took a chip from the bowl and scooped up some salsa. Instead of biting the chip, she licked away the salsa.

Mesmerized by the slow movement of her tongue combined with the steady flexing off her toes, he didn't realize he was gripping the edge of the pedestal table until it wobbled, nearly spilling their water.

Eileen smiled and spoke loudly enough that he could hear her. "A little tense, are we?"

"Nah." He willed his hands to relax on top of the table. "Totally in control."

"Too bad." She munched on her chip.

He cleared his throat and spoke distinctly. "You got the jump on me. Just wait until it's your turn on the hot seat." Even if someone overheard that, they'd have no idea what he meant unless they peeked under the table.

"Complaining?"

"Nope. Predicting."

"We'll see, won't we?" She picked up another curved chip and filled the slight depression with more hot salsa. This time she sucked it from the chip, all the while rubbing the ball of her foot right where it was guaranteed to drive him crazy.

As he became worried that she might actually make him come, he reached under the table and grabbed her foot.

Her eyes widened innocently. "Is there a problem?"

"Nothing I can't deal with." He massaged her foot and slipped his hand up her calf, but he couldn't reach where he wanted without some contortions that might be noticed by the waiter, who would arrive any minute.

Besides that, stroking her leg was getting him even more excited, so he'd be wise not to do that right now, either. Holding her foot with one hand, he put his other hand on the table and stared at the pattern of the tile over her left shoulder until the urge to climax eased.

"Have a chip," she said brightly.

He grabbed one from the bowl and bit the thing in two, not bothering with salsa. Salsa would only remind him of the way she'd sucked on that last chip.

The waiter arrived with their drinks in glasses the size of goldfish bowls. "Have you decided on your order?"

Shane realized that his menu lay untouched in front of him. He was so far from being ready to order it was pathetic. He might never be ready to order.

"I'll have the enchilada plate," Eileen said.

"Good choice," said Rick the perky waiter. "They're served with sour cream and the best guacamole you've ever tasted."

Shane was sure Eileen had ordered the enchiladas to torture him the same way she'd tortured him with the wraps during their rooftop picnic. He wondered how long he'd last before he had to pull her outside and into the van. He hadn't meant to do that, figuring they'd had enough van sex for one day, but tough times called for tough measures.

Unless…unless she had something else in mind. He hardly dared hope. He wasn't sure if this was all about teasing or not. If they scooted their chairs a little closer to the corner of the table, he could still manage some interesting maneuvers with her, but as for him…

"Shane, I'll bet you'd love the soft tacos," she said.

Whoops. While he'd been dreaming of sex in the van, the waiter had continued to hover, waiting for him to order. Eileen wanted him to have the soft tacos. No kidding. The counterpart to her rolled enchiladas.

"Sure." He glanced at her. "Soft tacos sound terrific. What do they, uh, *come* with?" He put just enough emphasis on the word to make her bite her lip to keep from laughing.

"Rice and our signature black beans," said the waiter.

"Sounds delicious."

"Very good. I'll be back with your order in a jiffy."

After he left, Eileen lifted her giant glass. "Here's to great…" She paused.

"Times," he said over the music. "Great times."

"*And sex,*" she mouthed carefully.

"Yeah." He smiled at her and gave her toes a little squeeze. "That, too." The margarita tasted cool and relaxing, the exact opposite to the way his body felt at the moment.

He decided maybe he should get a little proactive. He leaned in so he didn't have to shout. "You need to move your foot, so I can scoot my chair closer."

"Oh?" She licked the salt from the rim of her glass before taking another sip. "Why?"

"So I can reach you."

Her mouth curved in a saucy little smile. "Maybe I don't want you to reach me yet." She hunched forward until her lips were inches from his. "Remember how good it was up on the roof last night?"

His heart thudded faster. "Which part?" But he thought he knew.

"The part where you were lying on the quilt and I unzipped your jeans. And then I—"

Under the table, his penis surged to life again. "Okay, I know which part."

"Did you like it?"

He took a gulp of the cool margarita. "Silly question."

"What?"

He put his face close to hers. "I loved it, you incredible tease. You know I did."

"Want more of that?"

The blood rushed in his ears. He'd wondered how far she'd go. "H-here?"

She nodded. "Right...here."

13

SHANE GULPED. "I'm not exactly sure how you could—"

"Leave that to me."

He wanted her to try it. No doubt about that. But if they were caught, he was pretty sure that what she had in mind was illegal in your average metropolitan area. Getting arrested wouldn't do either of their careers a lot of good, and might convince her that adventure wasn't worth the price.

Well, they wouldn't be caught, that's all, because now that she'd suggested it, he wouldn't be able to live without the experience. As his penis throbbed in anticipation, their waiter arrived with two steaming plates.

"Here you are, folks," he said loudly. "Anything else I can get for you? Another margarita?"

"Not for me." Eileen raised her eyebrows in question as she looked at Shane. "But maybe you'd like a second one? You still look a little tense."

"I'm fine."

"Okay. Just thought you might want a little Dutch courage." She took a sip from her salt-rimmed glass and looked totally cool, as if promising to give her dinner companion oral sex in the middle of this restaurant was an everyday occurrence for her.

Because Shane's pulse was hopping around like a Mexican jumping bean, he couldn't resist trying to rattle her, just a little. He glanced at the waiter. "You could turn up the music, though,'' he said. ''I love this stuff. The louder the better.''

Eileen's mouthful of margarita spurted back into her glass.

The waiter laughed. ''Are you serious? It's already pretty loud.''

''I know, but if you'd crank it up some more, I'd be very grateful.''

''Sure.'' The waiter looked at him as if he still thought Shane was making a joke. ''I'll be back soon to check on you.''

''Take your time,'' Shane said. Then he looked over at Eileen, who was shaking her head and giggling. ''Can I help it if I'm a big mariachi fan?''

''And I thought I might have to talk you into this.''

He had to lean very close to make himself heard, because the music actually did seem to be louder now. ''Darlin', I would be a damned fool to talk you out of it.''

''I think so, too.'' Her mouth was tantalizingly close to his. ''But first, we need to eat a little, so we look as if we're having a normal meal.''

''I'm not hungry.''

''I am.'' She glanced down at her plate. ''Nice.'' She ran the tip of her finger along the length of one enchilada, gathering sauce as she went.

Shane groaned. ''Don't you dare....''

She dared. Bringing her finger to her mouth, she sucked on it.

He hunched forward and looked into her dancing eyes. ''You keep that up, and I'm liable to come before you ever start the main event.''

She took her damp finger out of her mouth and smiled at him. ''I don't think so. I've had sex with you, and I know you have better control than that.''

"I've never had to sit and watch you stroke an enchilada before."

"Poor baby. Take a bite of your food."

"Not interested."

"You'll have to pretend to eat, or someone might get curious." She took a mouthful of food and chewed slowly.

"You're going to make me wait for this, aren't you?"

"Not much longer. Eat something."

"Let me tell you what I'd like to eat."

"That's not on the menu."

"It will be, later."

Her eyes grew dark. Slowly she swallowed her bite of food. Then she ran her tongue over her mouth. "I can't believe how much I want you."

Every time she said something like that, he was filled with hope that they had a future. "I'm right here and, oh, so available."

"Oh, look at that. I dropped my napkin." She leaned toward the floor. "Whoops, still can't get it."

And before Shane could take a breath, she was out of sight under the table. Then...oh, dear Lord...she started unzipping his pants. He couldn't resist glancing around, to see if anybody, anybody at all, had a clue what was going on in this dark little corner of the restaurant.

To his amazement, everyone seemed totally unaware. They talked, laughed, ate and drank as if they had no idea that Eileen had worked his aching penis free and was stroking it with fingers slightly chilled by a frozen margarita glass. A fantasy didn't get much better than this.

Check that. It could get a hell of a lot better. Now she was using her tongue. And he was going quietly insane.

She'd told him to fake eating his dinner. He tried, but the fork clattered from his fingers onto the plate. Picking up his margarita in two hands, he gulped it down, every last drop.

But when she closed her mouth over the tip of his very happy penis, he put the margarita glass down. At this moment he'd be better off not holding anything breakable, because she was sliding her lips down, down, down. The subtle pressure of her tongue made him start to shake.

He didn't know what to do about the shaking. Or the moaning. Even the mariachi trumpets might not be loud enough. In a flash of inspiration, he grabbed his cloth napkin from his lap and pretended to be coughing into it.

She began to suck more deliberately, and he knew the day of reckoning was close at hand. His climax rode closer with every downward stroke of her tongue. Yes…there… oh…*yes.* He pressed the napkin to his mouth and shuddered as he erupted into the warmth of her velvet mouth.

As of now, mariachi music was his favorite in the whole wide world.

AFTER TUCKING, ZIPPING and generally getting Shane back together again, Eileen quickly emerged from under the table holding her napkin as if she'd only just returned from grabbing it. After she slipped into her seat, she glanced over at Shane.

He looked like a man who'd been hit by lightning. His eyes were unfocused and his lips were parted as he gasped for air. She'd be willing to bet he'd never had a sexual experience to equal this one.

As for her, she was totally proud of herself and unbelievably turned on. But from the looks of Shane, he wouldn't recover enough to help her out until a wee bit later, which was as she'd planned it. She'd wanted this restaurant adventure to be all about him.

Because he was so sexually generous, she loved being the same. Looking at him, she felt a rush of tenderness. That kind of emotion hadn't been part of the plan, but she couldn't help it. To think she'd started out looking for completely anonymous sex, and now...now it was intensely personal.

Giving Shane's elbow a nudge, she smiled at him. "What do you think of this restaurant so far?"

He cleared his throat and shifted in his chair, but his gaze was firmly fastened on her. "Outstanding."

"Glad you approve."

Just then their waiter popped over to their table and glanced at their plates. "Anything wrong with your food, folks? I'd be more than happy to get you something else if there's a problem."

"We're not as hungry as we thought," Eileen said. "How about boxing it up for us?"

"Good idea," Shane said. His voice was almost back to normal.

"Be glad to do that." The waiter whisked both plates away.

For the first time Eileen noticed that Shane's margarita glass was empty. "Whoa. You must have polished that off when I wasn't looking."

His grin was sheepish. "I couldn't eat while you were...under there. So I drank."

"So I see. Maybe I should drive to wherever we're going next. I've barely touched mine."

"I feel as if I could do anything right now, but maybe you're right. Between the tequila and you, I may not be fully in command of my reflexes." He glanced at her and shook his head in wonder. "You are one hell of a woman."

"Thank you." She beamed, willing to accept that compliment. She felt like one hell of a woman for the first time in her life.

Their waiter arrived with styrofoam boxes and a bill. Although it bothered Eileen to hold back and let Shane pay yet again, she knew he wouldn't want her to contribute and she didn't want to argue about money. At least tonight would be the end of his expenditures. And quite possibly the end of their time together. She definitely didn't want to think about that.

In the parking lot, Shane set the bag of food on the van's hood and unlocked the driver's door. "Let's get you in there and then we'll adjust the seat." He boosted her up and she settled behind the wheel.

Technically she probably shouldn't be driving a company van, she suspected, but Shane had already broken so many company rules that this one was insignificant. And he needed to let that margarita wear off.

"The adjustment's under here." He reached between her legs for the seat lever.

It made for a very tempting position, with his head nearly in her lap and his arm between her legs. She squirmed in the seat as little jolts of arousal taunted her.

Apparently he was thinking along the same lines. "This might take a while," he murmured. "God, but you smell good." He pulled the metal lever under the seat and it moved, but instead of going forward, it slid back. "That's better," he said.

Maybe he was drunker than she'd thought. "Um, Shane, I need it closer to the pedals, not farther away."

"You only think that's what you need." He let go of the lever and slipped his hand up under her skirt.

She gasped and closed her thighs over his hand. For good measure, she grabbed his arm with both hands. "Not here!"

He smiled up at her, his eyes sparkling in the overhead lights. "Why not? I know you want to come. Giving me that treat under the table must have had an effect on you, too."

"So what if it did? We can take care of me later, when we get to…wherever we're going."

"That'll take too long. Let me give you something to tide you over."

All he had to do was suggest such a thing and she was more than ready. But she had to consider the risks. "The place is well lit and…someone could come along."

"And all they'd see would be me explaining the idio-syncrasies of this van so you'll feel comfortable driving it. My body will block any view of you."

"I don't know." Her nipples grew rigid with excitement and she began to quiver.

"Sure you do. You know you want me to." He rubbed his cheek against the side of her breast. "Put your hands on the wheel and leave the driving to me."

"If anybody shows up…"

"I'll stop what I'm doing and start explaining the stiff clutch and how to handle it." He worked his fingers closer to her damp panties. "Come to think of it, you should be very good at handling a stiff clutch. You handled mine like a pro. That orgasm seemed to go on forever."

With a moan of surrender, she placed both hands on the steering wheel and unclenched her thighs.

"Good girl." He slid his fingers past the elastic.

Or maybe she was a bad girl, because at the first electric thrill of his touch, she spread her thighs even wider.

"Nice," he murmured. "And don't tell me you don't need this. You're on fire." He stroked her quickly, using his talent for finding the right spot and the right rhythm. "How's that?"

"Incredible." Her climax slipped closer with every stroke. Closing her eyes, she leaned against the headrest.

"Head forward," he said softly. "If you lean back, you'll look like a woman about to come, instead of a woman listening to automotive instructions."

She forced her head upright and hung on to the steering wheel for dear life. "I *am*…a woman…about to come."

"Good." He quickened the pace even more. "Let loose, woman," he said in a voice husky and intimate. "Show me what you're made of."

It seemed she was made of shooting stars and a shimmering rainbow. Pressing her lips together to keep from crying out, she slid over the arch of that rainbow, propelled by the urgent thrust of his fingers.

"That's it," he said softly, caressing her as she slowly returned from her wild and wonderful ride. "Fantastic."

With a long, quivering sigh, she sank against the seat. Then she looked down at him through eyes glazed with satisfaction. "Now…I don't know if *I'm*…fit to drive."

He eased his hand free and stood on the running board to give her a lingering kiss. "You will be. We'll sit here a minute, until you've recovered." Then he reached down for the lever and carefully moved the seat up again. "How's that?"

Her laugh was breathless. "When my legs are no longer made of rubber, it'll be fine."

He closed her door, walked around to the passenger side and unlocked it. After climbing in, he handed her the keys. "When you're ready."

"Where are we going?"

He grinned at her. "Where else? To paradise."

ONCE SHE'D RECOVERED from her climax, Eileen seemed more than willing to drive, so Shane tried not to feel guilty or guzzling his margarita and putting her in that position. He felt a little better after treating her to some fun, but, still, he didn't feel like a manly man with her behind the wheel and him riding shotgun.

On the positive side, because he wasn't driving he could spend a lot more time looking at Eileen, and that was a definite benefit. The light from the dash illuminated her profile, and he visually caressed her high, smooth forehead, her upturned nose, her full mouth and her endearingly firm chin.

She looked adorable at the wheel of the van. Competent, too. He had a sudden picture of her ferrying kids to soccer practice, and the image squeezed his heart. He wanted to be the father of her kids.

"Driving a van is kind of cool," she said. "I like being able to see over the regular cars. So, where do we turn off?"

He took a deep breath. He'd been expecting to drive, and he'd planned to keep her guessing, keep her talking until they were well on their way. He wasn't sure about this decision, but it had seemed like the right one at the time. "Not for a while yet."

"A man of mystery, huh?" She flashed him a smile. "We're running out of civilization fast, though. Are you looking for a lonely road so we can park?"

"Nope."

"I know, you've stowed a tent in the back."

"No tent. That might be fun sometime, though." He said knowing that theoretically they would be out of time after tonight. But if the next few hours went the way he wanted them to, they might have all the time in the world.

"Okay, no tent and we're headed out of town. You're sure we're not going to spend the night in the van?"

"I don't know about you, but that wouldn't be my idϵ of a fantasy."

"Maybe not for the whole night. Okay, Shane, my c riosity is killing me. Where are we spending the night?"

He was so worried that she'd think he was crazy f planning this, but he couldn't keep her in the dark foreve "In a cabin in the woods."

"We *are?* But there aren't any woods until we get to—

"Oak Creek Canyon." Suddenly he was sure he'd ma a huge tactical error. He should have taken her to one the many fancy resorts in Scottsdale. "I hope you don mind driving that far, but it's only about another hour the traffic stays light like this, and I thought it would fun."

She laughed in delight. "I *love* the idea! A cabin for on night. How crazy and silly and absolutely inspired. Tot seclusion so we can do whatever we want."

"Exactly." He sighed with relief. "I was hoping you have that reaction." And it proved he was beginning know her. Why go to a resort when they could be all alor in the woods? "It means we'll have to get up and leav early, so we can be at work on time."

"I don't care. The adventure is worth it. Does it have fireplace?"

"Of course."

"And we'll build a fire?"

"That's the idea. It's one big room, with a fireplace ar a peeled-log bed." He hoped she liked the bed. From t picture, it looked exactly like the one in his condo, ar someday he hoped she'd share that one with him, too.

"You've been there?"

"No, I saw this place on the Internet."

"The Internet? Oh, Shane, I love the idea. I really d But I'm even more worried about your job. I'll bet y

alked Rhonda into using the company computer to find this
place.''

"Not exactly." He'd used his own computer, but he'd
had to be cagey about it, changing screens whenever
Rhonda happened to walk into his office.

Eileen let out a breath. "Well, what's done is done, I
suppose. We have to make sure we aren't late tomorrow.
How did you get a key so quick?"

"Because it was such short notice, they sent a messenger
over with it." And that had really aroused Rhonda's curiosity.

"Now I'm worried about what this is costing you."

"Don't. Spending tonight with you is worth a hell of a
lot more than what I'm paying for this cabin."

"I'm getting something out of the deal, too, you know,"
she said quietly. "So I think you should let me help pay."

"Look, I haven't been dating much at all lately." At
least that much was true. "This week isn't going to break
me." Not financially, anyway. His heart might be a different story.

She was silent for several long seconds. "Okay," she
said at last. "But just let me say you're a very generous
guy, going out of your way like this, considering…"

He knew what she was thinking—*considering I'll probably dump you when my boyfriend gets back.* He didn't
want her lingering on that subject long. And he didn't plan
for it to happen, anyway. "Considering that you've treated
me to the best sex of my life?" he said, finishing her sentence in his own way. "I'd say generosity on my part is
called for."

"You've given me the best sex of my life, too," she
said.

"And I'm not even finished."

"Now don't start with that, or I'm liable to get all dis combobulated and wreck this van."

He laughed, happy to know that he had that kind of effec on her. "Then what should I talk about?"

"You can tell me about your job."

"I don't want to talk about my job."

"Then tell me about your family."

He was more than happy to do that. Part of his plan i driving up here was that they'd have enforced togethernes with no immediate chance of sex. The sex was terrific, an through that they'd begun to know each other in certai ways, but they were missing some important connections

So he told her about growing up in Phoenix, about hi older brother and the rivalry they'd always had. Then was her turn, and he found out that being an only kid ha built-in pressure to succeed, too.

Both of them, it seemed to him, had tried to live up t the expectations of others. In the process, they'd lost sigh of what they wanted, at least he had. He was beginning t figure out what he wanted, and it was all tied in with th woman driving this van.

The conversation took them up the Black Canyon high way and through the town of Sedona. The famous red roc formations that had made the town famous were silhouette against a night sky filled with stars as they drove alon U.S. 89 and into the wooded canyon beyond town.

"This next road should be it," Shane said after anothe ten minutes of driving. "Okay, right turn and down thi little lane. Here it is." A small log cabin with a tiny fron porch was barely visible in the darkness.

"I am *so* excited."

"Never had cabin-in-the-woods sex?" He'd counte on that.

"Never. And I've always wanted to."

Shane thought about all that he had in mind for this cozy little spot. "Darlin', you're about to have all the cabin-in-the-woods sex you can handle."

14

EILEEN HOPPED OUT of the van, not bothering to wait for Shane to come around and help her. Her shoes crunched on dried leaves and she took a deep breath, drawing in the scent of pine and oak. If she wasn't mistaken, that burbling sound nearby had to be Oak Creek.

She'd driven up here years ago with her parents. She'd meant to come back, but school, career goals and generally trying to be the model daughter had gotten in the way. She was beginning to realize how much of her true nature she'd denied while she'd striven to be a good girl.

The forest was so still, so secluded and dark. The forest would keep their secrets. A cool breeze caressed her bare arms and she shivered with excitement.

The sound of Shane opening and closing the back doors of the van seemed very loud in the quiet night. The liquid slide of water over smooth stones just beyond the cabin had a sexual quality to it. Someday she'd like to make love beside a gurgling stream. Or in a tent, as Shane had suggested.

Silly girl, she'd thought her need for adventure could be satisfied in three nights. Slowly she was coming to a conclusion. She definitely wasn't ready to settle down with Benjamin. She probably wasn't ready to settle down with anyone at all. There was a good chance that her love of sexual excitement meant that she shouldn't agree to any commitment, not now and maybe not ever.

"Let's go in." Shane appeared by her side carrying the two suitcases. "We have a date with a bearskin rug."

"There's a bearskin rug in there?" She closed and locked the driver's door and followed him onto the wooden porch.

"Fake bearskin. These are very environmentally friendly folks." He put down the suitcases and took a key out of his pocket. "But, fake or not, I want you lying naked on it while I lick you all over."

She wanted that, too. The drive up here had been just long enough to ratchet her craving to the combustible stage. Riding through the rugged moonlit landscape with Shane, being within touching distance and yet unable to touch because she had to concentrate on the road, had been a delicious form of torture.

He opened the door, which creaked on its hinges, and flipped on a switch just inside the door. "Not bad." He stepped aside to let her go in ahead of him.

"It's perfect." She walked into a room scented with freshly split logs. Two bedside lamps with parchment shades cast a buttery glow over a room right out of her dreams. Her gaze swept over log walls, a stone fireplace, and a bed that looked as if it had been put together by Paul Bunyan.

Through a door was a small bathroom, and along the cabin's far wall were a sink, a stove and a small refrigerator. Wood, cedar from the scent of it, lay stacked neatly beside the fireplace, along with a supply of kindling. And, sure enough, in front of the fireplace was a large furry white rug.

"I think it'll work." Shane put down the suitcases and turned to lock the door.

"I could live here." Eileen surprised herself by saying that. "I mean, if life was different, and I was different."

"You wouldn't have to be the slightest bit different."
Shane crossed to her and slipped his arms around her waist.
"But your life would."

She wound her arms around his neck and looked into his
hungry eyes. "You mean this could be the equivalent of
living in a grass hut and existing on mangoes and fish?"

"I mean when life is simpler, there's more time for
this." He pulled her close and covered her mouth with his.

His kiss was filled with the promise of what they'd do
in this cabin, and his mouth and tongue moved suggestively
as he teased her with unspoken possibilities. But woven
through the sensuality was something more, a bold male
assurance that he'd get whatever he wanted from her, because it was his right.

She couldn't deny the sensation of being claimed. She
shouldn't like that. But she did. At this moment, in this
remote cabin, she wanted to be taken on a fur rug in front
of the fire while outside the pines whispered in the wind.
For now, she belonged to this dark-haired, green-eyed man
who knew her better than any other person in the world.

He ran his hands down her back and cupped her bottom,
holding her tightly against his erection. Then, with obvious
reluctance, he pulled away from the kiss. "If I keep this
up, we'll be on the rug in front of a cold hearth. Can you
find something to do while I build a fire?"

"I think I might be able to."

"Use your imagination." He kissed her lightly and released her. Then he turned toward the hearth.

She swayed for a moment, still caught in the daze that
his kiss had produced.

Shane knelt by the empty fireplace, removed the screen
and open the flue. He was so damned sexy. She ached for
him with a fierceness that made her wonder how she'd survive without him.

But if they were to continue, it would be on different terms. Different terms might destroy the thrill. Now they were racing against time, but what if they had all the time in the world?

The idea made her body tighten with anticipation. She couldn't imagine ever getting tired of having sexual adventures with him. But she couldn't trust her judgment when he was so near and so unbelievably exciting.

She remembered that she was supposed to be making good use of her time right now, and all she'd done so far was stand and gaze raptly at Shane. He'd said he wanted her naked on that soft white rug, but she had another step in mind before that happened.

Because she understood his love of fantasy, she was pretty sure he'd enjoy seeing her in the transparent red slip she'd grabbed off the rack in a ten-minute raid on Victoria's Secret after work. She hadn't even taken the time to try it on. She hoped it fit.

While Shane stacked wood and kindling in the fireplace, she stepped out of her shoes and started taking off her skirt.

He glanced over his shoulder at her. "Hey, I like where this is going."

"Don't look yet. Just keep building the fire."

"Oh, babe, that's definitely happening. One look at you shimmying out of your skirt, and the temperature over here shot way up. I may not need a match."

"We may not need the fire, period." A flush had spread over her skin, warming her more than any fire could. Even though she was stripping down to nothing, she wasn't at all chilled.

"I know we don't need it to stay warm." He struck a match against the stone hearth and touched it to the dry kindling. "But I want to hear it crackling while I'm moving deep inside you. It's part of my mountain-man fantasy."

She'd guessed as much when he'd told her about this cabin. "Am I the beautiful maiden you've rescued from the marauding bear?" She zipped open her suitcase and pulled out the slip.

"Yeah, you are. If I could order up a snowstorm, I'd throw that in." He looked at the flames devouring the kindling. When they started licking the bigger logs, he replaced the fireplace screen. "That should hold us for awhile. Can I look yet?"

The slip was a little tighter than she expected, clinging to her breasts and hips and shimmering with every breath she took. She had no mirror, so she wasn't sure what the effect would be. "Yes, you can look."

Still on his knees, he turned. From the widening of his eyes and the slackness of his jaw, the effect was exactly what she'd been after.

She clasped her hands in front of her and batted her eyelashes like a heroine in a melodrama. "Thank you for saving me from the bear, you big strong man, you."

He swallowed. "Ma'am, I would battle twenty grizzlies to see you in that outfit."

"I'm glad you like it." Holding out her hands, she did a slow turn.

He groaned. "You do realize I can see right through it."

"Of course. That's exactly the point. I'm wearing something, but it's as if I'm wearing nothing." She turned to face him again.

"Damn, that's sexy, seeing your nipples through that red filmy stuff." He started unbuttoning his shirt. "Come closer. It's time for you to show me how grateful you are about that bear."

She sashayed over to him. "What did you have in mind, you rugged mountain man?"

He stood and gestured to the rug at his feet. "You,

stretched out on that rug.'' He kicked off his shoes. ''And me, claiming my reward for bravery.''

She sank to her knees on the rug, which tickled her skin. ''Will you be gentle?''

''Probably not.'' He disposed of his slacks and briefs, revealing an impressive erection.

''Good.'' She ran her tongue over her lips, remembering the taste of him.

He drew in a sharp breath.

Looking into his eyes, she thought he might be remembering how she'd made him come earlier that night. ''Would you like—''

''Not this time.'' His voice was hoarse, and his eyes hot. ''But I wonder if I'll ever look at your mouth without thinking of what happened in that restaurant.''

''Is that a bad thing?''

He smiled. ''Not when we're alone. Lie down, fair maiden. I'm about to enjoy the pleasures of your ripe and willing body.''

AS SHANE WATCHED his dream girl stretch out on the rug, he fought to keep from making love to her right that instant, without thought of birth control or consequences. She was everything he'd ever wanted, and he had the strongest urge to make her his in the most basic way, without barriers of any kind between them. That would mean she could get pregnant. He wanted that, too.

Complete insanity. That kind of momentous decision needed to be made by both of them, and he knew damned well she wasn't ready for such a step with him. Dropping to his knees, he fumbled for his slacks and dug out the condoms he'd stuffed in the pocket before he'd left his condo.

Laying them within reach, he braced both hands on either

side of her shoulders and gazed down at a vision that put to shame every centerfold he'd ever ogled. From her blond hair spilling over the white rug to her hourglass figure draped in transparent red, right on down her long legs to her hot red toenails, she was what every guy wished for and never imagined he'd get. And for this moment, she wanted him.

"How's this fantasy treating you?" she murmured, cupping his face in both hands and drawing him down to her full, red mouth.

"Can't complain." Then he closed his eyes and kissed that talented mouth, the same one that had taken him around the world inside a noisy Mexican restaurant. She'd offered to do it again right now. Saints be praised, she sounded as if she *wanted* to.

She wasn't shy about taking charge of that ever-ready bad boy. As if to prove that point, she reached down and curled her fingers around his penis.

Ah, that was good. As he sucked gently on her tongue, she flicked her thumb against the underside of his shaft. Next to them the fire popped and sizzled in time with his surging blood. She knew exactly how to touch him, and he wanted to stay right here, enjoying that steady motion of her thumb until his come poured over her hand.

And he would…another time…another night. There would be another night, if only because when he slept his dreams were filled with images of sex in every conceivable place, every conceivable position, always with her, the woman who shared his obsessions.

And she'd nearly petted him into oblivion this time. With a groan he caught her wrist. "Stop," he whispered against her wet mouth. "Or I'll lose it."

Her breath feathered his lips. "But you want to."

"More than you know. I love the way you touch me.

But now it's my turn...to touch you.'' He kissed his way down the curve of her throat, closing his eyes and breathing in her orange-blossom perfume.

Her skin was so warm. He pressed his mouth to the spot where her pulse beat while he slid one hand between her silky thighs. Her pulse became more rapid, fluttering against his lips as he pressed the heel of his hand against her curls and dipped two fingers inside her heat.

She clutched his shoulders, her fingertips flexing, her body starting to quiver.

He nipped the tender skin of her throat and slid his fingers deeper. "Are you close?"

"Always."

"Good." He slipped his hand free. "I want you to be close...on the edge. That'll make this next part more fun."

She moaned softly, as if in protest.

But he didn't take that protest seriously. She would love this.

He began with the tips of her fingers, licking each hand until she quivered. Then he moved to her wrists, the insides of each elbow, her inner arm. Next he caressed her feet, sucking each toe until she began to whimper and move restlessly against the fur rug. His tongue traveled to the backs of her knees and the insides of her thighs.

Then he slowly pushed the transparent material up over her breasts. He spent as much time as he dared licking her rigid nipples. He didn't want her to come, not yet, and her rapid breathing told him she might if he stayed there long.

His tongue took another journey between her ribs and over her belly. By the time he reached his final destination, she was shaking. And so very wet.

One swipe of his tongue and she arched into his caress, silently begging for more. And then, at long last, he gave her more, deepening that intimate kiss until she shuddered in the grip of her climax. He loved making her come, but it wasn't only her wild release that made his heart beat faster. At the peak of her pleasure, she called his name. He took that to signify something very important to him. He was her mystery lover no more.

While she was still gasping for breath, he lifted himself away long enough to grab a condom from the floor beside them. He put it on in record time and entered her, the last spasms of her orgasm stroking his aching penis.

He took a deep, quivering breath, fought back the on-slaught of his own climax, and began to thrust. "Eileen, open your eyes," he murmured, saying her name on purpose. The time for a meeting of anonymous bodies was long over.

Her lashes fluttered upward, and she looked at him. "Shane," she whispered. "Oh, Shane."

"I'm here, Eileen." He shoved deep. Unless heaven could give him pleasure like this, he didn't care if he never made it past those pearly gates.

He gazed down at the most beautiful woman in the universe while firelight flickered over her body, a woman whose thighs were spread so that he could plunge deep, again and again. He listened to the crackle of the fire as the steady friction brought him ever closer.

She grasped his hips and rose to meet his thrusts. And he knew exactly when she realized that she was about to come again. Her breath caught, and surprise flashed in her blue eyes.

"Yes," he said. "Together, this time."

Her grip tightened, but her body became more fluid. He felt her open up, welcoming him in a way that brought a groan of joy to his lips. He wondered if she knew this was about more than sex.

He drove home with a sureness that he'd never felt before. He didn't have to calculate how much longer before they'd both come. His body knew. Her body knew.

At the moment she arched with the first convulsion, he exploded, rocking forward in a shower of ecstasy. Nearly blinded by the pleasure of it, he still sought her gaze and saw the same wonder reflected there. She might not know it, but they'd passed the point of no return.

EILEEN HAD TO ADMIT that Shane had shaken her up with that last session. And she didn't want to talk about it, so once they'd recovered enough to speak, she'd announced that they should warm up their dinner and eat it. Shane had gone along with the suggestion readily enough, but she could feel him watching her as she borrowed his shirt, putting it on and rolling up the sleeves. She slipped on her panties, too, and he pulled on his briefs and slacks.

Up until now they'd had sex like two playful animals. But she couldn't pretend they'd only been playing this time. This time Shane hadn't simply been pushing her sexual boundaries. He'd made love to her.

But she wasn't ready to deal with that, so she bustled around finding plates in the cupboards and forks in a drawer. Because they hadn't thought about bringing anything to drink, they filled two glasses with ice and water. Then they used the small microwave to warm the food and took it over by the fire, sitting cross-legged and side by side on the white rug,

At first she made small talk about how surprisingly good the food was, even after all this time. She made a production of enjoying it, too, which wasn't difficult because she was hungry.

But gradually the food began to disappear, and she ran out of comments. Shane didn't seem inclined to make conversation, so they sat and ate in silence for a while.

Finally she motioned to the smartly burning fire. "You're good at that."

He swallowed a bite of his taco. "I used to be a Boy Scout. Earned enough merit badges to make me top-heavy."

She laughed. "I did the same with Girl Scouts."

"Just a couple of overachievers, I guess."

"I guess." She thought about all that Shane had told her while they were driving here about being in competition with his older brother growing up. And he'd obviously excelled at many things, including being a Boy Scout. Something about him wasn't adding up. "So didn't you ever think about going to college?"

"I went to college."

"Really?" She glanced at him. "But you didn't like it?"

He met her gaze. "I liked it fine. Got a degree in business, but I also messed around with some electrical engineering courses."

Gradually the pieces fell into place. She should have figured it out earlier. So that was why he wasn't worried about losing his job, and why he'd happened to be there when she'd called the office this morning. "Mercury is your company, isn't it?" she said stiffly.

"Yeah."

More than anything, she felt foolish for not catching on. But he hadn't wanted her to, apparently. She'd been worried about Benjamin's manipulative behavior in calling her mother, but what was this? She stared into the fire, trying to reconcile all the wonderful sex they'd had with a gross misrepresentation.

"You think I should have told you sooner," he said.

She swallowed a lump of anger. "Yes, I think you should have told me sooner."

"Would you have propositioned me if you'd known who I was?"

"No, but that's not the point!" Or maybe it was. He should have been truthful from the beginning, but that would have meant destroying any chance of acting out her fantasy.

"Forgive me for wanting you so much that I'd do anything, say anything, be anything you needed me to be."

She turned to look at him, and her anger softened at the pleading look in his eyes. "But you could have told me the next night. You could have told me while we sat in that cute little pub having drinks."

"You still had your blue-collar adventure going on. Our rooftop sex was all about the working man and the professional woman. Don't try to tell me it wasn't, because I know better."

She tried to hold on to indignation, at the very least, but she was having trouble doing that. He was right about her. Part of the thrill had been getting it on with a tradesman, someone who worked with his hands. She focused on the fire again, unable to face him. "I guess that makes me pretty shallow."

"No." He ran a finger over her cheek. "It makes you a woman fighting to get out of a straitjacket. Finding a man who wasn't in your normal circle made it easier to let go. And because you thought I was somebody else, I could let go, too. I needed that alter ego as much as you did."

"So why admit to it at all? I never would have had to know."

"I think you know why. Something's happening between us, and I—"

"Forget I asked that." She turned to him and cupped his face in both hands. "We're not going to have this conversation."

"Eileen."

"I'm a mixed-up woman who doesn't know what she wants." She stared intently into his wonderful eyes, determined to make him understand. "The man I thought I was going to marry, the man my mother is sure I'm going to marry, is flying home tomorrow night. I owe it to myself and him to meet his plane and figure out what to do about him before I start screwing up anybody else's life."

"I think you do know what you want."

She caressed his cheeks with her thumbs. "No, I don't. Not for the long haul. All I know is what I want right now. And I don't care if you own a company or dig ditches for a living. You're an incredible lover."

The corners of his mouth turned up in a faint smile. "Okay, I'll take that."

"So, can we…can we go to bed, now?"

His gaze smoldered. "Still have a craving for those doughnuts?"

"Guess so."

Questions lurked in his eyes, but at last he gave her a lazy smile as he got to his feet and pulled her up against him. "Then, darlin', you've come to the right place."

15

SHANE HAD KNOWN THAT he'd had to come clean about his identity. There was really no reason to hide his ownership of the company anymore. Once he'd seen Eileen's enthusiastic reaction to this rustic cabin, he'd known that she didn't care about whether a man was rich, poor or somewhere in between.

He had more to say regarding his job and how it might change in the future, specifically so that he could spend time with her. But she wasn't ready to hear that, not when he knew she was so confused about her own situation. He realized she had to deal with Benjamin before she could decide what to do about him.

It was sort of like one of those reality TV shows. The process of elimination had to be done in a certain order. In the meantime, he didn't blame her for wanting to lose herself in sex, considering they were tucked away in this cabin for the night. He couldn't imagine wasting precious time sitting around discussing whether he should restructure his life.

He was planning to do that, though. Tomorrow would be a big day for him, too. He was going to find out how to go about selling his company.

But right now, he had Eileen stretched out naked on a playground of a bed and he'd brought dessert in his suitcase. After shucking his pants and loading the bedside table with more condoms, he carried a small jar and a soft paint-brush over to the bed.

Her face lit with anticipation. "Toys?"

"I thought we could have a little fun with this. It's—"

"I know." She sat up and stretched out her hand. "Chocolate body paint. I have always wanted to try this, but…" Her voice trailed off. Then she wiggled her hand in eagerness. "Give it here. Let me look at it."

He held it out of reach. "My toy." He could imagine what she'd stopped herself from saying. Something to do with Benjamin being too finicky or repressed to try chocolate body paint.

She laughed and took hold of his erect cock instead. "Maybe I can talk you into sharing your toy."

"You can play with that one all you want. This body paint is mine. I'm in a decorating kind of mood."

She scooted closer and cupped his balls in her other hand, giving him a sensuous massage while she stroked his penis up and down. "Please, Shane?" She gazed up at him with those china-doll blue eyes. "Let me paint first. I l-o-o-ove chocolate."

"I want to suck chocolate off your nipples."

She licked her top lip. "I want to suck chocolate off your—"

"Okay." The briefest suggestion that she'd use that mouth of hers the way she had back in the restaurant, and he was her slave. Besides, he didn't want to be like finicky old Benny. And her slow massage down there was a real persuader, too.

"I thought you'd see things my way." She released him and held out her hand for the jar and the paint brush. Then she slid back across the mattress and patted the spot next to her. "Get ready to be my art project."

"And then I'll take a turn, right?"

She glanced at the small jar. "We'll see."

He wouldn't get a turn. He could see that. She'd lick chocolate off him until he came, and by then the chocolate would be all gone. So there was another thing to add to his wish list, painting Eileen with chocolate and eating it off.

By the time he'd stretched out on the soft sheet, she had the top off the jar and her finger inside it.

She scooped out a little and started to put her finger in her mouth. "Wanna taste?"

"Indulge me. Rub it on your nipple."

"I can do that."

If he'd been hard before, watching her rub chocolate on her nipple made his penis rigid as a crowbar.

She glanced up, her lips parted and her eyes growing dark. "That feels good."

How he loved watching her explore her sexuality. Apparently nobody had ever encouraged her before. "Then put on some more."

She did, dipping her finger into the jar and covering her nipple until it looked like a piece of Valentine candy. Then she sucked the excess from her finger, a dreamy expression on her face.

He cleared the huskiness from his throat. "Come here."

Leaning over him, she presented her chocolate-covered nipple for his enjoyment.

He took it in all at once, cupping her breast in both hands and fastening his mouth over this new kind of sugar treat. His mouth had never known anything to equal the double thrill of chocolate and Eileen. Closing his eyes, he concentrated on the taste and texture of his dessert.

The sweetness seemed to linger, and he wasn't ready to stop when she pulled back, dislodging her nipple. "That's...that's enough." Her voice was breathless.

He looked into her eyes, glazed with desire. "Again."

"No. Or I'll never get my turn."

"Sure you will." He kneaded her plump breast. "Put some on your other nipple. You said it feels nice when you do that."

"Too nice. It makes me want to try it…other places."

His breath caught. "Then put it other places. Forget about the paint brush. Rub chocolate wherever it feels good and I'll suck it off and make you feel even better."

She hesitated, as if the sensuous pull of his suggestion was almost more than she could resist. Then she shook her head. "No. I've never had a chance to try it on a guy, and I might never…"

"You can paint me with chocolate anytime you want." He refused to let her think that tonight would be the end of them.

"Then I think I'll do it right now."

"Sure. Go ahead." He wasn't going to argue with her about who put chocolate on whom. Either way, he'd be a winner tonight. But damn it, he wished he could guarantee what would happen after tomorrow.

"I think I'll start with your mouth."

"I thought you might start a little lower."

"No, that'll be my final masterpiece."

She looked so cute and serious as she dipped the brush in the jar. He realized that she really did want this body-painting experience, that she'd been curious about trying it for a long time, and she didn't want to miss out on the opportunity.

Although he didn't care about getting chocolate on anything but his stiff buddy down below, she wanted the whole shebang. Correction, maybe he wanted the whole shebang, too. When she stroked the brush over his lower lip, it was incredibly sexy.

He could see why she'd enjoyed putting chocolate on

her nipple. The creamy sensation combined with the irresistible scent of chocolate stirred him up more than he'd expected.

And then she started licking it off, and there was another wild feeling. He tried to kiss her while she was doing it.

"No." She moved away. "No kissing. Just lie there and let me get the chocolate off. That's what this is all about."

He ran his tongue over his lower lip.

"And you can't do that, either. Now I have to put on more."

He laughed as he caught her determined expression. "There are rules?"

"My rules. I've imagined how this would be and I want to do it that way. Now hold still while I paint your lip again."

"I feel like some doll you're playing with."

She giggled as she stroked the brush over his lip again. "My dolls never had equipment like yours. And you're way more fun to play with."

"I should hope so."

"I love playing with you," she whispered. Then she licked his lower lip perfectly clean.

Getting painted by Eileen turned out to be more wonderful than he'd ever imagined. The smooth glide of the brush made him aware of things about his body he'd never known before. He discovered that his nipples were erogenous zones, and he'd never thought so. But then maybe every inch of him was an erogenous zone when he was with Eileen.

She painted each individual rib and managed to use her tongue without tickling him more than he could stand. Then she outlined the muscles of his stomach. "A chocolate-covered six-pack," she murmured, and began to lick again.

Finally she was ready for her masterpiece, and he was

more than ready for her to create it. With the first stroke
of her chocolate-covered brush from the base of his penis
to the tip, he thought he might climax.

But he managed to control himself. By now he had a
good idea of her planned scenario, and he didn't want to
ruin it by coming too soon. No one had ever painted his
penis before, though, and the sensation was unbelievably
erotic.

Soon he was gulping for air. "About done?"

"Almost."

He clenched his fists as she swished the brush over the
tip.

"There. Done."

"Thank goodness."

And then she began to clean him up, and he was ready
to thank the makers of soft paint brushes and the producers
of chocolate. As she worked him over, and he meant that
in the best way possible, he was so glad he'd stopped at
the mall on his way to her apartment. When he finally
came, crying out with joy, he knew he'd never look at a
chocolate-covered banana in the same way again.

AFTER THE GREAT chocolate caper, Eileen took a wet wash-
cloth from the bathroom and sponged Shane down a little
so they could cuddle without getting sticky. She toweled
him dry and even thought to walk over and put another log
on the fire. She'd never had a fireplace, but she'd always
wanted one. Benjamin thought the only kind worth having
was gas, but then the flame would be so *predictable*.

She thought about predictability as she climbed back into
bed with Shane and he gathered her close. He was the total
opposite of predictable.

"That was spectacular." He held her spoon fashion, with

her bottom tucked into the curve of his groin and his hands cradling her breasts.

"Thanks for letting me hog the whole jar and for being my guinea pig," she said.

"I loved every minute of it." He drew her closer and nestled his cheek against her hair. "I thought I'd only care about having my cock painted, but I enjoyed it all."

"You're so easy to be with." The words tumbled out before she had time to think about how they might sound, or the kind of encouragement they might offer. She had to untangle herself from Benjamin before she could think about anyone else.

"You're easy to be with, too," he said.

She liked hearing that, but she had to admit that almost all they'd done was have sex. Sure, they were sexually compatible, maybe too compatible. If she and Shane hooked up for any length of time, life would be all about sex, and that wasn't a very responsible way to be.

They lay quietly for a while, listening to the crackle of the fire as they snuggled together on the huge bed.

"You're going to think I'm a maniac," he said at last, "but I want you again."

"Maybe we both are maniacs." She was beginning to wonder about herself, because all he had to do was say he wanted her, and moisture gathered between her thighs. She couldn't get enough of him, either.

He sighed happily as he caressed her there and discovered the truth of what she'd said. "So wet. I love touching you and finding you this way."

"I can't seem to help it."

"Me, either." He rolled her to her back. "And there's one thing we haven't tried yet. You might not want to."

She looked into his eyes. "If it involves you inside me within the next ten seconds, I'm game to try anything."

"It does." He reached for a condom and balanced on his elbows while he tore open the package. "It most definitely does."

"What is it?" She watched, her body starting to throb with excitement, as he put on the condom.

"Just this." Holding her gaze, he moved over her, probed gently with the tip of his penis and drove home.

"Nice." It was a gross understatement. He felt so darned good in there. Amazingly good, as if his body and hers had been specifically fashioned for each other's and no one else's. She gripped his bottom and felt the play of muscles as he began to thrust. Mmm. Delicious.

"We've sort of shied away from this," he said. "I mean, here we are on a bed in the missionary position. How boring is that?"

Not. In fact, she was heating up faster than a June morning in Arizona. The steady friction of his stroke, placed exactly where she needed it most, was heavenly. "Are you bored?"

"Can't say as I am." His glance roved over her. "You look good in bed."

"You look good in me."

He laughed. "I feel good in you. And I have a perfect view of your face. I'm going to watch you come."

"And I can watch you come, too."

"Yeah, but you're going first. That simultaneous stuff is fine once in a while, but I want to watch you climax without being distracted by my own."

She could feel that climax he was discussing edging closer, maybe even *because* he was discussing it. "Does my face scrunch up?"

"No." He increased the tempo. "First you start panting, like that, so your lips are open a little bit. If I kissed you now I could slip my tongue right inside, but I'm not going to kiss you. I'm going to watch you come.''

She moaned as the coil of tension inside her tightened another notch.

''That's it. You're really getting close. Your eyes are so dark and wild-looking, and your cheeks are flushed. And when you start making those little mewing sounds, I know you're almost there.''

She gasped. ''I…am.''

''If I move a little bit faster, you're going to come.'' He stepped up the pace. ''Like that?''

''Yes!'' The first spasm hit her.

''There you go, over the top. Oh, yeah. Yeah, holler if you want. Yell my name. I love that. I can feel you coming. And now…now, I…it's my turn. Keep moving, babe. Keep…oh, yeah…yeah…Eileen…*Eileen!*'' He shuddered and bucked against her as his eyes burned with green fire.

Then, when the storm had finally subsided, he slowly lowered himself to his elbows and settled his mouth on hers for a long, deep kiss. Lifting his mouth at last, he whispered ''Perfect'' and nestled his head against her shoulder.

Dazed, she held him tight, stroked his hair and fought tears of an intense emotion she didn't understand. She was a basket case. Why? There had been no unusual circumstances, no special position and no props. It had just been plain old ordinary sex. And it had left her totally shattered.

SHANE DIDN'T WANT to go to sleep. Their hours in the cabin were too precious to waste that way. But this last go-round with Eileen had left him so damned mellow, he had trouble keeping his eyes open.

He wondered if she'd felt all the unspoken love he'd put into the experience this time. Because love was what he was feeling for her, with liberal doses of lust mixed in. He thought her feelings toward him might deepen, too, if she'd only allow that to happen. But she was fighting it, thinking she had to deal with Benny first.

Benny would fall asleep at a moment like this, no doubt. So Shane decided he wouldn't, no matter how tempting the idea might be. He roused himself with difficulty and left the warmth of her body with great reluctance. In the bathroom he considered a shower to wake himself up, but that seemed like too much effort. And maybe Eileen wanted to sleep and he didn't want her feeling she had to wait for him to return.

He came out of the bathroom and stood by the bed. She lay there with her eyes closed and her breathing steady. Although he wasn't ready to make love right this minute, he knew if he stood looking at her incredible body for much longer, he'd want her again.

And the wonder of it was that she'd want him again, too. Her sexual appetite matched his perfectly. He sensed that she had a problem with that.

The longer he watched her, the more he became convinced that she was falling asleep, and that's what he should let her do. The fire popped, and he wandered over to the hearth to make sure everything was under control.

The fire was mostly glowing coals, with only a few tiny flames dancing among them. Perfect for roasting marshmallows. Perfect for snuggling with a hot mug of cocoa.

Shane wanted the time and space to do those things with Eileen. He decided that one thing he would do after selling the business was buy a cabin in the woods somewhere, one with a fireplace. Maybe he could get a job installing phone lines in a mountain town like Prescott or Payson.

He sat down on the white rug, which tickled his privates. Interesting sensation. If he and Eileen tried it with her on top, he'd have a whole different memory of sex on the rug.

But that might not be in the cards tonight if Eileen slept until morning.

Staring into the fire, he tried to picture what his life might be like with a nine-to-five job and a cabin in the woods. And Eileen. The image wouldn't lock into place. She'd never said a word about giving up lawyering, and she and her parents had put a lot into her education. She might have said she could live in a cabin like this, but the skills she'd trained for were best put to use in a big city like Phoenix.

They had so much to talk about, the two of them, and none of it had to do with sex. He was eager to start sorting out the details, but instinct told him that he had to wait or risk scaring her away completely. He'd hold off until after tomorrow night, when she spoke with Benjamin.

Shane didn't like thinking of her with Benny, though. Being with him was probably a habit with her, and once he was home, she might find it easier to fall back in with him than fight the status quo. He sensed that her mother was part of the net holding her fast, too.

"You left me all alone," she said softly.

He glanced up in surprise to see her standing beside him wrapped in the comforter from the bed. "I thought you were sleeping."

She gazed at him, as if trying to figure out a particularly thorny problem. "I…missed you."

His heart squeezed. It was a small admission, but he'd take whatever he could get. He started to get up. "Then I'll come back to bed."

"I have a better idea. Let's bring the pillows down here and sleep right beside the fire. It'll be like camping out."

"I was just wishing I had a couple of coat hangers and some marshmallows."

She smiled. "Yeah, that would be fun." She let the

comforter slip from her shoulders and handed it to him. "Here, you can spread this out while I get the pillows."

Looking at her standing before him with her high, full breasts, her narrow waist and the blond thatch of curls between her thighs, his mouth went dry. She was so gorgeous, and he was the lucky man spending the night with her. "Maybe you'd better grab a condom while you're at it."

Her eyebrows lifted. "You don't want to sleep?"

"Do you?"

She shook her head.

"Then you'd better bring a condom." As he watched her walk to the bedside table, his erection was already making itself known, and he wondered if there would ever be a time when he'd look at this woman and not want to make love to her.

Apparently that particular phenomenon wasn't about to happen to him tonight.

16

SHANE FOUND OUT what sex on the rug felt like when he was on the bottom, and it was a damned fine experience. He tried to stay awake to savor the aftereffects, but apparently he'd pushed himself as far as he could go. Bundled under the quilt with Eileen in front of a grate of glowing embers, he slept until a bird chirping outside the window woke him.

He sat up with a start. Pale light filtered in through the window. Damn, they'd have to get moving if they intended to be at work by nine. He'd thought about setting the alarm on his watch but had been so sure he wouldn't fall asleep.

Leaning down, he nuzzled Eileen awake. "We have to get going. It's morning."

She bolted upright and came close to cracking him in the jaw. He leaped back in time to save a collision.

"I should have set the alarm on my watch," she said, echoing his very thought as she scrambled to her feet. "Can I have the first shower?"

"Sure. I'll see if they stock any coffee in the kitchen. And don't worry. We'll make it." He hated that they had to rush out of here. Someday, by God, he would wake up in a backwoods cabin with Eileen and they could snuggle until they decided to get up…or until something else was up.

He glanced down and smiled grimly. Well, that didn't

take long to happen. One look at Eileen as she hurried naked into the bathroom, and the flag was up.

But they were out of time for fun and games. As he walked over to the cupboard in search of coffee, he knew they'd had enough sex in these three days to sway her opinion, but he wondered if they'd had enough time. He hoped he'd given her reason to dump Benny and come running back to him.

A can of coffee sat in the back of the cupboard, along with a pack of filters, so he stoked up the coffee pot. If he'd been thinking clearly, he would have brought at least bread to make some toast. Instead he'd brought body paint. Maybe that had been more important, though.

He wanted to take care of one detail now, while he was thinking about it. On the bedside table he found a small pad of paper and a pen. He jotted down his home address and phone number, so he'd have it handy to give to Eileen before they parted ways this morning. The next contact had to be up to her. He hoped and prayed it would come tonight, after she'd dumped Benny.

As the coffee perked, he ran a hand over his stubbled jaw. He'd shave and shower before they left, even if they were on a tight schedule. Although he could afford to do that at home and go in late, he wanted to be reasonably presentable when he said goodbye to Eileen. If her last image of him was of some scruffy-looking rogue, that might not stand up so well against a Harvard grad getting off a plane in a tailored suit.

Whenever Shane thought about Benny, his gut tightened in a familiar way. And in a flash of insight, he realized why. He was competing with the guy exactly the way he'd always competed against his older brother. That rocked him back. He hoped to hell he didn't want Eileen simply because he had to fight off a rival to get her.

Sure, he'd recognized early that the challenge had drawn him, but if this was all about the challenge, what would happen if she dumped Benny? Would this craving for her disappear?

When she came out of the bathroom looking like a goddess, with one towel wrapped around her head and another barely concealing her luscious body, he couldn't believe that he'd ever lose that craving. Wanting her seemed to be what he did best. But he had to admit they were in an unusual situation, one that could mess with their minds.

"I want you to know that my fingers itch to come over and yank that towel off," he said. "But I'm keeping my hands off you so I don't make you late for work. In other words, I want credit for being noble."

"Credit given." She smiled at him and then looked away. "And I'm ignoring that you're naked and magnificently aroused, so I don't make *you* late for work." She walked over to her suitcase and pulled out her clothes.

"So we're both incredibly noble." Her smile made him think of happy endings and forever afters. He wanted to go down on one knee and proclaim his love. But he needed to wait, both for her sake and his.

So he put down his coffee mug, grabbed his shaving kit and headed toward the shower. "Help yourself to coffee. It's all we have in the way of breakfast, I'm afraid. I didn't plan ahead very well."

"You planned beautifully," she called after him. "I love this place."

"Good!" he called back, cheerfully, as if his heart hadn't slammed to a stop when she'd started a sentence with *I love*. But she'd ended it with *this place,* not *you.*

Maybe he'd been secretly hoping she'd say the words before they left. In any relationship, somebody had to go first, and because she was the one with the prior commitment, he thought it needed to be her. Damn the time crunch, anyway. If he had one more day, one more night...but he didn't.

Twenty minutes later, they stepped out on the front porch and Shane locked the cabin door. He breathed in the scent of the canyon, a combination of cedar boughs above and dried oak leaves carpeting the forest floor. The sky was becoming bluer by the minute.

"I want to call in sick," Eileen said softly.

He was sorely tempted. She was back to her professional self, all done up in a gray pantsuit and her hair in a careful arrangement on top of her head. Her perfectly applied red lipstick glistened in the morning sunlight.

Not a thing about her suggested that she was the same woman who had taken off her clothes in the back of his van or covered his penis with chocolate. Nothing except the look in her eyes. He knew that with one touch, one kiss, he could turn her into a vixen again.

But he didn't think that was a good idea. For three days he'd been determined to prove that he was more than willing to bend the rules. Maybe he needed to show her he could abide by them, too.

He stroked a knuckle softly over her cheek. "I'd love nothing better than to stay here all day. But we both have things to do."

"I know. I just...hate to say goodbye to the fantasy."

He reached in his pocket and handed her the piece of paper with his address and phone number on it. "I'll still be just a phone call away." It was the most he'd allow himself to say.

She stared at the paper and swallowed. "You know I can't promise anything." Then she looked up at him. "I have to see Benjamin, and I have to...think."

"Yeah, I know. Maybe we both need a little thinking time."

"Do you suppose that it's good that we have to pull back for a little while?"

"Maybe." He just wished she wasn't about to interact with another man. "But I'll leave the timing up to you. If…if you want to contact me tonight, even late, feel free." He wouldn't be sleeping, anyway, knowing that she could be with Benny.

She nodded and tucked the piece of paper in her pocket. "We'll see."

"Right." He wouldn't ask her for more of a commitment than that. "Let's saddle up. It's late."

"Okay." She cast one more look at the cabin before heading toward the van.

After he helped her into the passenger seat, she squeezed his hand and gazed down at him. "No matter what, these three days have been the most—"

"You don't have to say it." And he didn't want her to. It sounded too much like a speech you made when everything was over. "I know."

"I hope so."

"Yeah, I do." He looked into those eyes one last time. Then he brushed a kiss over the back of her hand before releasing it. He refused to consider the possibility that what they'd had was ending.

SEDONA'S RED ROCKS glowed in the morning sunlight as Shane and Eileen took the road back to the main highway. Eileen noticed hikers winding their way to the top of one of the massive rocks. She and Shane could do that, and if they picked their time carefully, they could have some fun when they got up there.

She didn't mention the idea to him. That would be unfair,

considering that she didn't know where they were headed in this relationship. He wasn't even sure himself, obviously, if he needed thinking time, too.

During the drive back to Phoenix, several more sexual fantasies occurred to her, all of them tied in with Shane— one of them involving tying *up* Shane. She kept them to herself. She wondered if he was having the same problem, because he didn't speak much, either. Where once they'd felt free to say whatever sexy thing entered their minds, now they had to censor their speech. It felt very unnatural.

She was almost relieved as they reached the outskirts of Phoenix. Without meaning to, she sighed.

Shane glanced at her. "If you're hungry, I can pick up something quick at a drive-through."

She gave him an automatic smile. "No, no. I'm fine. But go ahead if you're hungry."

"Nope. I'm okay."

She thought about the food that had been a part of their sexual adventures. Now they were reduced to discussing fast food from a drive-through. Maybe that's what real life did to fantasies.

She looked over at him, and his jaw seemed tight. This couldn't be fun for him, either. He'd dressed in jeans and a Mercury Communications T-shirt again this morning. Now that she knew he owned the company, she wondered about that. "Are those your normal work clothes?"

He looked down, as if he'd forgotten what he was wearing. "Uh, no."

"So this was your outfit to keep me thinking you were only an installer."

"Yeah." He cleared his throat. "Are you still bothered about that?"

"No. You're absolutely right that we wouldn't have got-ten together at all if you'd been up-front about your position with the company. Everything would have changed, and I...wouldn't want anything changed about our time together.''

Some of the tension left his shoulders. ''Neither would I.''

''But you've been out of touch for several hours.'' She glanced at his cell phone in its holder on the dash. ''Is that on?''

''Nope. I turned it off when I got to the parking lot of your apartment building. And the pager's sitting on my desk. I figured we deserved to get away from those contraptions.''

She worried about the reckless note in his voice. He'd built a thriving business, but she didn't think he'd done it with this kind of attitude. ''Maybe you should turn the phone on again.'' She reached in her purse and pulled out hers. ''We both should. I didn't tell anyone I was leaving. Did you?''

He shook his head. ''No, and it felt wonderful to play hooky for a change. I've given that company my heart and soul for way too long. If everything went to hell in a handbasket while I was gone, so be it.''

''Well, I'm turning on my phone, so be forewarned.''

With a heavy sigh, he reached for the button on his. ''Okay, we're reconnected to the world.''

Eileen's was the first one to ring.

It was her mother. ''Oh, sweetie, I'm so glad to hear your voice! I tried to get you at home last night and left a couple of messages. Then I tried the office, thinking you'd worked late, but you weren't there. Then I tried again early this morning, and when I still didn't get an answer, I didn't know what to think!''

Eileen settled for the truth. ''I spent the night in a cabin up in Oak Creek Canyon. I'm on my way back to the office now.''

"A cabin in Oak Creek Canyon?" She made it sound as if Eileen had taken a rocket ship to Mars. "What in heaven's name for?"

This was the point where she decided a little fiction needed to be woven in with the truth. "You know that project I told you I was so heavily involved in? I needed some quiet time to work on it."

Beside her, Shane snorted with laughter, and Eileen quickly covered the mouthpiece in hopes her mother wouldn't hear and get suspicious.

Apparently her mother was already suspicious. "All the way up there? You've been acting very strangely this week. Is there something wrong?"

"No, Mom. Nothing's wrong. What did you call me about?"

"Well, it has to do with your father and Benjamin. I just—"

"Mom, I'm not going to talk about this right now." She couldn't imagine having the conversation with Shane listening.

"Are you driving? Do you want to call me back when you get to the office?"

Eileen didn't want to talk to her mother about Benjamin at all today, because, by tonight, he could be a dead issue. But she wasn't going to tell her mother that.

As she was debating what to say, Shane's phone rang. He answered it.

"Eileen?" her mother said. "Are you there? Listen, if you can't talk now, please call me from work. I want to talk to you before you pick Benjamin up at the airport. This is important."

"I'm still here. Listen, Mom—" She broke off as she

heard Shane talking to Ken, the man who'd called him yesterday during their sexual escapade in the van.

Talk about being thrown back into reality with a capital *R*, riding down the road with each of them talking on their cells. It was enough to give Eileen hives. "Mom, I'll try to call, but I can't make any promises. Bye." She hung up and switched off the phone.

"Ken, I'll be happy to get back to you within the hour, but I'm not in my office so I can't go over those figures with you right now." He paused. "Absolutely. Please do check out the competition. Right. Goodbye." He hung up. "I'm turning it off again, Eileen. I'm just not ready to—"

"I turned mine off, too," she said. "At least we can have a few minutes of peace."

"Maybe we should call in sick and turn the van around."

"Don't tempt me."

He laughed softly. "I thought that was my job description."

She blew out an impatient breath. "Do you see what happens? We let ourselves get used to living in a fantasy world, and now we don't want to meet our obligations. This proves my whole point."

"Or maybe we just need to cut down on our obligations," he said quietly.

"And when you say things like that, you really start to scare me, Shane. It's one thing to throw caution to the wind for a few days, but I get the impression you're ready to make a career of it. You may want to sabotage the business you've worked so hard to build up, but I'm not about to let all those years of schooling go down the drain so I can live in a cabin in the woods."

"Don't be scared," he said. "I'm not nearly as radical as I sound. I can understand why you're panicking a little.

You just talked to your mother, and all her expectations are pulling at you right now, but—''

''It's not my mother talking. It's me! I don't want to become some lazy person living off the fat of the land while I indulge myself in sexual fantasies. I can't do that, Shane.''

''I'm not asking you to.'' His voice was tight. ''I'm just saying—''

''I don't think we should discuss this. We don't look at things in the same way.''

''Oh, yes, we do.''

''No, we don't!'' She didn't want to shout at him, but she was doing it, anyway. And she was afraid, very afraid. Because every time she looked at him, she felt like giving up all she'd ever worked for, all the things her parents had ever wanted for her, so that she could spend the rest of her days having sexual adventures with Shane.

But that wasn't his fault. After all, she'd been the one who'd originally seduced him. ''I'm sorry,'' she said. ''I'm sorry I yelled at you. I owe you a lot, and I'm sounding very ungrateful.''

He was silent for several long moments. ''You don't owe me a damned thing,'' he said at last. ''But you owe a hell of a lot to yourself. I hope you don't forget that.'' He braked the van, and she discovered to her surprise they were in the parking lot of her apartment building. She'd been so busy battling her fears, she'd become oblivious to her surroundings.

He opened his door. ''I'll take your suitcase upstairs for you.''

She glanced at her watch. ''Never mind. I'll just stick it in my trunk and leave. If I do that, I should just make it to the office on time.''

He paused, one hand still on the wheel. ''Look, if you're

afraid to let me into your apartment, afraid I'll try to kiss you or something, then—''

"I'm not." She put a hand on his arm. "I trust you not to deliberately sabotage me. Besides, I'm capable of doing that all by myself," she said wryly. "I just don't want to take the time to go back to my apartment."

"Okay." He sounded mollified. "Then let's get you on your way."

Moments later, she unlocked her car and popped the trunk so Shane could lift the suitcase inside. She waited until he came back to the driver's side of the car, but she left the door between them, more to keep herself in line than out of worry that he'd haul her into a passionate embrace.

With his sunglasses on, she couldn't see the expression in his eyes. That was just as well, because she was a sucker for those sexy green eyes.

He ran a finger up and down the sleeve of her jacket. "I need to know that I'll hear from you again," he said. "If not tonight, then sometime soon."

She nodded. "You'll hear from me."

"We have more business to transact, you and I."

The sexy undertone in his voice made her shiver with longing. But she didn't trust her response to him. She didn't want to look back one day and discover that she'd ruined her life for a few stolen hours of great sex.

"You'd better go," he said.

"You, too."

He leaned forward and brushed his lips over hers. "Till next time." Then he walked back to the van.

She got into her car quickly, as if lingering another second would be disastrous. It might. One little whisper of a kiss from him, and she was ready to forget work, forget

Benjamin, forget everything and drag him up to her apartment for more wild and satisfying sex.

Quivering, she started the car and drove out of the parking lot. Several blocks later, the dinging noise from her dashboard registered, and she fastened her seat belt. Driving without a seat belt. That pretty much summed up the way she felt whenever she thought about Shane.

17

SHANE DROVE STRAIGHT to the office, even though he could have gone home to change into slacks and a dress shirt. He didn't need to. His jeans and T-shirt would work fine for what he'd planned today—Operation Getting His Life Back.

He walked in only about ten minutes late. Not bad, considering that he'd been in Oak Creek Canyon three hours ago. But the thing was, he'd never been late before.

Jack Lansky, one of the salesmen, was heading out to an appointment. "Hi, Shane." He glanced at Shane's T-shirt and jeans. "Are we doing casual Fridays now?"

"No, just didn't have time to change." Shane gave him a smile and tried not to think about abandoning Jack, his wife and two kids to a new owner. "Have a great day." Because on Monday, everything will be different.

Rhonda was on the phone, juggling all three incoming lines. She handed him a wad of messages and gave his outfit the once-over before she returned her attention to her caller.

"I need you to come and see me when you get through there," he said.

She nodded and continued talking on the phone.

When Shane stepped through the door of his office, he looked at everything as if seeing it for the first time. The small room seemed stuffed—piles of papers on his desk, stacks of trade journals on top of a bookcase, boxes of

experimental equipment creating a tower in one corner.
Once upon a time he'd been excited about this office. Not
anymore.

He had no window because when he'd partitioned off
the leased space, he'd decided to make the reception area
open and inviting, so it had both windows. For lack of a
window, he'd hung up a picture of a forest with a snow-
capped mountain in the background.

He'd spent a lot of time staring at that rugged landscape
while talking to customers on the phone. No wonder he'd
taken Eileen up to Oak Creek Canyon. It was a small mir-
acle he hadn't driven to Montana.

Gazing at the picture, he could almost smell the freshness
of the evergreens. In that cabin with Eileen, he'd felt truly
relaxed and free for the first time in years. He laughed as
he realized that the cabin hadn't come equipped with a
telephone. Perfect.

He desperately needed out of this box he'd put himself
in. No matter what happened with Eileen, he wasn't going
to live this way any longer. His employees would be disappointed if he sold the business. He'd affect their lives,
no doubt about it, but if he didn't get out of this trap, he'd
go crazy, and that wouldn't help anyone.

"You needed to see me?"

He turned to find Rhonda standing in the doorway, a
notepad and pen in her hand, her expression openly curious.

"Yes. Have a seat. I've come to a decision, and I want
you to be the first one to know." He sat down in his desk
chair, but felt too imprisoned by it, so he got up and came
around the desk, propping his hips against it.

"If you're instituting a new dress code, I don't have the
figure for wearing a T-shirt and jeans. I could see about
getting the company logo silk-screened on a jumper, i'
that—"

"I'm going to sell Mercury."

Her eyes widened. "Why?"

"Because it's slowly killing me. My whole life is controlled by this company. I can't get away from it, not even for an evening. That's nuts."

Rhonda settled back in her chair and tapped her pen softly against her notepad. Then she cleared her throat. "I'm only your secretary, so I probably shouldn't be voicing an opinion."

"You're much more than a secretary, and you know it. I don't expect you to be happy about the decision, but my mind is made up. I can't live like this."

"I don't think you should, either."

He looked at her in surprise. "You don't?"

"Nope. You're, what, thirty-three years old? Most men your age have a wife and kids by now. Until Eileen came along, you didn't even have a steady girlfriend. I think you've put way too much time into Mercury and way too little into your personal life. But it was none of my business, so I kept quiet about it."

"So you're okay with me selling? I can't guarantee that the new owners will—"

"No, I'm not okay with it. I think that's plain dumb, if you'll excuse my saying so."

Shane blew out an impatient breath. "I just finished explaining that I'm fed up to here with being on call day and night."

"And whose fault is that?"

He laughed, because she sounded so much like a mother. "What do you mean, *whose fault is that?* It's nobody's fault. If you run a business, you have to spend a lot of hours at it. Quite a few of my customers, especially the ones who've been with me from the beginning, expect me to handle their problems personally. If I didn't, there's a good chance they'd be offended and take their business elsewhere. Before long the company would suffer.''

During this speech, Rhonda had been doodling on her notepad, drawing little hearts and flowers. She glanced up. ''I'm going to make a leap of logic here and conclude that you're serious about Eileen and want to spend more time with her. Would I be right about that?''

He felt his cheeks grow warm. ''Yeah, but that's not the only reason behind this decision. Being with her helped me see what I had to do to get my life back.''

''Have you told her you own the company?''

He nodded.

''That's a start. Did you also say that you plan to sell it?''

''Well, no.'' He hesitated. ''She'd probably have a fit.'' And that's why he wanted to set things in motion before telling her.

''As well she should. No woman wants to hook up with a flaky man.''

Shane didn't mention that Eileen already considered him a little flaky. This move would only add fuel to the fire. But he hoped to make her understand why he had to take this step, once she'd disposed of Benny and they could talk again. *If* she disposed of Benny. He didn't like to consider the possibility that she wouldn't.

''Well, if you're determined to sell the company, of course that's your right,'' Rhonda said. ''But before you throw the baby out with the bathwater, I have a suggestion to make, if you're interested in hearing it.''

''I want to buy a cabin in the woods and spent most of my time there,'' Shane said. ''Just to give you an idea of how serious I am.''

''Sounds nice. Why not? Let me run your company.''

He stared at her in shock. Then he tried to think how

best to tell her that wouldn't work without hurting her feelings. "Rhonda, you're smart and capable, and you'd do a terrific job. I'd even trust you to take care of the other employees the way I would. But you know how guys like George Ullman are. They're used to dealing with me."

Fortunately, she didn't look upset by that news. "And you're terrible at delegating."

"That, too."

"Would you like to take a crack at learning how to delegate? Specifically delegating to me?"

He sighed. "It's too late for that. I've conditioned these clients to expect me to handle everything, and I don't think we can retrain them at this late stage."

"I think we can. Are you serious about Eileen?"

"Yes." He didn't have to think about that one.

"As in marching-down-the-aisle serious?"

"Yes, but I don't know if she is."

"That's okay. You've built a business from scratch, so I believe you'll get this girl if you want her badly enough. Anyway, here's the strategy. Once you're engaged—and I'll take as much work off your shoulders as possible so you can work on that—you invite all your old customers to the wedding." She sat back and smiled, as if that solved everything.

"I don't get it."

"These people have taken advantage of you because you've encouraged them to, and because they know you're single, and because you've never demonstrated a need for a personal life. They treat you almost as a member of the family. Am I right?"

"I suppose that's true." He thought about it. "Or like the next-door neighbor you're always asking to come over and help fix something."

"Exactly." Eileen beamed at him. "So make them part

Rhonda

of your happy event, explain that you're a family man now who needs to spend time with his wife and, eventually, his kids. Therefore you're turning over a large part of the responsibility to me. They'll be thrilled for you and they'll become invested in the outcome.''

Shane gazed at her in admiration. "That's brilliant. I'm beginning to understand why you have such great kids.''

She rolled her eyes. "I do, but Kevin just switched majors for the fourth time. And Jeremy's in love with an older woman.''

Shane grinned. "So am I. You.''

"You like the plan?'' Her brown eyes glowed with eagerness. "I'll need a big fat raise, you know.''

"Name it. But are you sure you want this kind of responsibility? I'm telling you, it's a killer.''

"Ah, but unlike you, I know how to delegate. You don't think I cooked and cleaned while the boys sat around watching TV, do you?''

Shane laughed and shook his head. "Guess not.''

"But now, with the boys off doing their thing, I don't have nearly enough to keep me occupied. If you don't let me do this, I might have to take the class in needlepoint my sister's heckling me about, and I hate sewing. I always prick my fingers.''

"Then let me be the one to save you from a life of bloody fingers.'' His grin faded. "All this hangs on convincing Eileen to marry me, you know. That's not a done deal by a long shot.'' His chest tightened just thinking about how uncertain his chances were.

"I'm not worried about that.'' Rhonda gave him a glance of supreme confidence. "She'd be a fool to turn you down. Oh, and if you need an excuse to wander over to the Traynor and Sizemore offices today, the receptionist—Linda, I think it is—called about a little glitch in their phone system.

You could send Ralph over, but I thought you might want to handle the problem yourself.''

''Thanks.'' Shane had wondered how he was going to make it through the day without seeing Eileen. ''I think I'll do that.''

EILEEN DID HER LEVEL BEST to concentrate on work, but it was tough. Either she'd think about meeting Benjamin at the airport and her stomach would churn, or her mind would wander back to a certain cabin in the woods, and her body would hum. Then she'd think about Benjamin, and feel guilty all over again.

Her lack of concentration only proved how dangerous and distracting sexual adventures could be. She was so far gone that at about eleven in the morning she imagined Shane's voice in the outer office. No, wait, that wasn't her imagination. That was definitely Shane's voice drifting in from the reception area.

''I think it would be a good idea if I checked them all, just to make sure,'' he said.

''Not a bad idea,'' Linda said. ''No one else has had a problem, but you might as well take a look while you're here.''

Eileen's heart began to race. Her fantasy man was about to make an appearance in her office, the very office where they'd had wild sex on Tuesday night. She wondered what he was up to, coming here this morning.

But then that's what excited her so much about Shane. He was unpredictable. And he was striding down the hallway, exactly as he had on Tuesday night...except, this time, there would be no sex on the desk.

He appeared in the doorway wearing his tool belt and looking like every woman's dream of the hunky repairman.

She leaned her chin on her fist and waited to see what he'd say.

His expression was bland and businesslike, but his eyes told a different story. They were sparking with excitement. She imagined hers were, too, and she hoped nobody happened to wander down the hall right now.

He cleared his throat. "Excuse me. Can I interrupt you for a minute? I need to take a look at your phone." Then he waggled his eyebrows at her.

She smothered a laugh. "O-okay."

As he walked toward her desk, his gaze swept the room and lingered on the bouquet he'd given her. "Nice flowers."

"Thank you."

"Your receptionist had a little static on her phone, so I thought I'd better check them all, just in case." He held her gaze.

"Linda called you?"

"She called Rhonda. Amazing, huh?"

"Amazing." Although she found it hard to believe that Linda's phone had so conveniently gone berserk, Shane couldn't have booby-trapped it last night, because he'd been with her the whole time.

"So have you been having any problems?"

"Not with static."

He picked up the receiver and listened, all the while looking into her eyes. "But you've had other problems?"

"Uh-huh."

"Can you describe them to me?" He broke eye contact as he put down the receiver and picked up the entire phone, turning it over and taking a screwdriver out of his tool belt.

She lowered her voice. "I have a persistent little…"

"Yes?" He leaned over the desk while he continued taking screws out of the bottom of the phone.

"Ache," she murmured.

"I see." He put one of the small screws in the palm of his hand and held it out toward her. "Maybe you need one of these."

She covered her laughter by coughing into her hand.

"You might be able to get one during your lunch hour."

She wanted to take him up on that, but she didn't dare. She'd already lost too much time today, thanks to day-dreaming about him. "That's a great suggestion, but I'll be having lunch at my desk today."

"That's too bad." He took the bottom off the phone and studied the inner workings. Then he glanced into her eyes. "But I have to say, you have a great desk."

"You'd better finish with my phone," she murmured. "Or we're both going to be in a lot of trouble."

"Yeah, I know. Sure you can't get away?"

His gaze was so mesmerizing that she was ready to say yes. Then Mildred knocked on her open door. "Any chance you have a minute to brainstorm with me about the Palmer appeal?"

"Of—of course! Come on in, Mildred."

"I'll be out of your way in no time," Shane said.

"No problem," Eileen said, trying to sound casual even though her palms were sweating. Mildred already knew she was involved with a guy from Mercury Communications, so it wouldn't take much imagination on her part to figure out this was the man.

"Before you two get into your discussion," Shane said, "let me just say that the phone is okay." He set it back on Eileen's desk. Then he smiled at Mildred. "I'll need to check yours, too. Maybe while you're in here talking with Ms. Connelly would be a good time for me to do it."

"I guess so." Mildred surveyed him with obvious interest. "But I haven't had any trouble with it. I think it's fine."

"Probably is. Never hurts to double-check, though." Without another glance at Eileen, Shane headed out the door. "By the way, I really like that picture you have on the wall," he said as he left.

He was a devil, she thought as she fought to control a blush. And she was seriously going to kill him. With great effort she brought her attention back to Mildred and the Palmer appeal. "I think the way to go on Palmer is—"

"He's gorgeous, Eileen."

Eileen's face went from warm to hot as she stuttered and stammered, unable to think of a single appropriate response.

"I didn't come in here to talk about the Palmer case. I heard that someone from Mercury was checking the phones, and I had a hunch it would be your guy." She smiled. "I couldn't resist testing my theory. All I had to do was watch you two hunched toward each other over the desk, and I had my answer."

Eileen swallowed. "I don't want anyone else to know."

"I realize that and I won't tell. But I don't know how in the world you could choose Benjamin over him. Compared to this guy, Benjamin's as exciting as watching a cactus grow."

Eileen couldn't help laughing, although she felt disloyal.

"And this guy likes your sexy picture."

Eileen gaped at her. "You think it's sexy?"

"Of course. But it's subtle. A man like Benjamin wouldn't have the imagination to appreciate it." She paused. "Or appreciate you, for that matter." She stood. "Well, I've poked my nose in your business quite enough for one day."

"Thanks for keeping quiet, Mildred."

"You're welcome. I've never liked office gossip." With that, she left.

Eileen couldn't settle down to work, knowing that Shane was still in the suite of offices. But she didn't want him to leave, either. She was pitiful.

Finally he walked past her door, paused briefly to give her a little salute, and disappeared down the hall. She listened to his cheerful banter with Linda, and then the outer office door opened and closed. He was gone.

The rest of the day dragged by as she slogged through her workload. She considered calling her mother back, but didn't have the energy to deal with another conversation about moving in with Benjamin. At long last she turned off her computer, grabbed her purse and left the office. She was ready to get this meeting with Benjamin over with.

Just her luck, his plane was an hour late. She spent it pacing the area outside the security gate and watching the monitors. By the time they flashed the news that the plane had landed, her nerves were frazzled and she still hadn't figured out the best way to break the news about Shane.

She wanted to tell Benjamin right away, to get the unpleasantness over with, but that wouldn't be very considerate. Benjamin would be tired and jet-lagged. He should probably have a chance to eat something, maybe have a drink and unwind before she hit him with bad news.

When he came striding past security, a huge grin on his face, her stomach immediately knotted up. He looked surprisingly fresh, but then he'd been in first class getting special things like the heated face-cloth treatment. He liked to dress well for plane flights, so even his red power tie was still in place and his suit jacket unwrinkled because, no doubt, he'd had the flight attendant hang it up for him. He carried the overcoat he'd worn while in Switzerland, and had his leather briefcase on a wide strap over one broad shoulder.

Eileen was aware, as usual, of the envious looks other women sent her way when they realized this guy was headed in her direction. But she'd always suspected Benjamin was aware of them, too. He carried himself as if he'd already won an election.

He swept her up in a bear hug. "Damn, but you look good! Have you put a different color on your hair or something?"

"No, not a thing." She hoped if she kept talking, he might not try to kiss her. "Come on, let's go get your luggage. And then we'll stop for something to eat. I'm sure you're hungry."

"Not especially." He kissed her hard on the mouth. "Just eager to hear what you have to say for yourself."

At least the kiss didn't last long enough that she would have been forced to pull away. She realized now that she'd never liked kissing Benjamin. She'd talked herself into doing it because you couldn't consider marrying a man you didn't want to kiss on a regular basis.

After the week she'd been through, she had the experience to understand that Benjamin's kisses were way too efficient. They had a certain predictable rhythm, a quick three beats, and then they were over and he was ready to move on to the next part of the program. But Shane...no, she couldn't think about Shane's kisses. Not now.

"I take it your trip went well?" she asked as they rode the escalators down to the baggage claim area.

"Very well. I think Emory and Cecil will be pleased." Benjamin called Emory Traynor and Cecil Sizemore by their first names, and with Benjamin it seemed to work.

Eileen had never moved past addressing them as Mr. Traynor and Mr. Sizemore. As she stepped off the escalator ahead of Benjamin, she remembered Traynor's comment about she and Benjamin becoming a power couple. Well, it didn't look as if that would be happening.

They found the baggage carousel for Benjamin's flight, but the luggage hadn't yet arrived. That left them standing there staring at nothing, which made Eileen very nervous. Without something to do, they had to talk. She knew that time had to come and she really did want to get past the moment of revelation, but she was still dreading it.

Benjamin slipped an arm around her waist. "I can't get over how wonderful you look. Did you join a gym this week?"

"No, no gym." She kept watching the carousel, willing the buzzer to sound and the bags to start spilling out of the chute. How interesting, though, that Benjamin had paid her more compliments in the past ten minutes than he normally did in a week. Maybe she did look different. If so, it was all Shane's doing.

"It looks like we're going to be stuck here a while until the luggage shows up." He hugged her closer. "So don't keep me in suspense. I know your lease is almost up, so you might as well make it official and say you're moving in with me."

Her heart beat frantically as she slipped out of his embrace and turned to face him. "There's something I have to tell you."

"I know." He smiled at her, looking like the all-American guy that any woman would be crazy to dump. "Don't look so scared. It's what we both want and need."

She gulped. "While you were gone, I had an affair."

18

EILEEN BRACED HERSELF, waiting for Benjamin's disbelief, fury and pain to erupt. Maybe a crowded baggage terminal surrounded by strangers wasn't such a bad place to make her announcement. Benjamin wouldn't allow himself to get too upset in public. Then, to her total amazement, his eyes began to twinkle.

"Is that what you've been so uptight about ever since my plane landed? Some silly affair?"

She wasn't sure how to describe her affair with Shane, but whatever words she'd use, *silly* wouldn't be one of them. "I'm trying to tell you that I can't move in with you, because—"

"Because you had a little fun while I was gone? Don't be ridiculous. I did the exact same thing."

She stared at him in shock.

"Don't look so surprised." He chuckled. "After all, you're the one that kept saying we weren't exclusive. But I figured we would be when I got back, and the opportunity presented itself, so I thought, why not?"

She was stunned. He'd done precisely what she'd felt she needed to do while he was gone—have a fling before settling down for the long haul. His affair must not have shaken his world the way hers had. Otherwise he'd be telling her he wasn't ready for commitment, either.

At first, words failed her, but eventually she realized that she had to erase his impression that their affairs canceled each other out. "I don't know what went on in Switzerland, and I don't want to know but, in my case, I've discovered that I'm not ready to move in with you, to make that commitment, to start the process of becoming a 'power couple,' as Mr. Traynor seems to think of us."

"Sure you are." Benjamin gripped her shoulders and looked into her eyes, his expression benevolent.

She almost expected him to give her a little shake, the way you would a balky child. She met his gaze. "I don't think so. Not anymore."

"Oh, come on, let's not be melodramatic about this. We have a great future ahead of us. We both stepped out of character for a few days. So what? I'm sure it's healthy."

He wasn't taking her seriously, but then he never had. He'd seen the Eileen he wanted to see. The depth of their relationship, or its shallowness, suited him fine. Her parents had nearly divorced when a third person had come on the scene, but Benjamin thought such an occurrence was no big deal.

Eileen decided it was time to ask the million-dollar question, the one she already knew the answer to. But maybe bringing it out in the open would get him to understand. "Benjamin, do you love me?"

For the first time he lost some of his jaunty confidence. "You want the truth?"

"Yes, please." *The truth, the whole truth and nothing but the truth.*

"I've never been sure what that means, to be *in love* with someone. I like being with you and I think you'd make a great wife and mother. Your parents like me, and I'm sure mine will like you, when I finally get you back to Connecticut to meet them. We're each other's logical choice, and I'm ready to spend my life with you. Does all that add up to being *in love?* I don't know."

"I do." More than anything, she felt sad for him. He might never know the kind of love she was searching for, because he didn't allow himself to get that emotional. She'd thought he was steady, but instead he was shallow. "It doesn't add up to love, Benjamin. And you've described the way I feel about you, too, except that I don't want to spend the rest of my life with you. I think that would be wrong for me."

His grip tightened, and his gaze intensified. "No, it wouldn't. Look, I know our sex life hasn't been very hot. I especially realize that after the trip to Switzerland. And I'm picking up hints that you expanded your repertoire, too. It's easier to do with a relative stranger, and the thought of you with another guy excites me, to be perfectly honest. I think we can build on—"

"Ick." She backed away from him. "You actually *like* the fact I had an affair? That's gross."

He straightened and cleared his throat. "I didn't say I liked it, exactly." His tone had turned almost parental. "I'm trying to make the best of the situation, that's all."

"You *did* say that." She pictured him as a politician, evading the tough questions. "You said it turned you on."

His glance grew haughty. "Then maybe that's because I'm a little more sophisticated than you. In some circles—"

"Just because I had an affair doesn't mean I want to move in those circles. But the fact that you're even talking about it tells me what I might have been in for in that perfect future you were describing." She was beginning to realize that Benjamin might not need fantasies to get him excited. He might need something a little more concrete, like threesomes and couple-swapping. The thought turned her stomach.

"You know, there always was something kind of small

town about you, Eileen, but I was hoping, given time, that you'd get the necessary polish. Apparently I was wrong.''

"Apparently I was wrong about you, too. I thought you were just boring. Now I see you're also a little bit twisted. And for the record, I'm not the least turned on by the news that you had *fun* in Switzerland.''

"Obviously." His eyes grew cold. "But then, if you hadn't felt obliged to share your news, I would never have told you. I had a feeling you wouldn't be able to handle it.''

She wanted to get as far away from him as possible, but she'd promised him a ride home from the airport. At least the luggage was now plopping onto the carousel. "You might want to start looking for your bag," she said. "I'll get my car and bring it around by the door.''

"Don't bother." His voice was clipped and cool, the way he spoke to people who didn't particularly matter to him. "I'd rather take a limo, anyway.''

She gazed at him, astonished that she'd ever imagined a life with him. At least they were having this conversation now instead of ten years down the line. "All right. Goodbye, Benjamin.''

"Goodbye, Eileen." He turned away from her.

She started toward the automatic doors that opened onto the street and the nearby parking garage. Before she walked through them, she turned back, just to see if he was watching her leave. Surely he had some sadness about this. But if he did, he wasn't showing it. He was already talking and laughing with a tall brunette who seemed only too happy to have his attention.

ALTHOUGH SHANE LEFT HIS cell phone on in case Eileen called that number, he also hung around his condo, not wanting to miss a possible phone contact there, either. Or maybe, if he got really lucky, she'd drive over.

He hated knowing she was with Benny, hated it worse than he'd expected to. And although he told himself it wouldn't happen, couldn't happen, he was tortured by images of Eileen deciding to stay with the guy. If she decided to stay with him, then tonight she'd...no, that was unthinkable.

He wished that he'd memorized Benny's arrival information when he'd noticed it on her blotter. Without that info, he couldn't call and find out if the plane had landed. He could be worrying for nothing, because the flight might have been delayed and Eileen wasn't even with Benny yet.

He had no way of knowing...anything. What a damned helpless feeling. Prowling his apartment, he ate potato chips and drank cola because he didn't feel like sitting down and he could carry the bag and the can with him. Besides that, chewing worked his jaw, which kept tightening up on him.

By nine o'clock he was a total mess, full of caffeine, sugar and salt. He might as well switch to beer and get wasted, because no doubt Eileen had made up with Benny and they were back in Benny's condo naked. And if that was happening, there wasn't a damned thing he could do about it, so getting drunk was the best way to deal with the problem. He was—

The doorbell made him jump. He ran to answer it, his fourth can of cola in one hand. All the while he prayed that Eileen would be standing on the other side of the door.

She was, still wearing the gray pantsuit she'd put on in the cabin this morning.

He drew in a long, trembling breath. ''Thank God. You have no idea what I've been thinking. Come in. Please come in.''

''Thanks.'' She walked into his living room and looked

around. "Good thing I found out you owned Mercury, or I'd say you were living *way* above your income."

"I'm glad you found out, too." *For many reasons.* He set his cola can on a table beside the sofa. She was finally here, and suddenly he was very nervous. "Can I get you anything? What happened? Was he upset? Did you—"

"Yes." She walked over to him, slid her arms around his waist and gazed up at him, her expression soft. "Benjamin and I are finished. I'm sorry if this was rough on you."

"Nah. Piece of cake." He felt like shouting and shooting off fireworks, but he settled for wrapping his arms around her, which felt so good he forgot about being triumphant. But, man, was he happy.

"I would have come over sooner, but I needed to stop by my parents' house."

"So you told them?" That reminded him that he needed to meet her parents, and she'd need to meet his. But he didn't want to rush that, especially with her folks, who had just lost the guy they'd thought would become their son-in-law. But *he* would become their son-in-law. The thought sent off sparks of excitement in his stomach.

"I told them I'd broken up with Benjamin, but I didn't go into detail as to why. I just used the catch-all phrase and said we were incompatible. My mom thinks I blew it."

He drew her closer. "What do moms know, anyway?"

"More than you think. She suspects I've met someone and that's the reason she's had trouble getting in touch with me."

"But you didn't confirm it." He almost wished she had, even if it was too soon to trot out the new husband candidate. He was eager to become a solid presence in Eileen's life.

"No, I didn't admit to anything. But the interesting reaction came from my dad. It turns out he's been trying to like Benjamin because he thought I did, and because my mother was so enthusiastic, but he's never actually much cared for him.'' She sighed and nestled her cheek against his chest. ''Oh, Shane, I came so close to making a terrible mistake.''

''But you didn't.'' *And now you're here with me, and all's right with the world. Oh, and I'm crazy about your dad already.* ''I suppose Benjamin was pretty upset.'' He could almost feel sorry for the guy, now that he was mashed into the pavement like a warm pile of doggie-do.

''That was the creepy part.'' She hugged him closer. ''He thought it was kind of cool that I'd had sex with someone else. He did the same thing in Switzerland. I guess thinking of me with another guy turned him on.''

''Yuck.'' Shane closed his eyes and held her tight. Benny was more like a warm pile of doggie-do than he'd thought.

''Yeah, I know. I hate to think of what our life together would have been like. I might be into fantasies, but not that kind.''

''Don't think about it.'' Shane stroked her hair, wanting to do something for her, but not sure if she wanted what was on his mind. ''Are you hungry? Thirsty?''

''My parents insisted I eat something before I left, which is why I'm as late as I am.''

''Then I only have one thing left to offer you.''

There was a smile in her voice. ''What's that?''

''Doughnuts.''

EILEEN HAD BEEN ACHING for Shane all day, so she didn't have to be asked twice. She lifted her gaze to his. ''Where?''

He laughed. ''You're the only woman I know who

wouldn't automatically assume that we'd go upstairs to the bedroom.''

''Bedrooms are nice.'' She remembered how much they'd enjoyed that bed in the cabin and felt herself go all warm and liquid at the thought of playing on another king-size mattress with Shane. If she'd worried that taking away the threat of Benjamin and the element of secrecy would squelch her need for him, she'd been wonderfully wrong about that.

Shane smiled down at her. ''Tell you what. I'll give you a tour of the house, and then you can decide where.''

''That sounds like fun.''

''If a spot appeals to you, we can make out a little while there and see if you want to stay.''

''That sounds like even more fun.''

He turned her toward the furniture grouped around his fireplace. ''This, for example, is my living room. I don't know if you noticed, but the sofa is plenty big enough for sex.'' He guided her over toward it.

She eyed the plump cushions covered in blue-and-white stripes and battled a flash of jealousy. She didn't want to think of him having sex with another woman on that sofa in front of a crackling fire. ''Do you know this for a fact?''

''I know I can stretch out on it with my head on the armrest, which means you could straddle me with no problem. Other positions might be a little dicey, but it would be fun trying. If you're asking if I've tested it, the answer is no. I told you my personal life has been destroyed by work recently.''

She thought of his recent attitude toward his job and felt guilty for the way she'd distracted him. ''And now your personal life is screwing up your work.''

''Nope. Not at all.'' He slipped her suit jacket from her

shoulders. "But we can talk about that later. Here's option A, sofa sex." Then he kissed her.

Now this was a kiss, she thought as her surroundings melted away. When Shane's lips touched hers, it was the beginning of something special. He took his time fitting his mouth to hers, and then he had a way of moving, adjusting and sensuously caressing her mouth that made the connection even more magical.

Only when he'd totally settled in did he gradually bring his tongue into the equation. The first foray was subtle, but as her body heated, so did his kiss, until she was churning with the need to strip off her clothes and get horizontal. When he eased his mouth from hers, she was ready to suggest that.

"So there you have the option of sofa sex," he murmured. "Want that?"

"Yes."

"But you haven't had a chance to consider kitchen-table sex, or kitchen-counter sex, or stairway sex—one of my personal favorites because of the interesting positions possible—or hot-tub sex, or—"

"You have a hot tub?"

He nibbled her lower lip. "Upstairs in the bathroom. Wanna go up there and check it out?"

She moaned softly. "I want it all. I'm like a chocoholic in the Godiva store. I don't know where to start."

"Then let's bow to tradition this once and start with my bed, because in the nightstand drawer is a full box of condoms. Then we can branch out from there."

"I have a feeling I'm going to love this place."

"I'm counting on that. Come on. Let's go upstairs while I can still walk."

Navigating the stairs took a while because Shane paused every couple of steps to kiss her. She began to wonder if they'd have stairway sex, after all, but instead he used each kissing session to eliminate another piece of clothing, either his or hers. By the time they got to his bedroom she was down to her panties and he wore only his jeans and briefs.

Even though he'd worked her into a lather, she noticed through her sensual fog that his bed was a clone of the one in the cabin. His house was masculine and substantial, an invitation to earthy sensuality. Then they were rolling and tumbling over the king-size mattress, and she noticed nothing except his clever mouth, his wonderful hands, and what she needed more than anything else, the firm thrust of his penis.

She came almost immediately. He followed soon afterward, murmuring her name over and over as he shuddered in her arms.

She held him close, marveling at how great the sex was between them, even after all the times they'd had it. At some point she'd have to start controlling this runaway passion, or their lives would be in chaos. Maybe he was ready to surrender completely to a sense of adventure, but she wasn't.

Although Benjamin hadn't turned out to be the sensible, solid influence she'd thought, she still needed a guy with that quality. She'd had a moment alone with her dad tonight, and she'd asked him how he felt about being married to a practical woman like her mom. He'd said her mom was the best thing that had ever happened to him, that she kept him anchored.

He'd only confirmed what Eileen had believed for years. Like her dad, she needed a mate who would help curb her recklessness. Shane was wonderful to be with, but when it came to seeking adventure, they were too much alike. Someday in the future, she'd have to give him up.

But not right this minute. The weekend stretched ahead

of them, and judging from the possibilities he'd laid out for her, and the full box of condoms in the nightstand drawer, they wouldn't have to leave the house unless they chose to. She'd indulge her need for fantasy sex for a little longer. Just a little.

Shane stirred and eased away from her. "Don't go away. I'll be right back."

"Going to fill up the hot tub, by chance?"

He leaned down to nuzzle her ear. "I thought I might. I've never used that tub the way I think it should be used."

"Mmm." The merest touch of his mouth along with a sexy suggestion, and she was excited again. "I'm a virgin when it comes to hot-tub sex, so you'll have to show me the ropes."

He gazed down at her, a smile on his lips, a challenge in his eyes. "Ropes? Did I hear someone mention ropes?"

Oh, this would be some weekend. "Get in there and run us some warm water, you bad boy, you."

He grinned. "At your service, m'lady. Your pulsating, climax-producing jets will be operational shortly." Then he slid off the bed and went into the bathroom.

Not long afterward, the sound of water thundering into the tub was accompanied by Shane's out-of-tune whistling. Eileen smiled. She was regaining the sense of freedom she'd had in the cabin and, apparently, so was he.

As the water continued to run, he walked back into the bedroom and sprawled next to her on the bed. "It takes a little while to get to the top, but that's when you get the best jet action, which is what I want for your ultimate enjoyment," he said and waggled his brows. "So I'll just hang out here awhile."

She rolled to her side and stroked his back. "I'm happy to have you here."

He held her gaze. "I'm happy to have *you* here. Extremely happy."

"I, um, don't have any particular plans for the weekend,
but you might need to—"

"If you're saying you can spend the weekend with me,
I would love that."

She still needed reassurance that he wasn't ruining his
business because of her. "I keep thinking about your work,
though. You said before that you've had no personal life
because of the company, and that means you've been working nights and weekends. I don't understand how you can
suddenly stop doing that."

He smiled. "Because I've worked it out."

"How?"

Propping himself on one elbow, he reached for her hand.
"I need to thank you for setting the wheels in motion. At
first I was all set to sell the company, but—"

"Omigod! No!"

He squeezed her hand. "Take it easy. I'm not selling.
Rhonda, who is much more of an asset than just my secretary, came up with a perfect plan. I'm going to let her
run the business so that I can have a life."

Eileen frowned. "That seems way too simple. I mean, if
you can just do that, why wouldn't you have thought of it
before? I mean, if you've been unhappy about the workload, you could have given her more to do before this."

"Spoken just like a lawyer. The reason I didn't think of
it was because I've been terrible at delegating, which means
most of my customers, especially the ones I've had forever,
expect to deal with me all the time. Even though I'm ready
to learn to delegate, I was afraid clients would leave if I
stopped baby-sitting them."

"So what's changed?"

"You." He brought her hand to his mouth and kissed it

softly. "The possibility of spending time with you makes me want to learn to delegate, and Rhonda's come up with a way to retrain my clients to think differently."

"Like what?"

"Well, up to now they've looked at me as a single guy with no life, but if they know that I'm serious about someone, if they know that I have other obligations to consider then—"

"Shane, what are you saying?" Her tummy was telling her she wouldn't like what would come next.

He closed his eyes and groaned. "Well, damn, I didn' meant to lead into it like this. I wanted everything to be romantic, and here I am, stumbling into what should be a special moment."

He's going to propose. She sat up in a panic. "Listen, we need to get something straight. The sex has been fantastic, but that doesn't mean I'm ready to enter into some permanent agreement."

He sat up, too, his smile gone. "You ditched Benny, and then you came over here. You just said you can spend the weekend with me."

"I know!" Her stomach churned with anxiety. "But I never in a million years thought you'd want to get married!"

His voice grew very quiet. "Why wouldn't I?"

"Because…because married people don't have wild sexual adventures, Shane! What do you want to do, ruin everything?"

19

"LET ME GET THIS straight." Shane's head was buzzing. "You don't want to marry me because I'm too good in bed?"

"I know that sounds ridiculous," Eileen said. "But think about it."

"It's so ridiculous that I can't possibly think about it! How can you not want to spend our lives having great sex? What's so terrible about that?"

"Did you hear what you just said? *Spend our lives having great sex.* Where does that leave room for all the other important stuff, like taking care of kids, and earning a living, and…and…*voting?*"

"We would vote!" He couldn't believe they were having this conversation. "You think I'd let sex stop me from being a responsible member of society?"

"Not just you—both of us. Don't you see? We're too much alike. When we're together, we turn into a couple of overgrown kids who encourage each other to spend all our time fooling around. Who would be the steady one? Who would say enough's enough, it's time to put food on the table?"

"I'm sure we could work it out! We wouldn't just let our world go to hell while we got our jollies. We would stay on top of things. We—"

"Is that right?" She looked over his shoulder. "Then

After Hours

what about the water flooding your bathroom? How did that happen?''

"Shit." He leaped from the bed, crossed the wet carpet and splashed through the puddles on the bathroom floor to shut off both faucets. The overflow drain was sucking water madly, but he'd turned the taps on full blast to fill the tub quickly, and the overflow drain hadn't been able to handle the volume.

He threw towels on the floor to sop up the mess, but he could already tell he'd need a professional cleaning company to come in and dry the bedroom carpet where the water had seeped through the doorway. How had things gone from terrific to terrible in a few short minutes?

Eileen was making absolutely no sense. He'd never heard of a woman turning down a marriage proposal because the groom drove her crazy with lust. Wasn't that what women were supposed to want?

Well, he wasn't through with this discussion. Once he decided the bathroom was under some kind of control, he stepped over the soggy towels and onto the squishy bedroom carpet. "Okay, obviously we've had a little lack of communication, but—" He paused to stare at her. She had her panties on. "You're getting *dressed?*"

"Yes. I think it would be better for both of us if I went home."

"Speak for yourself. I was planning on a weekend losing ourselves with each other."

"Exactly." She headed toward the bedroom door. "That's what happens when we get together. We're lost to the world." She leaned down and picked up her slacks.

Shane grabbed his pants off the floor and started putting them on. "It's supposed to be a good thing," he said, hopping on one foot, "to enjoy each other so much." He followed her out of the bedroom, zipping up as he went.

"Up to a point." She found her bra draped over the stair railing and put it on. "But I've never known anybody as wild about each other as we are."

He hadn't, either, but he counted it as a plus. He shoved his hands in his pockets to keep them from shaking. "We'd probably lose some of that intensity as time went on."

"I thought we might once Benjamin was out of the picture." She snatched her blouse from the bottom step and pushed her arms into the sleeves. "But if anything, I wanted you even more tonight."

He blew out a breath. "Okay! You want one of us to be the responsible one in this relationship? I'll be that person. You won't believe how responsible I'm going to get."

She found her shoes at the bottom of the stairs. "No, I'm going to be the one, and I'm making the move right now. I'm going to have the grit to end this while I still can."

He latched onto that last part. "Meaning that if you stayed around, you might not be able to leave me?"

"Maybe not." Her eyes glimmered with unshed tears. "Don't get me wrong. I think what we've had has been amazing. But it's not real life. I still want the house and the kids."

"So do I, damn it!"

She shook her head and looked very sad. "I think we'd make a mess of that. Goodbye, Shane." She picked up her jacket and purse and walked toward the door.

"Eileen, please don't go. Please don't."

"It's for the best." She unlocked the door.

"Eileen! Listen, don't go, because—" The door closed. She was gone. "Because I love you," he whispered into the silence.

SHANE SPENT THE WEEKEND at the office taking care of all the things he'd let slide the past week. When he wasn't immersed in work, he went over and over what Eileen had said, looking for a way to convince her that she was wrong. But he couldn't figure out how to do that. For the first time in years, he was up against a challenge he didn't know how to meet.

Apparently he'd done a hell of job convincing her that he loved sexual adventure. She thought that was all he was about. He didn't know how to erase that impression. He'd need months, maybe years, to prove that they could create a life that included great sex plus all the other elements they both wanted. If she didn't believe it was possible, he was finished before he started.

Maybe even the plan with Rhonda had turned Eileen off. She might have seen him as the kind of man who would shove responsibility off on someone else so that he had more time to fool around with her. She didn't understand that Rhonda welcomed the opportunity, one she wouldn't have if he hadn't built the business in the first place. And he'd done that by being responsible, damn it! But he hadn't exactly wowed her with his work ethic this past week, and that was part of the problem.

Monday morning he arrived at the office ahead of everyone else and dove into the paperwork with a vengeance. He couldn't turn the business over to Rhonda at the moment. He needed the mind-numbing comfort of the job for a while longer. Eventually he'd get over the pain of Eileen leaving, and then he could proceed with the plan of having a life again.

The plan had little appeal anymore, though. He'd assumed that he was clearing a place in his life for Eileen. She didn't want to be there, so what was the point in anything?

By the time Rhonda came in, he'd already gone through a pot of coffee and was wired and irritable.

She poked her head into his office. "I'm surprised to see you here early."

He glanced up. "You'd better get used to it. The girl said no."

"What?" Rhonda came in and sat down in a chair in front of his desk. "You asked her to marry you already?"

"Sort of." He wasn't proud of the way he'd sidled up to the subject, but he'd been so sure of where he stood with her that he'd forgotten to be careful.

Rhonda looked disapproving. "Most women don't react well to offhanded proposals."

He sighed and threw down his pen. "I screwed it up, no question. But it wouldn't have mattered. She doesn't think we're a good fit." He smiled grimly at his choice of words. Eileen was the only woman who'd ever fit him perfectly, both physically and mentally.

"Do you mind me asking why?"

He wondered if he could say it in a way that wouldn't embarrass both of them. "Our relationship started off in a very...physical way. Lots of chemistry. She thinks all that chemistry would keep us from...from leading normal lives."

Rhonda's eyes widened. Then she looked away and pressed her lips together. Finally a snort escaped her, then another one. Before long she was laughing so hard tears ran down her cheeks. "I'm sorry," she said, gasping. "I'm so sorry to laugh. I know this is terrible for you." Then she burst into a fresh set of giggles.

"I don't blame you. I wish I could laugh about it, too. I've never been in such a ridiculous spot. Ever."

Rhonda took a tissue from the pocket of her skirt, dried

her eyes and blew her nose. Then she cleared her throat "Um, she thinks you're that undisciplined?"

He shrugged. "I guess."

"You sure must have pulled the wool over her eyes You're the most disciplined thirty-three-year-old guy know."

"That's just it. I kind of...kicked over the traces this past week. That's all she really knows about me. It's no like we have a long history."

"I see." Her eyes twinkled, as if she did, indeed, see.

Shane found himself blushing. "I think that's about al the discussion on this topic that I can handle right now Rhonda. Just give me some time, and I'll be fine. You know me. Resilient."

"I do know you. And I have every confidence that you'l be fine." She got up and walked out of his office.

Shane wished he had the same confidence. He felt as i he had a big black hole in his chest where his heart use to be.

BY MONDAY AFTERNOON, Eileen's determination to ac normally was wearing thin. She'd spent Saturday at the mall shopping with Suz, Saturday night at her parents house, and all day Sunday washing and detailing her car Sunday night she'd gone to a comedy at the multiplex, an then she'd stayed up late reading, hoping exhaustion woul allow her to sleep.

But for the third night in a row, she'd tossed and turned Consequently she hadn't been in very good shape to fac Benjamin at the office today, but she'd be damned if she' have let him know that. She'd maintained a cool and col lected facade whenever she'd happened to encounter him He'd treated her with casual indifference.

Therefore, the day had been generally crappy so fa

She'd had one moment of satisfaction a moment ago when, as predicted, her neighbor Miranda had stopped by the office to expose Eileen's infidelity. Eileen had waylaid her before she'd made it to Benjamin's office. Eileen had taken great pleasure in announcing that he already knew everything.

Miranda had looked disappointed not to be the tattletale, but encouraged when Eileen had said Benjamin was now a free man. As Miranda walked down the hall towards Benjamin's office murmuring something about needing a legal opinion on her condo contract, Eileen found herself thinking that Miranda had been the right match for Benjamin, all along. She was a mover and shaker, like him, and she'd never impressed Eileen with her depth.

Eileen had to give herself credit for some moxie, though. She might have set some kind of record by dumping two extremely eligible men within the space of four hours. She wondered if Ripley had a category for that.

She stood gazing at the flowers Shane had given her and thought she'd better get rid of them before they made her cry. Then her phone buzzed. She jumped, as she had been doing all day. She didn't want Shane to call, but she thought he might, and each time someone contacted her, she half-expected it to be him.

Instead it was Linda. ''There's a woman named Rhonda Ferguson here to see you. She doesn't have an appointment. Can you talk with her now, or should I make an appointment for later?''

Rhonda. Eileen couldn't believe it could be Shane's Rhonda. Still, a little tingle went down her spine at the thought that it might be. ''Sure. I can see her.''

Moments later, a plump fifty-something woman with very red hair walked into Eileen's office. She paused as Eileen stood.

Eileen had the distinct impression she was being evaluated. She'd had potential clients do that before, as if they'd heard one too many blond jokes and weren't sure they could trust her with their legal problems.

Apparently Eileen passed muster, because the woman gave a quick nod and marched over to Eileen's desk. "Rhonda Ferguson," she said, holding out a manicured hand.

"Eileen Connelly." Eileen shook her hand and found herself liking the directness of the woman's gaze. "What can I do for you?"

"Just listen to me for a little while," Rhonda said.

"Of course. Please sit down."

Rhonda took a seat in front of Eileen's desk and glanced around. "I'll bet you had to work hard to get to this point."

"I did." Considering how miserable she felt today, she wondered what the hell she'd been working for. All she wanted was a good job and a family of her own, including a nice husband—not too boring, not too kinky and certainly not so sexy that she'd be tempted to forget everything else.

"I admire hard work," Rhonda said. "It's not easy to set goals and then do what's necessary to achieve them. It takes character."

"Thank you."

"I'm glad to see that you have that kind of character, but I'm not surprised. You came highly recommended."

"Oh, really? Do you know one of my clients?"

Rhonda settled her attention firmly on Eileen. "I'm Shane Nichols's secretary."

Eileen knew she was getting red, but she had no way of controlling her blush. "And you have a legal matter you'd like me to take care of?"

"Actually, I will, in a few weeks. Shane and I are drawing up a new contract of employment, detailing how my duties will change as he shifts more responsibility to me. I wouldn't be worried about it, because I trust him completely, but he's insisting on some legal protection for me, in case something happens to him and someone starts questioning my authority.''

Eileen was impressed. When Shane had tossed out the idea of letting his secretary run the business, she'd thought it sounded crazy, but Rhonda looked perfectly capable of doing the job. And Shane was putting far more thought into the transition than Eileen had given him credit for.

"But that isn't why I'm here today," Rhonda said. "Shane would kill me if he knew I was sitting in your office. I told him I had an appointment for a root canal, and I hated like anything to make up a lie. But if I'd told him I was coming here, he might have fired me. And he wouldn't fire me lightly, so that gives you some idea of how upset he would be.''

"I won't tell him," Eileen said. It was an easy promise to make. She didn't plan to see him again. But she had an uneasy feeling about why Rhonda might have come. "But if you're here to suggest I reconsider my relationship with Shane, then you've wasted a trip.''

Rhonda nodded. "I thought you might say something like that. Listen, you're a lawyer, and I know you're taught to go by the evidence. From what I gather, you've only heard one side of the case when it comes to Shane.''

Eileen felt her blush return. She wondered how much Rhonda knew about her reasons for leaving Shane.

"Don't worry," Rhonda said. "I don't know a single detail. But I do know that you think that the combination of you and Shane equals chaos, and you don't want that.''

Eileen pressed her fingers together to stop them from trembling. "I guess that's fair to say.''

"So I want to enter more evidence into the record, if

that's how they say it in the courtroom. You've known Shane for a few days. I've known him for eight years. I don't think you can make the kind of decision you have, based on so little information.''

Eileen blinked. Rhonda could have been her mother talking. Rhonda was sounding extremely levelheaded, and she was insinuating that Eileen had gone off half-cocked. Acted impulsively. That was exactly the trait she'd been fighting ever since she'd turned ten. What a twist of irony if she'd acted impulsively in order to become more responsible.

She took a deep breath. ''Okay, I'm listening.''

Rhonda proceeded to describe how a young man with very little capital had worked night and day to build Mercury Communications, how he'd treated his customers with such care and courtesy that word had spread. As the business had grown, he'd hired employees, people he treated with the same respect as his customers. He'd labored for eight years, without a break, and his business was now a success story.

At last Rhonda folded her hands in her lap. ''Is this an irresponsible man?'' she asked, her eyes bright with pride.

''No. No, of course not.'' Eileen's heart had softened with every word, and yet…Shane had seemed so ready to put their sexual games ahead of everything else. ''But what if…he's changed?''

''He hasn't changed. When Shane does something, he goes all out. He loves nothing better than a challenge. For the time being, he was focused on winning you. That's the part of him you saw.''

''Yes, but—''

''Let him achieve that goal, and you'll see him get his balance again. In fact, that's exactly what he's trying to do by shifting company responsibility to me. He knows his life's been out of whack. He wants a family. And he desperately wants you. Don't punish him for giving that goal everything he had.''

A lump stuck in Eileen's throat. She had punished him for doing his best to win her. He'd pulled out all the stops, and she'd made that the reason for her leaving. She couldn't listen to the words of a loyal, capable woman who'd worked closely with Shane for eight years and still pretend that he was a flake with no ability to self-correct when he leaned toward excess.

''When he did his best and it came back to bite him, he didn't know what to do. He's stymied right now. But all he needs is a challenge he understands, like figuring out how to juggle the responsibility of having you, a family and his work, and he'll be a happy man. He's up to that challenge, if you'll give him a chance.''

Eileen swallowed and blinked back tears. Poor Shane. He must be so confused.

''I can see by the expression in your eyes that I've gotten through.'' Rhonda pushed back her chair. ''So I'd better go. That root canal would be about over by now.''

Eileen stood. ''I...I'm not sure what to do next. What's the best way for me to let him know that I—''

''Have you ever been to the Mercury Communications office?''

Eileen shook her head. And that seemed like a serious omission, now. She'd judged Shane without ever seeing the business he'd built.

''I'd suggest you come by early this evening. I can guarantee he'll be there working late. The way he always does, except for a few days last week,'' she added, with a significant glance at Eileen.

''I will go there, if nothing else, to apologize.''

Rhonda smiled. ''It's a start.'' Then she left the office.

SHANE WAS GLAD THAT Rhonda had left for a dental appointment this afternoon. The more he thought about it, the more he regretted telling her anything about his problem with Eileen. He'd never forget how Rhonda had cracked up on learning that he was such a stud that he'd driven Eileen away in a panic.

Maybe someday he'd be able to laugh the way she had. He could appreciate that it was all exceedingly funny, if you weren't the guy dealing with it. Hilarious, no doubt.

But for the time being, he preferred to forget that he'd ever met Eileen Connelly. So he'd covered himself in work, doing battle with every piece of paper in his office and stealing back some of the ones he'd turned over to Rhonda last week.

Rhonda had returned from her dentist's appointment in an annoyingly cheerful mood, so cheerful that he wondered if she had a crush on her dentist. He liked Rhonda and thought she deserved to find a nice guy, but not today. Today he couldn't be happy for anybody hitching a ride on the love train.

Considering that Rhonda kept giving him solicitous looks for the rest of the afternoon, he was glad to see her leave at five, taking her good cheer and mothering behavior with her. That left him free to wallow in his gloom.

He heard the outer door open again about fifteen or twenty minutes later. God, he hoped she hadn't brought him dinner. He didn't want her treating him as if he was in need of coddling.

"You work too hard," said a voice from the doorway, a voice he'd been hearing in his dreams for three straight nights.

His head came up with such a snap that he wrenched a muscle in his neck.

Eileen looked as if she'd just left work. Except that this

suit was green instead of navy, the combo was the same one she'd worn the night they'd met—short skirt, white blouse and crisp jacket, along with pointy-toed heels that matched the outfit. Her legs looked amazing in that kind of getup.

She looked amazing. If the past three days had been tough on her, Shane couldn't see the evidence. She was radiant.

"Hi, Eileen." He wanted to jump her immediately, but damned if he'd let on. This was a perfect opportunity to prove that he wasn't the sex maniac she took him for. "What can I do for you?"

She walked toward his desk. "Forgive me."

In a heartbeat. Anything. You name it. "For what?" His pulse started hammering. If she was here to make up, he had to take it slow. One false move and she might hang the sex maniac sign on him again.

"For jumping to conclusions about the kind of man you are. For thinking that all you care about is sex."

"I do care a lot about it."

"So do I." She propped her hip against the edge of his desk. "But I didn't get through law school because I lack discipline."

"I didn't think you did." He gripped the arms of his desk chair and willed away the arousal that threatened, but the way she was perched on his desk reminded him of the way she'd leaned against her own desk that first night.

"And you didn't create this business by being undisciplined." She scooted up on the desk, crinkling papers in the process. "We're very much alike in that way, both working hard to be the success others expect us to be."

He clenched his jaw. He could smell her perfume from this distance. He was getting hot, but this wasn't the time.

She was probably testing him, to see if he could control himself.

She leaned toward him, and her blouse gaped a little, revealing the lace of her bra. "I drew some stupid conclusions from our time together. You have a right to be upset. But I was wondering if…that offer is still open."

"Which offer?" To make love to her until they both collapsed from exhaustion? That was the only offer he could think of right now, especially when she ran her tongue over her lower lip like that.

Uncertainty flickered in her eyes, followed by regret. "You're right. I blew it." She started to slide off his desk. "I shouldn't have bothered you."

"Wait." He grabbed her wrist. He wouldn't pounce on her, but he wasn't letting her get away, either. This moment was turning into something excellent.

She paused, looking into his eyes. "Shane, I'm so sorry. You gave me a chance any woman would love to have, and I threw it back in your face. I've probably said this all wrong, but I want you to know that I…I'm honored that you once thought…" She stopped speaking and swallowed nervously.

"That I love you?" he murmured, rubbing his thumb over her galloping pulse. "I still do, you know. And I can't imagine a better life than being married to you."

"Y-you love me?" She looked ready to cry.

"Uh-huh." Heart pounding, he left his chair, but he held on to her wrist as he circled the desk to stand in front of her.

"Did I ruin everything?"

"No. But I don't want to ruin everything now, either. Are you trying to see if I'll snap, seeing you perched on my desk like that?"

"No!" She looked horrified. "Did you think I was *testing* you?"

"The thought crossed my mind. After all, you did say that—"

"You must think I'm awful."

"I think you're wonderful. But you're also so damned sexy that sometimes I forget myself. I'll admit that."

"I feel the same about you. And it's a good thing, both of us feeling that way." She gazed up at him, her eyes luminous. "I was being an idiot. An idiot who couldn't even recognize that…that she'd fallen in love, and love can make anyone act a little crazy."

He searched her expression, almost afraid to believe what he was hearing. "Are you sure? Because there has to be more than sex between us. And if that's all you think we have…"

Her smile was tremulous. "Oh, we have a lot more than sex. We have trust. We couldn't have had the wonderful sex without it. I've never trusted anyone with my fantasies before. How strange that I could do that, and then not realize I could trust you with my dreams, too."

His throat tightened. "You can."

"I know that, now. Will…will you marry me, Shane?"

With the emotion crowding his chest, he struggled to respond. "Absolutely."

"And we'll have a house and kids and…and we'll vote."

His vocal cords worked, but barely. "Definitely vote."

"And have sex, lots of sex."

He looked into her eyes. "You're sure? You don't think that I'm too focused on—"

"Look at the evidence." She cupped his face in both hands. "I've been in this office for a good ten minutes, and you have yet to suggest desktop sex."

He wrapped her in his arms. "I've been restraining my self."

"Well, don't."

Grinning, Shane lifted her to the desk. "Will you have desktop sex with me?"

"Yes, and hot-tub sex, and kitchen-table sex, and picnic table sex, and—"

"Picnic-table sex?" He wedged himself between her thighs. Damn, but that felt good. "I don't have a picnic table."

She drew him close, her lips nearly touching his. "I'll ask my parents to give us one as a wedding present."

A wedding. They were getting married. He kissed her eagerly, and was so flooded with happiness that he could almost consider giving up the idea of having sex right now. They had fifty or sixty more years to have lots of sex. He lifted his mouth from hers, needing to say the words again. "I love you so much."

"I love you, too. Desperately, with all my heart. And I really wish you'd put your hand up my skirt."

Then again, they might as well enjoy every minute, beginning with this one. He slid his hand between her thigh and discovered there was no lace barrier between him and heaven. "Eileen?"

She laughed softly. "Let the adventure continue, darlin'."

Epilogue

A year later

ON A NARROW TRAIL winding up the side of one of Sedona's many red rock formations, Eileen stopped to drink from her water bottle. Shane hadn't noticed and kept hiking. Eileen didn't mind pausing so she could better admire her husband in shorts, his muscular legs flexing as he climbed, his firm buns making her salivate. Still. After ten months of wedded bliss.

The plan was to hike to the top of this formation and have sex. They'd picked a weekday and a seldom-traveled trail. Eileen was wearing a tank top and a pair of men's boxers with no panties underneath, which would give Shane immediate access once they'd chosen a spot.

However, Eileen had never noticed before how many helicopters and small planes flew over Sedona. The helicopters were particularly bothersome, because they swooped near the rocks to give tourists inside a thrill. She didn't want that thrill to include a closeup of the locals getting it on.

But she didn't want to abandon the idea of having a sexual adventure on this warm sandstone, either. Glancing around, she noticed a cleft in the rocks right beside the trail that looked high enough and wide enough to give them some privacy.

She laughed to herself as she made a megaphone of her

hands. She'd been waiting months for a legitimate chance to do this. "Shaaane! Come back, Shaaane!" Her voice echoed in a very satisfying way.

He turned and gazed down at her, his dark hair ruffled by the breeze, his eyes protected by sexy shades. He grinned. "I'm impressed you've waited this long to try that out."

"That's not something you want to waste in the grocery store. It needed someplace where it would resonate."

"So do you really want me to come back, or are you just goofing around?"

"I want you to come back. I have an idea."

"Always a good sign." He started down toward her.

What a gorgeous guy, she thought as he drew closer. Every day she had to pinch herself to make sure she wasn't dreaming that she'd married this hunk last November. To think she'd ever had any doubts about him.

In a matter of months they'd created paradise, alternating between his condo in Phoenix and the cabin they'd bought in Oak Creek. She'd left Traynor and Sizemore and opened a small individual practice. She had clients in Sedona and in Phoenix, but she limited her caseload, leaving plenty of time for adventures such as they'd planned for today.

Rhonda had Mercury Communications well in hand, and Shane had begun a home-based consulting business. He'd vowed to keep it small, and he'd done that, turning down clients when his schedule became too crowded. They'd built the perfect life for themselves.

Well, almost perfect. But one thing was missing. Eileen smiled as she thought of the surprise she'd planned for today.

"You're looking extremely pleased with yourself," Shane said as he stopped in front of her. "What's going on in that fertile brain of yours?"

Her brain wasn't the only thing that could be fertile, she thought with glee. "I'm rethinking our plan to have sex on the rocks. Too many flyovers going on."

"But you have an alternative, I'll bet. You look way too happy for a woman who's decided to forgo an orgasm this afternoon."

She gestured toward the cleft in the rock. "I think we can go into that space. You know, me braced up against the rock."

"One of my favorite positions," he said softly. After glancing at the spot, he nodded. "I'm picturing your tush against one rock, your feet planted against the other, and me between your legs. Is that how you have it figured?"

"Yep." And her moist and ready body wanted her to get on with it.

Shane slipped the light backpack from his shoulders, put it on the ground and dropped his sunglasses beside it. "Come on, you hot woman. I don't think I can wait a moment."

"So you don't care if we don't climb all the way to the top?" She took off her sunglasses and put them and her water bottle next to his backpack.

"Are you kidding? You think I was going up there for the view? I was going up there to get laid." He maneuvered her in between the rocks. Then he cupped her bottom in both hands. "I'll hold you until you're sure you won't fall."

"Okay." Pressing the small of her back against the rock, she walked her feet up the side of the opposite wall, her heart racing in anticipation. If he didn't like her surprise, then that was okay, too, but she thought he might. "The rock's warm," she said.

"I'll bet you're even warmer." He leaned forward to kiss her, moving his tongue sensuously against hers. Then he nibbled her lips as he squeezed her bottom. "And you taste wonderful."

She wound her arms around his neck and enjoyed the kiss as she savored the thought of what would come next. "You, too."

"Are you braced? Can I let go of you to get the condom?"

"You can let go to unzip, but as for the condom…let's forget it."

He drew back, and a new kind of excitement flared in his eyes. "Did you say what I think you said?"

"I did. Does it freak you out?"

"God, no. I've been thinking about it for months, but I didn't want to rush you."

She smiled. They were doing exactly as they'd promised each other, balancing impulse with planning, and here was the perfect example. "And I didn't want to rush you, either. But I have this fantasy—you coming inside me and us…us making a baby."

His gaze grew tender. "I love that fantasy."

"I was hoping you would."

"I want that fantasy." He stepped back and unzipped his shorts.

She lowered her gaze. "And I want *that*," she said, taking in the view of his fully erect penis.

"And you're getting that." His voice was roughened by desire. "Finally, finally, we'll have sex without latex." He found the opening in her boxers. "Ready?"

"More than you know."

Grasping her hips, he slipped in partway. "How's that?"

"Mmm." She closed her eyes. "Wonderful."

"Okay, you gotta open your eyes for this next move. I want to see them get all dark and excited."

She looked into his eyes, hot with lust. "Go for it."

He thrust all the way in and gasped with pleasure. "Oh…this is…outstanding."

"I'd have to…agree." And she'd thought sex between them couldn't get any better. "Now let's make that baby," she whispered.

"Yeah, let's." He began to pump slowly. "Are we making a boy or a girl?"

"I don't know." She gazed into his eyes as her heart overflowed with love. "But one thing I do know."

"What?" He shifted his position and stroked her more deeply.

"This…" she said, as she felt her world coming together, at long last "…this is my favorite adventure of all."

Is your man too good to be true?

Hot, gorgeous AND romantic?
If so, he could be a Harlequin® Blaze™ series cover model!

Our grand-prize winners will receive a trip for two to New York City to
shoot the cover of a Blaze novel, and will stay at the luxurious Plaza Hotel.
Plus, they'll receive $500 U.S. spending money!
The runner-up winners will receive $200 U.S.
to spend on a romantic dinner for two.

It's easy to enter!

In 100 words or less, tell us what makes your boyfriend or spouse a true romantic
and the perfect candidate for the cover of a Blaze novel, and include in your submission
two photos of this potential cover model.

All entries must include the written submission of the contest entrant, two photographs of the model
candidate and the Official Entry Form and Publicity Release forms completed in full and signed by
both the model candidate and the contest entrant. Harlequin, along with the experts at
Elite Model Management, will select a winner.

For photo and complete Contest details, please refer to the Official Rules on the next page. All entries
will become the property of Harlequin Enterprises Ltd. and are not returnable.

**Please visit www.blazecovermodel.com to download a copy of the Official Entry Form and
Publicity Release Form or send a request to one of the addresses below.**

Please mail your entry to: **Harlequin Blaze Cover Model Search**

In U.S.A.	In Canada
P.O. Box 9069	P.O. Box 637
Buffalo, NY	Fort Erie, ON
14269-9069	L2A 5X3

No purchase necessary. Contest open to Canadian and U.S. residents who are 18 and over.
Void where prohibited. Contest closes September 30, 2003.

HBCVRMODEL1

HARLEQUIN BLAZE COVER MODEL SEARCH CONTEST 3569 OFFICIAL RULES
NO PURCHASE NECESSARY TO ENTER

1. To enter, submit two (2) 4" x 6" photographs of a boyfriend or spouse (who must be 18 years of age or older) take no later than three (3) months from the time of entry: a close-up, waist up, shirtless photograph; and a fully clothe full-length photograph, then, tell us, in 100 words or fewer, why he should be a Harlequin Blaze cover model and he he is romantic. Your complete "entry" must include: (i) your essay, (ii) the Official Entry Form and Publicity Relea Form printed below completed and signed by you (as "Entrant"), (iii) the photographs (with your hand-written nam address and phone number, and your model's name, address and phone number on the back of each photograph), an (iv) the Publicity Release Form and Photograph Representation Form printed below completed and signed by your model (as "Model"), and should be sent via first-class mail to either: Harlequin Blaze Cover Model Search Conte 3569, P.O. Box 9069, Buffalo, NY, 14269-9069, or Harlequin Blaze Cover Model Search Contest 3569, P.O. Box 63 Fort Erie, Ontario L2A 5X3. All submissions must be in English and be received no later than September 30, 200 Limit: one entry per person, household or organization. **Purchase or acceptance of a product offer does not improve yo chances of winning.** All entry requirements must be strictly adhered to for eligibility and to ensure fairness among entrie

2. Ten (10) Finalist submissions (photographs and essays) will be selected by a panel of judges consisting of membe of the Harlequin editorial, marketing and public relations staff, as well as a representative of Elite Mod Management (Toronto) Inc., based on the following criteria:

Aptness/Appropriateness of submitted photographs for a Harlequin Blaze cover—70%
Originality of Essay—20%
Sincerity of Essay—10%

In the event of a tie, duplicate finalists will be selected. The photographs submitted by finalists will be posted on th Harlequin website no later than November 15, 2003 (at www.blazecovermodel.com), and viewers may vote, in ra order, on their favorite(s) to assist in the panel of judges' final determination of the Grand Prize and Runner-up winni entries based on the above judging criteria. All decisions of the judges are final.

3. All entries become the property of Harlequin Enterprises Ltd. and none will be returned. Any entry may be used f future promotional purposes. Elite Model Management (Toronto) Inc. and/or its partners, subsidiaries and affiliat operating as "Elite Model Management" will have access to all entries including all personal information, and ma contact any Entrant and/or Model in its sole discretion for their own business purposes. Harlequin and Elite Mod Management (Toronto) Inc. are separate entities with no legal association or partnership whatsoever having no pow to bind or obligate the other or create any expressed or implied obligation or responsibility on behalf of the other, su that Harlequin shall not be responsible in any way for any acts or omissions of Elite Model Management (Toronto) In or its partners, subsidiaries and affiliates in connection with the Contest or otherwise and Elite Model Management sha not be responsible in any way for any acts or omissions of Harlequin or its partners, subsidiaries and affiliates connection with the contest or otherwise.

4. All Entrants and Models must be residents of the U.S. or Canada, be 18 years of age or older, and have no pri criminal convictions. The contest is not open to any Model that is a professional model and/or actor in any capacity the time of the entry. Contest void wherever prohibited by law; all applicable laws and regulations apply. Any litigatie within the Province of Quebec regarding the conduct or organization of a publicity contest may be submitted to the Rég des alcools, des courses et des jeux for a ruling, and any litigation regarding the awarding of a prize may be submitt to the Régie only for the purpose of helping the parties reach a settlement. Employees and immediate family membe of Harlequin Enterprises Ltd., D.L. Blair, Inc., Elite Model Management (Toronto) Inc. and their parents, affiliate subsidiaries and all other agencies, entities and persons connected with the use, marketing or conduct of this Contest a not eligible to enter. Acceptance of any prize offered constitutes permission to use Entrants' and Models' names, ess submissions, photographs or other likenesses for the purposes of advertising, trade, publication and promotion on beh of Harlequin Enterprises Ltd., its parent, affiliates, subsidiaries, assigns and other authorized entities involved in th judging and promotion of the contest without further compensation to any Entrant or Model, unless prohibited by law

5. Finalists will be determined no later than October 30, 2003. Prize Winners will be determined no later than Januar 31, 2004. Grand Prize Winners (consisting of winning Entrant and Model) will be required to sign and return Affida of Eligibility/Release of Liability and Model Release forms within thirty (30) days of notification. Non-complian with this requirement and within the specified time period will result in disqualification and an alternate will selected. Any prize notification returned as undeliverable will result in the awarding of the prize to an alternate set winners. All travelers (or parent/legal guardian of a minor) must execute the Affidavit of Eligibility/Release of Liabili prior to ticketing and must possess required travel documents (e.g. valid photo ID) where applicable. Travel da specified by Sponsor but no later than May 30, 2004.

6. Prizes: One (1) Grand Prize—the opportunity for the Model to appear on the cover of a paperback book from t Harlequin Blaze series, and a 3 day/2 night trip for two (Entrant and Model) to New York, NY for the photo shoot Model which includes round-trip coach air transportation from the commercial airport nearest the winning Entran home to New York, NY, (or, in lieu of air transportation, $100 cash payable to Entrant and Model, if the winning Entran home is within 250 miles of New York, NY), hotel accommodations (double occupancy) at the Plaza Hotel and $5 cash spending money payable to Entrant and Model, (approximate prize value: $8,000), and one (1) Runner-up Prize $200 cash payable to Entrant and Model for a romantic dinner for two (approximate prize value: $200). Prizes are valu in U.S. currency. Prizes consist of only those items listed as part of the prize. No substitution of prize(s) permitted winners. All prizes are awarded jointly to the Entrant and Model of the winning entries, and are not severable - priz and obligations may not be assigned or transferred. Any change to the Entrant and/or Model of the winning entries w result in disqualification and an alternate will be selected. Taxes on prize are the sole responsibility of winners. Any an all expenses and/or items not specifically described as part of the prize are the sole responsibility of winners. Harlequ Enterprises Ltd. and D.L. Blair, Inc., their parents, affiliates, and subsidiaries are not responsible for errors in printing Contest entries and/or game pieces. No responsibility is assumed for lost, stolen, late, illegible, incomplete, inaccura non-delivered, postage due or misdirected mail or entries. In the event of printing or other errors which may result unintended prize values or duplication of prizes, all affected game pieces or entries shall be null and void.

7. Winners will be notified by mail. For winners' list (available after March 31, 2004), send a self-addressed, stampe envelope to: Harlequin Blaze Cover Model Search Contest 3569 Winners, P.O. Box 4200, Blair, NE 68009-4200, refer to the Harlequin website (at www.blazecovermodel.com).

Contest sponsored by Harlequin Enterprises Ltd., P.O. Box 9042, Buffalo, NY 14269-9042.

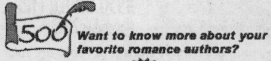

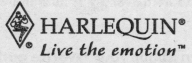

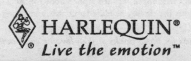

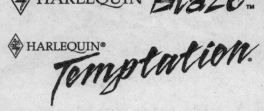